I0639182

THE KEEPERS OF MEN

CLARICE MONTGOMERY

THM

Copyright © 2025 by Wild Buffalo Novels, LLC.

All rights reserved.

No part of this book may be reproduced in any form or by any electronic or mechanical means, including information storage and retrieval systems, without written permission from the author, except for the use of brief quotations in a book review.

Ten Hut Media
tenhutmedia.com

This is a work of fiction. Names, characters, businesses, places, events and incidents are either the products of the author's imagination or used in a fictitious manner. Any resemblance to actual persons, living or dead, or actual events is purely coincidental.

ISBN: 978-1-964007-29-8 (Paperback)

To my love, Russell

PROLOGUE

Excerpt from the *All Things Golf* Podcast with Drake Jones
Released on July 3, 2022

Drake: Frankly, I'm a bit surprised by Vegas's betting odds going into the Desert Invitational.

Britney Gibson: What's surprising?

Drake: It just feels like there's a bias against the players who were expelled from the Professional Golf Association when they joined the new tour. You don't see any of those guys as favorites to be in the top five, much less as picks for the outright win.

Britney: Well, I guess it makes sense to me. If they're factoring in the assumptions and rumors surrounding the new league, then I don't see how they could rank them higher. All the analysts seem to believe that while the new league is pulling some big names, and no doubt incredible talent, these guys are over the hill, so to speak. The thought process behind it is that maybe they're still competitive but their best days are behind them.

Drake: That's insane to me when I look at some of these players.

Britney: I don't disagree, but it makes sense.

Drake: Well, there won't be any excuses next weekend. Desert Invitational is open to everyone who qualified, so those PGA guys who have been stirring the pot with those "over the hill" statements better come ready to play.

Britney: For sure. I think we're in for a good show this weekend. Not just for the golf, but also the potential drama...

Drake: What drama?

Britney: Rumors surrounding the practice rounds are that PGA players are avoiding the new league guys and refusing to practice near them. It's like the field has severed itself, essentially. A lot of long-standing friend-ships and competitor acquaintances seem to have dissolved overnight and it's causing problems for everyone in charge of organizing practice rounds.

Drake: God, I hate this <EXPLETIVE>.

Britney: I know you do, but drama makes for good ratings.

Drake: Maybe among women.

Britney: I do love watching grown men behave like middle school girls.

Drake: I hate to sound old, but it used to be that the guys who were winning brought in the good ratings. Speaking of winning, who do you have as a favorite coming out of practice rounds?

Britney: I've got my eye on Jared Farmer this week.

Drake: You always liked the underdog.

Britney: I don't know if that description is entirely fair here. This kid has been playing his whole life and really got going last year with two league wins and five top ten finishes. He's focused, healthy, and has all the momentum in the world behind him leading into Desert Invitational. I think he's a force to be reckoned with.

Drake: I'll believe it when I see it.

Britney: Who do you like this week?

Drake: I'm going to disagree with you and Vegas here and pick Andy Bell.

Britney: <Laughs> I should have guessed that.

Drake: Hear me out. He's been in the top fifteen of world rankings almost his entire career—

Britney: He hasn't been ranked in the top five since 2019.

Drake: I don't care about that. You mentioned momentum and I think all Bell's performances recently in the new league were building up to something spectacular for the weekend. He really thrives under pressure, and the hyper competitive environment of Desert Invitational is a perfect place for him to rise to the occasion.

Britney: It's like you said earlier; there won't be any excuses.

1

SARAH
SATURDAY

Sarah is ready to have an excellent day.

Not right at this moment, as the security guard at the entrance to the course waves his metal detecting wand across her body while another one digs through the tampon and lip gloss stash in her backpack. Even as the wife of one of the players, she isn't excused from the strict safety measures. She just hopes that they let her through in time for her to see Jared before he begins his warm-up. After that, she'll lose direct access to him until after he signs his scorecard.

"She's clear. No phone," the guard in charge of her bag says.

She grabs her transparent plastic backpack and steps farther into Desert Invitational. One of the most elite majors of the year, spectators are forbidden from having a cell phone in hand, even if it's off. Any distractions for the players are sacrilege. This is where the best of the best come to compete.

Moving farther into the country club lawns, Sarah maneuvers around merchandise and refreshment tents so she can get another glimpse of the scenery before finding her husband.

Vast swaths of desert roses and tulips, as well as other dry climate shrubs decorate the course. It is like walking through a Southwestern botanical museum, and a far cry from the terrain in which she'd grown up.

Born and raised in Ottawa, Kansas, most of the topography to which she'd been accustomed was farmland. Certainly, there was a natural beauty to the Midwest, but the past year had given Sarah a chance to see more of the United States than she'd ever dreamed of visiting.

But in her opinion, so far nothing has compared to the flowers of Desert Invitational.

Reminding herself she'll have a full two more days to admire the landscaping while Jared competes, Sarah begins her search for him in earnest. When she married her high school boyfriend, part of her had been resigned to a quiet life in their rural community. That is typically where small-town relationships end—right where they started. Jared was different in that way. He had always been ambitious and competitive beyond what success in Ottawa required and spent a decade fine tuning his skills as a golfer. Extra hours on the range after practice ended and early morning workouts were the bare minimum for him.

Sarah would have followed him anywhere. While a smaller life in their hometown suited her just fine, when he expressed his desire to focus on golf, she'd thrown herself headfirst into making sure that dream came true. His hours on the practice putting green mirrored hers at both the small women's boutique in town and as the beverage cart girl on their local course on the weekends.

Taking two jobs was nothing. Sarah had also toiled domestically to ensure their home was a place Jared could rest. It was always clean, functional, and worry free. He could spend both his mental and physical energy focused entirely on becoming an elite competitor on tour.

Those outside their relationship might look at Sarah with a critical eye, saying she sacrificed too much for him. If asked, she would say she felt like she wasn't doing enough.

Whatever their combined efforts had been, they were finally getting a return on their investment. Jared Farmer was on the leader board for Desert Invitational three years after officially going pro.

Sighing again at the greenery around her, Sarah takes a breath and focuses on finding Jared. She should have left at the same time as him, but she'd taken longer than usual to get ready. It might already be too late to wish him good luck.

"You don't have to do all that," he'd said that morning as he tucked in his shirt. He was alluding to the heavy hand she'd taken with her make-up. "It's gonna be a high of 103 today. Might as well be comfortable."

"It all feels the same to me," she'd lied. "I'll meet you there, I'm just going to be a few more minutes."

Forty minutes later, she'd boarded a crowded shuttle that drove spectators from the hotel to the course. Sarah had honestly not expected to be as late as she is, and now she is paying for it battling the crowds.

She moves with more purpose now, light panic setting in as more time passes with no sign of her husband. He would be disappointed not to see her before he tees off. Jared would never admonish her, but she wouldn't be able to forgive herself if she missed out on the one thing he'd verbally requested of her for this tournament.

"Excuse me," she approaches an eager teenage boy volunteering at the water station. "I'm Jared Farmer's wife. Do you know where I could find him?"

A wide smile breaks out across his face. This is why so many men and boys volunteer at professional golf events—free access to the greatest in the game. "Sure, just follow me!"

They move through the crowds and Sarah hopes they stop at the clubhouse, where Jared might be getting breakfast or changing his shoes in the dressing room, but no. The volunteer moves quickly past the main building, farther into the competition area.

Her heart sinks when she sees Jared already stretching on the range. She can't approach him now, he's in the zone.

Sarah regrets not leaving with him, but she doesn't know what she could have done differently. For all the hard work they both put into his playing golf full-time, there were certain aspects she hadn't considered or prepared to encounter.

Specifically, cameras. Everywhere.

Jared won his first tournament eight months ago. Immersed in the excitement, Sarah had rushed out to hug him without a thought in the world besides how proud she'd been. She had a framed photo on their mantel of them embracing on the eighteenth green next to his trophy from that day.

She did not, however, appreciate the published action shots of her jogging toward him. They had been...well, unflattering was an understatement.

Having never given much thought to her own form, Sarah had been devastated. At a size six—fine, sometimes eight—she was basically a rural Kansas beauty queen. But this was the big leagues, and her appearance was another item to keep track of on her never-ending list of things she imagined she needed to support Jared. As a professional athlete's wife, she'd known she needed to step up her game.

This is why she couldn't think of anything she would have skipped as she got ready that morning. The make-up, the subtle jewelry, the curled ponytail, even the horrid shapewear were all pieces of her new and improved puzzle. With the right amount of high coverage foundation and skipped meals, she was very close to being competitive with the other wives.

Jared had been right, though. It is hot today.

Spectators have already claimed all the premium shade under larger trees and the sun is beating down relentlessly on those less fortunate. Sarah won't survive very long this way, having already sweated through the Spanx under her tennis skirt. Cameras or not, she needs to change something before walking along with Jared for all eighteen holes.

After a full bead of sweat tickles her along its path from her clavicle to her belly button, Sarah turns to walk back to the clubhouse. Locker rooms are reserved for the players, but a few air-conditioned restrooms inside have been courteously set aside for their families, a luxury not seen at all tournaments. The blast of cold air coming out of the vents is tempting Sarah to change her mind, but she doesn't pause on her way to the women's room.

Pushing the door inside, Sarah checks under all the stalls and finds them empty. She chooses the accessible stall then dumps her backpack on the ground.

Despite the vents on full blast, the sweat on her skin hasn't dried yet, and she wrestles off her tennis skirt. It sticks to her the whole way down as she girds herself to peel off her shapewear. This is going to be a nightmare.

After several frustrated grunts, she finally stuffs the dreaded undergarments in the tiny restroom stall trash can and replaces her tennis skirt. If she hurries, she can purchase a few bottles of water before watching Jared warm-up for his first swing. He's in third place, the second to last tee time.

Sarah throws open the door and freezes at the sight of a tall blonde woman fixing her lipstick in the mirror.

Shoot. She'd thought she was alone.

The woman's eyes meet hers in the mirror and Sarah is surprised to see a genuine smile as she moves toward the next vanity. The woman is Cassandra Bell, wife to Andy Bell who is leading the tournament, daughter of Senator Collins from Montana, and somehow more lovely in person than she is on camera.

Sarah has met a few dozen tour wives, but not Cassandra yet. Andy's decision to move to the new league means that they haven't been able to compete in any of the PGA events that Jared qualified for last year, only attending the majors hosted by the USGA.

Walking closer to the mirror, Sarah moves to wash her hands just so she has something to do. She didn't actually relieve herself in the stall, but it would look weird to exit one and not wash, she thinks.

"It's Sarah, right?"

"Yes," she says, surprised to be identified. Jared has some limited fame these days, but no one really recognizes Sarah. She turns off the faucet and pulls a paper towel to dry her hands now that she's trapped in a conversation.

"I'm Cassandra," she replies easily. "Andy has been really impressed with Jared this year. You guys should be proud of how well he's doing."

Sarah smiles. "That means a lot. Jared would be thrilled that Andy knows who he is," she halfway jokes. Jared would be ecstatic, but she isn't sure she trusts Cassandra. Their husbands are competitors now, and the other woman is frankly too pretty to be friends with Sarah.

Cassandra points behind her. "Do you mind if I get something for you?"

"Get what?"

Ignoring her, the woman reaches beneath Sarah's backpack and pulls at the tennis skirt. In her haste to get ready, she'd accidentally tucked it into itself, exposing her spandex covered rear.

Oh God. How humiliating.

"It's not a big deal," Cassandra smiles kindly. "I would just want someone to catch that for me if they saw it."

"Thank you," Sarah says. She is genuinely grateful to the woman now, competitors or not, but the gratitude makes her uncomfortable, so she turns toward her reflection.

She cringes at the mascara already collecting under her eyes and pulls her backpack around to find her setting powder. She knew she'd need it for touch-ups throughout the day and had thrown it on top.

As she works, she sees Cassandra turn toward her fully and set her left hip against the sink. The attention is unnerving, but Sarah doesn't know what she should add to their small interaction.

She shouldn't have worried since Cassandra speaks first. "It can be a lot to keep up with, you know?"

"A lot of what?"

The woman moves her hand in a vague swirling gesture which could include anything. "All of this. The weight of being seen, the travel, the winning and losing. Not to mention the drama," she continues with a wink. "It can be overwhelming to try and cover all your bases, is what I'm trying to say. Doing it all means inevitably missing a few steps. But do you want to know a secret?"

"Sure," Sarah responds, attempting not to cringe at her own eagerness.

"All they really want," Cassandra explains with a nod toward outside, "is to know that we believe in them. Our guys need to understand that we're their biggest cheerleaders out there, and that we trust them to win. Everything else is secondary if it even matters at all."

A pregnant pause follows the woman's statement. Sarah tries to understand, she really does. Yet in the face of Cassandra's flawless hair and smile, her somehow sweat-free attire, not to mention her quiet confidence, Sarah can't help but feel that there's no way the other woman understands what she's thinking. It is impossible to imagine her as anything less than perfect in most circumstances.

"That makes sense," Sarah offers, after pretending to think about it.

Cassandra smiles knowingly, as if she doesn't believe the façade. "We better get going," she turns to the exit and holds the door open for Sarah. "I think our husbands' tee times are right next to each other, so we'll probably get a chance to catch up later on the course."

Sarah dreads the idea of being photographed next to Cassandra but gives a pleasant yet noncommittal reply to the offer. They move quickly toward the practice greens in silence as the noises of the pro shop take over.

Outside, Sarah is once again assaulted by the heat and congratulates herself for not changing her mind on the underwear swap. This day was going to be unbearable.

"Mrs. Bell? Mrs. Farmer?"

They turn toward the speaker, who appears to be a high-level volunteer. She worries that something has happened to Jared, but a quick glance in Cassandra's direction lets her know that she shouldn't express concern yet.

"How convenient, I thought I'd have to hunt down both of you separately," the man says. His hair has some grey in it, and his thick mustache reminds Sarah of one of her dad's friends from when she was a kid. She's always hated mustaches and thinks they look cartoonish on almost every man.

"What do you need?" Cassandra's voice is kind but unyielding, clearly seasoned in handling these kinds of approaches diplomatically.

"You're both needed at the press tent. There's a message for you, but I don't have any more details."

Sarah's plan to continue looking nonchalant falls apart when she glances at Cassandra. It's clear now that this is something out of the ordinary, something the other woman didn't anticipate either. Confusion is apparent in her expression, but she covers it quickly.

She's a pro, after all.

"Thank you for letting us know," she replies easily. "We ought to get going then. Shall we?"

It wasn't a question, not really. Something is wrong, and Sarah has no way of knowing what it is, so her only option is to follow.

She takes the entire five-minute walk to ruminate on how wrong it might be.

2

WHITNEY

Like most little girls, Whitney spent many hours of her childhood daydreaming about her wedding. She loved all things feminine from the dresses to the flowers to the sparkling chandeliers. She had picked songs for each dance before she even began dating, and, as a teenager, her wedding themed Pinterest board boasted almost a quarter of a million followers. Every vacation would include recon on what kind of event venues the area offered. On more than one occasion, she spent Halloween in princess gowns reminiscent of Disney cartoon nuptials. Whitney was determined to be an extravagant, traditional bride.

One segment of the traditional wedding didn't appeal to her, though. Whitney hated the portion of the vows declaring "til death do us part," or even its sanitized brother, "as long as we both shall live." Why would she want to think about death on the happiest day of her life? It seemed perverse, and never having outgrown that feeling, she insisted on alternative vows for her own wedding several years back.

I promise to love you forever.

She often wonders if she jinxed herself with that decision.

"Thank you so much for being here, Mrs. Silver."

Whitney turns to look at the man speaking to her, bringing her back to the present. She's already forgotten his name, despite hearing it mere moments ago. Living in a fog for over a year now, she doesn't let the memory split bother her.

"It was no problem at all," she replies. "I wasn't expecting the invite, I'll admit."

"Are you kidding? This was the least we could do," he counters. "We thought it was important to give Rowan some kind of memorial. He's deeply missed by players and fans alike and, even after a year, people are still mourning the loss. I can't imagine what you've been through."

Whitney stares back at him silently. Her husband was dead, that's what she'd been through.

He rubs the back of his neck, reacting to her silence, then speaks up again. "Not to mention all the charity work you've done this year, with children's outreach, making golf accessible for everyone. It would be a sin not to honor you both."

Her smile is tight but genuine. "Well, the only way to move is forward, and it was what Rowan would have wanted," she says. Rowan had loved golf, both its competitive nature and the tradition of the game. He had been ruthless in his desire to win but sportsmanlike to all. Watching him compete had been like watching one of those nature documentaries with a giant wildcat following a gazelle by a small pond. Steady, focused, and patient in the beginning, then ending with a swift and efficient kill.

Whitney wishes every day that he was still with her, but a small section of her mind is glad that he isn't around for all the changes. He would have been intensely disappointed with the state of the sport. All the drama around new tours, pros being banned from the PGA, and the infighting between players who used to be friends would have broken his heart. He would have tried not to take sides, likely sticking with the PGA but not disparaging the new league. Not many players can walk that line, though. The media's pestering questions and internet message boards stirring up drama have forced most men to take a side and defend it openly. Few golfers have avoided the infighting.

Yes, it is a small blessing that Rowan can't see what's happening to his beloved game.

"If you need anything," the man interrupts her thoughts, "don't hesitate to ask any of the volunteers. We want to make sure you get to enjoy the tournament while you're here."

Whitney thanks him and walks toward the action. She hasn't been to a tournament since Rowan's passing, and the environment allows her to pretend briefly that he's still here. The wound of losing him is fresh, like it happened yesterday. Her family assures her that time would help, that with patience it won't hurt so much. They say that she will always love him, but that it will get easier, that maybe someday she'll meet someone else. But they don't know what it's like, to wake up every morning hoping that every-thing that happened was just a nightmare, to roll over in bed and find it still cold and realize you can't breathe all over again.

Honestly, she doesn't want to heal. In a way, her pain keeps him alive.

When she really wants to hurt, Whitney will reminisce on the memory of identifying his body. She'll fixate on the glass shards in his skin from the broken front windshield and passenger window, the bruising, the blood. His normally tanned skin, pale with lifelessness, unnaturally firm with death. She'll think about how his eyes will never look back at her, how his hand will never warm hers again.

When she wants to feel angry, she'll think about the fact that the driver fled the scene and is still out there, living freely, safe in their anonymity.

But that's not why she was invited to the tournament, so she buries negative thoughts and focuses on her surroundings. Whitney attended to watch the competition, yes, but specifically she was invited to tonight's gala dinner for the competitors and their wives. Those in charge of the dinner are doing an in memoriam for Rowan and gifting her an award for her charity work this year. She doesn't need to be a weeping mess when she walks across the stage.

No, she has an image to portray while she's here. A widow in mourning, silent and resilient in her strength. She has the world's pity right now, and she doesn't want to squander any goodwill from the public by making a scene in front of everyone attending. It would be a disaster if the public knew how little she'd moved on.

A sweaty spectator bumps into Whitney's shoulder, ignoring her. Irra-tionally, she tells herself that it's because she's no longer recognized, a thought that's obviously untrue with all the media coverage she still gets.

That creature never would have run into me if Rowan were still here.

They met when she was twenty-four, two years into her career as a cheerleader for the Dallas Cowboys. The job had been life changing, for both her and her mother, who raised her alone. Her income was able to support them modestly. It also felt good to give back just a fraction of what her mother had provided to her as she grew up.

Another perk of the role had been more personal. As a pretty-faced, sexually desirable redhead in her early twenties, she now had almost unlimited access to professional football players. That was where the real money was. Whitney had dated strategically, only opting for the men who offered more than just a onetime visit to their hotel room in the night. She stayed away from the married ones, an approach sometimes lost on her fellow cheerleaders. She required actual dates from her paramours, and due to her looks and easy laugh, she got them often.

But she grew tired of football players, more quickly than she'd expected. Most were too showy and bordering on neanderthal in their personalities. A date with one, of course, meant you were spoiled by their spending, but that usually meant bottle service at clubs rather than a nice quiet dinner. One could hardly get to know a potential lover while bombarded with the sounds of deep bass and squealing co-eds.

"Is this seat taken?"

Whitney had stopped running her index finger around the rim of her glass of wine long enough to look up and see Rowan standing behind her at the bar the night they met. "Sure is," she smiled back, "by you if you want it."

He grinned, revealing a row of straight, white teeth, a contrast against his darker, Mediterranean skin. "I want it."

Rowan had been eons away from her former boyfriends. Refined, classy, almost unapproachable. When he sat next to her at the hotel bar where they'd both been staying, she assumed he was waiting for someone else, like she was. He had asked to buy her a drink and introduced himself. She couldn't believe how easily they connected. When asked about their relationship in interviews, Whitney always declared that it had been love at first sight for her. She adored how gentlemanly he was compared to what she'd grown used to, and she was almost unable to comprehend how a man could be so beautiful but still so masculine.

If her football-playing ex-boyfriends were sledgehammers, then Rowan had been a beautiful, jewel-encrusted dagger.

"Mrs. Silver?"

A volunteer, different from the one who greeted her, has just spoken to her. Whitney needs to be careful, getting lost in her thoughts as she is. If she's going to survive this weekend, she must have her wits about her.

"Yes, that's me," she replies.

"You're needed at the press tent."

The press tent? They should be busy with players and analysts, focused on the competition itself. She couldn't fathom why they would choose that location to bring her, even if they wanted an interview with a woman who didn't have a husband competing anymore.

Whitney decides to engage the young man as they walk. "Do you know why I'm needed?"

The young man shrugs, "I wish I could tell you. All I know is that there's some kind of message for you, but it's not supposed to take long."

Whitney sighs and puts her sunglasses back in her purse. It's a small diversion, and it's not like she has a specific tee time to follow today.

3

HILLARY

Hillary hates New Mexico. She grew up in the state, and every time she's forced to come back for her husband's career it feels as painful as having to spend the day at a packed DMV. With all the golf courses in the world, all the beautiful locations and resort getaways available to the tours, there is literally no reason to bring any event to New Mexico. Also, whoever had the genius idea to have a major golf tournament in the desert *in the middle of the summer* ought to be sent to jail. This heat combined with these crowds is criminal.

Hillary's husband has already teed off for the day, but she wasn't there.

Most wives, if they attend the tournaments, watch their husbands from start to finish. It's typically a show of support, along with a genuine desire to be near their husbands. There's also the added benefit of scaring away any groupies, underdressed women seeking one night with a famous player. But Hillary isn't motivated by any of those things today. Why should she have had to wake up early, just to watch Steven limp across the finish line? He had been more than obvious about the fact that he wasn't taking this seriously, either.

Steven barely made the cut yesterday. After two double bogeys to start his back nine, there had been a stretch where Hillary was sure he wouldn't turn it around. With five holes left, he'd needed to play one under par, and nothing about his game leading up to that point indicated he could pull it off.

He had, but it was too close. She remembers the text thread from her half-sister yesterday just to punish herself.

Gwen: What the hell was that?

Hillary: Nothing, he made the cut.

Gwen: He better. You owe me.

It was good to keep in mind how much she had to lose. After receiving the messages yesterday, Hillary had set out for the practice green, looking for her husband. Her frustration reached a boiling point when she couldn't find him in the short game areas or on the range. She'd seen most of the men who made the cut, and some who hadn't, fine tuning areas of weakness after the round. That's what it took to be great—the time commitment, the extra repetitions, the near insane drive to not only be good, but to be the best.

But Steven wasn't that guy, and after exhausting the respectable locations available, she found him where she usually found him.

At the bar.

Hillary was typically skilled in lying—or to be more diplomatic, hiding her emotions—but seeing Steven hunched over the bar with three empty Budweiser tall boys in front of him had been infuriating.

He saw her approach, unaware of her temper or maybe already drunk, and smiled lazily at her. "Sweetie, you made it," he drawled. "Have a drink with me to celebrate."

"Steven, what the fuck?"

He frowned. "What's wrong? I made the cut."

"Barely," she'd hissed at him. "Shouldn't you be practicing? There are two more rounds in case you forgot. At this rate, you won't even place."

Which was simply unacceptable. She needed the money that would come from at least a top thirty finish. They certainly weren't suffering, far from it, but keeping her payouts to Gwen hidden from Steven was easier when they were flush with winnings and lately that had been harder. Their accountant had mentioned her frequent shopping and beauty treatments, offered up a budget suggestion to her husband. He'd laughed it off, saying his wife didn't need an allowance.

While his lackadaisical attitude toward money gave her more cover, bringing that attitude to the tournament wasn't helping her mood.

"You know, I don't need this from you," he countered. "Why can't you support me? I don't get any kind of encouragement from you."

"I *encourage* you," Hillary leaned close and whispered into his ear, "to go outside and practice."

He reeled back, glaring at her, then turned like a child back toward the bar. "Fuck you too, Hillary," he'd replied, then finished beer number four.

She'd assessed him briefly before storming off. Steven wasn't overweight or unattractive, but he didn't have the dialed in physique one usually associated with a professional athlete. He drank more than he exercised, and it showed. Hillary took in the slouched posture, the severe tan lines, the sweat stains. She walked away before resentment could build further.

It was her fault, really. She'd married into the only sport she could think of where one could remain competitive after several drinks and a pack of cigarettes. In fact, she was pretty sure professional poker players and bowlers took better care of themselves than her husband did.

So here she is, Saturday morning of Desert Invitational. Steven is probably on hole three by now, but Hillary is in no hurry to cheer for him or follow along with his group in this heat. She'll wait for the last five holes or so, when the cameras can catch her being supportive as he finishes.

She's pretty sure she loved him once, in the beginning. Steven had an easy way of making her laugh, and her gratitude toward him overpowered anything unsavory for a long time.

"You should have held out," Gwen lectured her when she learned of Hillary's marriage. "There were wealthier men available to you."

Gwen was probably right; she is, humiliatingly, almost never wrong. But holding out for something better hadn't mattered when she was with Steven at the beginning.

Steven, for a long time, had been her savior, and thus had earned several early years of marriage in which she turned a blind eye to his vices but had been genuinely happy.

Hillary looks around, still in the air-conditioned clubhouse. Her ice water remains untouched, its condensation running down the side of the glass and collecting on its small bar napkin. Not for the first time, she wonders why she's so miserable when she's gotten everything she's ever wanted.

Well, got everything she was told she should want.

A crowd erupts in a cheer somewhere on the course, and Hillary checks the television screen above her. One of guys in an early tee time just after Steven's, she thinks, has holed out a greenside bunker shot for birdie. Good for him.

She sighs and stands up, prepared to suffer in the heat intermittently. Hillary has practiced for many years now the face of a supportive wife, and she knows she can't avoid that chore the entire day.

"Mrs. Torre?"

Hillary turns at the sound of her married name. Getting to dump Gwen's last name had been another perk of marrying Steven, and she's never tired of hearing it.

She smiles at the volunteer. "Yes?"

"You're needed in the press tent," he says, trying and failing to keep his eyes directed at her face.

Hillary grins knowingly. She isn't shy with her wardrobe, and it never hurts to have her hard work in the gym validated. A few subtle surgeries funded by her husband give her a face and body with which few mortal women could compete.

"Lead the way," she replies. In her satisfaction with making the teenage volunteer nervous, she forgets to question why she is being called to the press tent in the first place.

4

SARAH

Sarah follows Cassandra, who follows the volunteer, in an accidental single file line. Ceding authority to the veteran wife, she doesn't feel comfortable speeding up to walk next to her for some reason.

The other woman either notices this and doesn't wish for Sarah to feel slighted or she is ignoring it entirely, slowing so they walk evenly. The volunteer leading them is far enough away that they can whisper without being heard. Cassandra speaks first.

"I have to admit, I have no idea what this is about."

"Really?" Shoot. Sarah had been hoping for a clue, something to help prepare her for this. It appears that she has no choice but to go in blind, just like Cassandra. "Why us, though?"

The other woman shrugs. "Our husbands are leading, maybe they just want some quick sound bites about how proud we are."

"And this is common?"

"No," Cassandra replies easily. "This weekend isn't about us, but I can't think of anything else."

They walk in silence for a few more steps before she speaks again. "At least my mother-in-law is with us this week. Otherwise, I'd be dragging three unruly kids with me to whatever this is."

Sarah tries to laugh, but it sounds choked instead of lighthearted. Oh well. They've arrived at the tent, so she doesn't have to worry about a witty reply.

The volunteer moves them past the tables, the camera crews, and the panel interview stage to the back corner of the tent where another gentleman waits with two other women.

As they approach, Sarah feels the casual air that had previously surrounded Cassandra harden almost imperceptibly. She doesn't look any different, her expression hasn't changed, but whatever camaraderie she'd offered Sarah earlier wouldn't be present for this confrontation.

"Hillary, Whitney," Cassandra says, already having met them before. "Good to see you this morning."

Sarah hasn't met the women, but she recognizes them. The redhead, Whitney, is wearing a black sleeveless polo shirt and a black tennis skirt. She is Rowan Silver's widow and hasn't been photographed in another color for a full year since his death. Sarah isn't sure why she's here, since obviously her husband isn't competing.

The brunette, Hillary, is almost as recognizable as Cassandra. As Steven Torre's wife, she's known primarily for being unbelievably beautiful. Like Cassandra, she is also inexplicably more stunning in real life than on camera, but unlike the senator's daughter, Hillary's appearance has a slight cheapness to it. The teal dress she wears is skintight and could only be defended as golf course appropriate with its tiny collar around her neckline.

"Hi Cassandra," Whitney offers. Hillary seems perturbed at the presence of the other women and says nothing, but neither her nor Whitney bother introducing themselves to Sarah.

It stings a little, but she isn't surprised.

"Sorry to interrupt your morning, ladies," the elder volunteer between them says. "I'll make this quick so you can get on your way. I've got these," he holds up a small stack of envelopes, and Sarah counts four, one for each of them. "These were left for each of you."

The sealed envelopes have each woman's name on them, so he passes them out accordingly. "That's all I've got, so I'll leave you all to it."

The volunteer walks away before any of them have a chance to open the cards, and Sarah thinks this may be on purpose. She looks at Cassandra, then Whitney and Hillary. None of them show signs of understanding what's going on, but when they move to open the card, she follows, not wanting to be left behind.

No one reads aloud, but Sarah can tell they have all reached the end of the letter when Hillary speaks up first.

"What the fuck?"

Hello friends,

You don't know me, not yet at least. But I know you four, better than you think. I see your comfortable, happy lives. I see your families and wealth. So in love with your husbands it's adorable. You might think you're living a life other people envy.

But what if it's all a lie?

For one of you, I can promise that it is. You see, I've had an affair with one of your husbands. Out of the four of you, one has been betrayed, and by the end of the weekend, the whole world will know when I bring my story to the press.

Now, which of you is it?

Excerpt from Post Practice Round Panel Interview with Andy Bell
July 13, 2022

CBS: Mr. Bell, how has your game changed since leaving the PGA?

Andy: My game is as good as it's ever been. I think if anything has changed, I've gotten sharper and more focused on the tasks in front of me. My mind doesn't wander like it did when I was younger, so I definitely feel more dangerous than I used to.

Fox Sports: What did preparation for Desert Invitational look like the past few weeks?

Andy: As far as tournament prep goes, I just did the same things I always do. Really grind at the gym and with the fundamentals, especially short game, then spend time with my family.

ABC: In what ways would you say that becoming a family man has helped your game?

Andy: Oh, in every way I can think of. I made the same mistakes anyone would make with the notoriety and money I had in my twenties. Booze, parties, women, gambling, you name it. I knew I had to make some changes. Maybe you can get away with living fast like that when your career has an expiration date, like in heavy contact sports. But I wanted to play golf professionally for as long as possible, so I couldn't keep doing that. I began cleaning up my lifestyle and image, taking better care of my mind and body. When I met Cassandra along the way, something just clicked for me. I thought I was getting better for myself. Turns out I was getting better for her.

<Soft laughter from the press>

Fox Sports: Do you have any regrets about leaving the PGA for the new tour in what was arguably a very controversial decision?

Andy: I don't see it as controversial. Look, this was extremely straight-forward for me. I was going to be offered more money in exchange for less travel, more time with my wife and kids. Any man in my position would be a complete moron to pass on that offer.

CBS: What would you say about the talk that those who defected to the new tour are past their prime?

Andy: Anyone saying that better come ready to play. Writing checks you can't cash, and all that. The greatest players in the world are here competing this weekend, PGA and otherwise. Everyone watching will know that the new tour guys are as deadly as anyone playing right now. So, we'll see what happens.

CBS: The general consensus around you and the other new tour players is that you all sold out. Do you have any response to that?

Andy: Honestly? I don't give a [EXPLETIVE].

5

HILLARY

"What the fuck?" Hillary thinks, or possibly says out loud, not that she cares. She hasn't read the whole thing, that would take too long, but she has gathered that someone is trying to scare her. Furious at having her time wasted, she just wants to get away from these women. She doesn't care for female friendship or acknowledging any kind of sisterhood amongst the other wives. Hillary is a one woman show.

She's not as confident as she pretends to be given the circumstances. Is Steven cheating on her? Unlikely, but not impossible. She can recall no signs of it from him despite their marriage loosening like a rubber band without its elasticity. Not with a bang, but a whimper.

While Hillary is certain the note's words aren't true for her, there are other implications at play. The press catching any wind of her marital problems could cause an entire avalanche of secrets to come undone, and that's a mess she can't think about right now, especially with Gwen breathing down her neck.

The letter can be technically false but still instigate a multitude of issues for her, and this makes her nervous.

"Is this some kind of sick joke?"

Whitney's statement pulls her away from her own thoughts. Oh, right. Three other women received the same letter.

Whitney has already crumbled her letter, pretending to be unaffected. It's not the most convincing act. "Obviously, this is a mistake or a cruel prank."

Hillary feels perspiration gather on her own palms as she nods along, showing her agreement with the widow. Rowan Silver died in a car wreck last year. Everyone knew that. This knowledge did nothing to alleviate Hillary's growing discomfort, though.

"It must be a prank," Cassandra Bell inserts. "I don't believe this for a second. It's ludicrous."

Of course she's not worried. Perfect Cassandra, shiny blonde Cassandra, kind to all Cassandra, everyone loves Cassandra. Bleh.

"But what if it's not fake?"

The mousy voice pulls Hillary back to the present again. She has completely forgotten about the fourth woman, who she doesn't recognize. She's young and appears unused to their world. She doesn't have any of the confidence forged with time spent married to a professional athlete that they all wear like armor. If Hillary was feeling uncharitable—and she usually is—she might call the girl chubby. It isn't a fair description, but the girl is standing next to Whitney Silver, Cassandra Bell, and Hillary Torre. Those three could make Ingrid Bergman look dumpy.

"And you are...?" Hillary asks the girl by way of introduction.

Her tone has the intended effect of belittling. "I'm Sarah," is all the girl replies.

How is that helpful? Hillary doesn't give a shit who Sarah is.

"She's married to Jared Farmer," Cassandra interrupts, moving to face Hillary more directly. "Our husbands don't tee off for over an hour. Speaking of," the woman looks at her watch, "shouldn't you get going? Steven must be halfway done by now."

It was an exaggeration, but not far enough from the truth for safety. Hillary keeps her face impassive but fights an urge to glare at Whitney, who appears to be enjoying the put-down most out of the four of them.

Jared Farmer's wife is still staring at the note, the only one who hasn't schooled her features.

It makes sense. She's not used to the cameras yet.

Though, if the women are aligned on one thing, it's that nobody wants this going to the press. Even false rumors getting percolated through gossip rags could harm families, hurt relationships.

After focusing on the new girl, Hillary remembers reading about Jared recently. An article detailed his rise in the league and his childhood in Kansas. He had attributed much of his success to his wife, Sarah, whom he'd started dating in high school.

Hillary thinks this was short-sighted of him. Jared had clearly been talented early on, and waiting to choose a wife until after he became a professional would have increased his marital options. He was now handsome, successful, wealthy, and famous.

No wonder Sarah is worried.

Cassandra is looking at her, and she decides to move on from the squabble.

"Steven is doing fine," Hillary says, her smile just as lethal as the other women's. "I'm going to find that volunteer and figure out who left these." She waves the note over her shoulder and walks straight through the group.

Hillary knows not to look back as she walks away. That kind of insecurity is unforgivable.

Before she approaches the press tent's entrance, she glances again at the note. It's written by someone who declares they know her, but that can't be true. Other details give that away—talk of happy lives, comfort, families. Whoever this person is, they know her peripherally at best.

Hillary can't relax in the comfort of understanding Steven wouldn't cheat on her. This note has wider implications for her than that.

Her eyes scan the tent, and just beyond its borders through the open flaps. She can find no sign of the man who delivered the notes anywhere. She knew him as a regular volunteer on tour who often works with the golfers for private events as well. It shouldn't be hard to find him.

"Excuse me," she asks one of the teenage volunteers, a new one this time. He straightens at her attention, ready to deliver on whatever she might ask. "I'm looking for a man I just spoke to a few minutes ago. He had a shirt just like yours, a thick mustache, salt and pepper hair," she continues. "Does he sound familiar, and do you know where I could find him?"

The kid furrows his brow, taking the task seriously. This irritates

Hillary; if he knew who she was asking about, it shouldn't take this much work.

"I'm sorry ma'am," he says. "Everyone on my team is pretty young. And it's a golf tournament, you see. Guys with salt and pepper hair are all over the place."

She thanks him with a tight smile and moves through the exit of the tent. Hillary knows the kid is right, but with nowhere else to store her annoyance, she places it firmly on his shoulders.

One last time, she searches the crowd, trying to find the man who gave them the notes. Hillary sees a multitude of men fitting the description, but not the volunteer.

6

SARAH

"Is this some kind of sick joke?"

Sarah hopes it is. She hasn't even considered an affair to add to her other insecurities. She and Jared travel together, after all. When would he have had the time or opportunity to be unfaithful?

She doesn't bother looking at Whitney, or the other women. Seeing them would only make her feel worse about herself, so she focuses on the note.

This does not help.

Sarah wishes she had Cassandra's confidence, but she's gone numb. All the other things that worried her this morning seem insignificant now. This is a nightmare she hadn't even considered.

She glances at the other women. Why Whitney? Even if it's true, giving the note to her seems unnecessarily cruel, like grounding your heel into someone's already broken bone. Her husband is gone—just let the assumptive affair die with him.

Cassandra appears confident, barely sparing a second glance at the note she's now placing in her purse. Hillary seemed nervous, but that can't be right. They all look to be operating under the assumption that the note isn't a serious threat, or if it is, it means something other than what it says.

Perhaps they're just better at feigning confidence than she is.

Once Hillary has left the group, Sarah looks up at the other two women. Whitney and Cassandra share a tense look. As if exchanging information without speaking, though she didn't know they were friends.

"Well," Whitney breaks first, "I'll get going. I can only move forward, so this changes nothing for me."

As she leaves, a weight goes with her. Sarah didn't understand the extra intensity of the moment, but she sees it now as Whitney walks. Her grief falls off her like a chemical weapon. No one is unaffected by the sadness the widow brings everywhere with her.

"Come on," Cassandra pulls her hand. "Let's get outside to the practice greens."

"Shouldn't we, you know, do something about this?" Sarah doesn't know what that would be, but ignoring the note seems unwise. Volunteers, media personalities, and behind-the-camera types move out of the way for Cassandra as if they don't even know they're doing it. She keeps to her path, unobtrusive but unbending.

The other woman is already leading her outside, the oppressive heat unchanged from earlier. "No. Focus on what you can control," Cassandra replies, sounding like Sarah's high school counselor when she failed an exam. "Jared is competing, and you have no proof that anything in that note is real. What were your plans for today before you read it?"

That seems like years ago now. "I was just going to walk with his group," Sarah says.

"Then that's what you'll do," Cassandra replies.

Sarah knows she needs to get it together. Jared's tee time is approaching, and she can't be on the verge of losing it with so many eyes on her. Though she thinks she could probably pass off her anxiety as game day nerves if asked.

She looks back at Cassandra. "What are you going to do?"

"The same as you," she smiles.

"Mrs. Bell," a voice calls from behind them in the tent. "Do you have a couple minutes to talk about Andy with CBS Sports?"

Cassandra answers the man in the affirmative with a confident smile that hides the nature of their conversation, then turns back to Sarah. "But first I need to handle the press." She gives Sarah's arm a squeeze and turns, inviting no further discussion on the matter. The other woman embracing the short interview also gives Sarah a chance to dart out of the tent, avoiding any press who might corner her for information on Jared.

She doesn't want scrutiny right now.

Admitting that the other woman's refusal to be perturbed is helpful, Sarah doesn't feel as off balance as she had when she received the note, now safely tucked into her backpack. Cassandra's initial reaction had been to laugh it off, at least outwardly, while Sarah's first instinct had been to call her mother. This was a bad sign.

Sarah doesn't go to her mother for marriage advice. A sharp woman with an academic disposition, she was lovely to look at but harsh. Sarah would approach her mother for help with homework or advice on extracurriculars growing up. Petitions for affection or love she brought to her father.

No longer married to each other, her parents had split years ago. Her father has a second wife now, while her mother elected to remain on her own. As a result, any relationship advice coming from her was shaded with distrust and bitterness.

"You can't marry your first boyfriend. Don't you want to see the world?"

"Why aren't you going away to college? Jared will be here when you get back, or he won't. Then you'll know for sure."

"You should keep separate bank accounts, just to be safe."

"Don't you want to date around? It's what young people are supposed to do."

"I cannot believe you're passing on a pre-nuptial, Sarah. I mean really, it's 2018 for Christ's sake."

Sarah had no idea what the current year being what it is had to do with her desire to not get divorced, but she typically took her mother's words with a half-smile and noncommittal response. Her mother's own marriage having failed meant that Sarah would try to do the opposite of her advice in most cases. There was no pre-nuptial agreement, they had one bank account, and they had refused to go their separate ways for college. As a result, she and Jared had been happy, or as happy as two young people with no money can be.

Well, she thought they had been.

The note this morning was a crack in that happiness for Sarah. She didn't think Jared was capable of cheating on her, but she was rattled at her own response. She knows what she'll hear from her mother if she brings this up: a big, fat "I told you so."

Good thing she doesn't have her cell phone. Desert Invitational had protected her from the potentially disastrous impulse to ask her mother's advice.

Determined to be strong like Cassandra, Sarah makes her way to the first tee, where Jared is standing back with his caddie. With the spectator risers and media presence, she can't get too close, so she moves down the crowded pathway a few dozen yards. From here, she can watch his first shot then make her way quickly to his second.

With nothing left to do but walk, Sarah allows her mind to consider the note in as detached a manner as she can. Who writes something like that? Having taken measures to calm herself, her reaction feels a bit silly now. She shouldn't have jumped to conclusions about her husband so quickly.

She looks at him now, tries to see him as others might. In high school, he'd been small for his age, leaving golf as one of his few options for competing in sports, though he grew taller by junior year. Even then, Jared had been lanky, and his charm had come primarily from his ability to make Sarah laugh. She adored him, but in the back of her mind, she had always seen her affection for him as a gift when they were young. There were other boys in Ottawa who would have liked her, and she'd chosen him.

The announcer on the first tee calls Jared's name and Sarah watches as his caddie hands him the driver. Jared has scored birdie and par on this hole his first two rounds, respectively. He approaches the tee with confidence, his shoulders back, his mouth a firm line.

He's different now, she admits. He isn't the lanky high schooler anymore. On his quest to compete professionally in his chosen sport, Jared has filled out, gaining a significant amount of lean muscle mass. He's more serious but still quick to smile. His determination has made a man out of him in ways she doesn't understand, sculpting himself into something handsome and formidable.

Sarah sees his practice swing, then his stance over the ball. The spectators are silent on hole one, the only noises a distant crunching of steps and a cheer coming from somewhere on the back nine.

Jared draws his club back, pausing at the top, and whips his swing through the ball towards the fairway.

She isn't surprised at all to see it land center-left, bouncing exactly where he told Sarah he wanted to place it for his approach to the green. Her husband waves graciously at the crowd and she joins in the soft cheering and clapping until she's distracted by something shrill.

Across the fairway, a group of what looks to be college girls is screaming Jared's name mixed with declarations of love for him as they jump around. His attention is pulled there just as Sarah's is, and she fights anger and jealousy when he gives them a courteous wave and a wide smile.

Jared's smile is full, carefree, framed by dimples on both sides. It's a smile Sarah is belatedly realizing she must share with the rest of the world now.

His caddie is already pulling him back into the game, notebook out as they walk down the fairway. As they discuss which club to hit next, Sarah watches the girls ogle her husband.

The smile, the blond hair, his body, his fame. Of course, Jared has options other than Sarah if he wants them.

What if he has already strayed? What if she is too late in her realization?

Nothing to be done about that right now. If Sarah wants to protect her marriage, she needs to start playing offense. In her mind, it's imperative that she transform herself into a Cassandra or Whitney. There cannot be a single hair out of place if her competition is, well, all women.

She suddenly regrets ridding herself of the shapewear earlier.

As she walks along the fairway, she tries to catch Jared's eye and is unsuccessful. Sarah ignores the pain, the small crack in her heart at the possibility she's too late and resolves to fix what she can.

First, she needs to find out who wrote that note. Whether it's a woman who has already stolen her husband's affections, or someone simply trying to, she needs to eliminate that threat. How? She doesn't know. Sarah has never understood female diplomacy or dirty tricks. The way girls talk to each other without saying anything always went over her head, but she is determined to learn those games as soon as possible. Whoever wrote the note is going to have to deal with a new and improved Sarah.

Second, and she is less sure of this decision, she concludes that she should not share the note with Jared. Sarah wouldn't tell him about it during the round even if she could, but keeping the note from him through the end of the tournament feels like the right call. This is a nightmare, but it's one she can handle herself. She doesn't want Jared distracted during the final round with worry for her.

Or guilt over his own actions.

No, this is a secret Sarah is going to keep from her husband. Just this one time.

~

Interview with Jared Farmer for *Golf Now Magazine*
Published May 31, 2022

Jared Farmer is quickly becoming one of the most recognizable names in professional golf. For the casual observer, he may appear to be an overnight success, having won his first title within the last nine months. However, Farmer disputes that description.

Jared: Overnight success? My mom would certainly argue against that, with all the dinners I accidentally missed for a late practice in high school. <Laughs>

Golf Now: So, would you say that's when you started taking golf seriously, as a teenager?

Jared: There's never been a time when I didn't take it seriously if I'm being honest. Did I always think I would play professionally? Probably not. But ever since I could understand the game, I've worked towards mastering it.

Golf Now: Does one ever master golf?

Jared: Of course not <laughing> where would be the fun in that? Let me put it this way: I can't think of a single time I stood over a putt and was content to miss it or just get it close. Since I've started playing, the only good putts are the ones that go in.

Golf Now: Well said. I don't think I've heard it explained that way before.

Jared: Maybe not, but everyone competitive in the league has that same attitude.

Golf Now: Speaking of competitive, Desert Invitational will be your first opportunity to play against some of the bigger names that moved to the new league. Who do you see as your biggest competitor this weekend?

Jared: Everyone and no one, I guess. I don't like to underestimate the other guys; I always try to assume that the man next to me on the first tee is going to be at least as strong as I am, have practiced longer hours than I did. That mindset really drives me in the weeks leading up to the competition, with my preparation. Day of, though, there's no competitor besides myself. If I'm confident in the work I've been doing, I try and shut everything out when it comes to the tournament. As far as the new league goes, they've got strong contenders. It would be foolish to write them off.

Golf Now: Are there any players that you hope to get paired with, or that you idolized growing up?

Jared: Absolutely. I feel immense gratitude for all the men who came before me and playing alongside any of them would be an honor.

Golf Now: Unfortunately, we'll be missing one of those men this year. As you know, we are coming up on the one-year anniversary of Rowan Silver's death. Was he one of the men you admired?

Jared: Well, sure, but not specifically.

Golf Now: Really?

Jared: I guess. Look, obviously what happened was a tragedy. I wish he was still here, and I can't imagine what his family went through. But I do think his career is being misremembered to an extent. He was a strong golfer, but not really Hall of Fame material and I believe that his untimely passing has made everyone look back on his record with rose colored glasses.

Golf Now: That's an unusual take.

Jared: <Laughs> I'm an unusual guy.

Golf Now: Let's move on then. There were some rumors a few months ago about talks between you and the new league.

Jared: Is that a question?

Golf Now: Were the rumors true?

Jared: Not in any serious way. Obviously, I brought it to my wife, Sarah.

The money would have set us up for a while, but she told me to do what I needed to do, and I knew that for now it's best for me to stay with the PGA.

Golf Now: Not every wife would be comfortable passing up that kind of money.

Jared: Good thing I didn't marry every wife, I married Sarah. She trusts me.

7

CASSANDRA

"Mrs. Bell, this is Andy's fifteenth Desert Invitational. How confident is he that he can pull off a win at this advanced stage in his career?"

Advanced? It's golf. Men win tournaments into their fifties.

Outwardly, she smiles graciously with a full set of teeth. "Extremely confident. He's near the top of the leaderboard and I've never seen him in better shape. Andy's very dialed in this weekend and I fully expect him to play some of his best golf yet."

The reporter she's talking to right now is just taking notes, but the tent itself is outfitted with several dozen cameras belonging to any number of news organizations. Instinctively, she flexes her neck muscles while she speaks, so none of them accidentally film an unflattering angle of her profile.

"Do you lend any credence to the theory that since joining the new league, he's out of practice with true competition?"

Cassandra freezes briefly, not because she can't answer, but because she's momentarily confused by both the audacity and stupidity of the question.

"Of course not," she quickly recovers. "As I mentioned before, he's among the leaders today. In fact, if he scores even with what he's done the first two days, Andy is on track to have one of the lowest ranking scores in tournament history. I believe your channel covered that this morning."

The reporter at least has the decency to look embarrassed. "Thank you, Mrs. Bell," he says, putting his notepad away, indicating the end of his questions.

She accepts his thanks and moves to exit the tent. As she walks, her smile never moves, and her shoulders never slump. She almost caves into the sigh she is tempted to release when a wave of hot, dry, desert air hits her face. This weather is harsh enough to ruin anyone's mood, and Cassandra doesn't have much patience left for politics.

Checking her watch, she sees she has enough time to leave the grounds for a phone call before her husband tees off.

Andy is in the last group, making it slightly easier for Cassandra to blend in with the crowds than usual. His group has the most spectators, but the same two wives following, so her chances of having to engage in an unpleasant conversation are limited.

Things are different for them since Andy left the PGA.

Sure, mostly it's much better. Financially, they are set up for life, having invested most of his signing bonus for joining the new league, and his regular income is an allowance that would change the lives of most middle-class families. She will never have to work and each of their three kids has their own 529 college investment fund. And the vacation properties don't exactly hurt Cassandra's feelings either. Her husband is nothing if not an excellent provider.

Not to mention the fact that he is a perfect partner to her, and a flawless father to their children. The new league demands far less of his time and a reduced amount of travel compared to the PGA. Andy has never been more available to their family, and the Bell household flourishes under these changes. Grades are up for each kid, they are enrolled in soccer, and family dinners are a regular staple. All these improvements, and Andy still has energy and affection for Cassandra at the end of the day when it's just the two of them.

"Hi, Patricia," Cassandra says to one of the other wives walking past her on the cart path. Her husband isn't on this hole, so she must be returning to the clubhouse for some reason.

The other woman nods slightly, but doesn't slow down to speak, doesn't smile. "Cassandra," is all she says before hurrying along, almost as if embarrassed to be seen having even that small interaction.

The fact that Cassandra expected the snub doesn't make it hurt less.

This is the price she pays for Andy leaving the PGA, though he no doubt pays a higher price socially among the men. In her opinion, men who golf have some of the most womanish, gossipy and catty behaviors she's ever seen—her own husband not included, of course. The divided tours split the players now, like the boy versus girl sides of the room at a middle school dance. Andy doesn't bring his troubles home to Cassandra. She thinks he had a hard time with the practice round pairings, though he'd never admit it to her.

"Don't worry about me," he whispered before they fell asleep the other night. "I have everything I need and more."

"Me too," she replied.

No, a snub is what she can expect these days. Some of the wives have more tact than others, but it was an intense and resounding message to receive right after Andy signed his contract.

You're no longer one of us.

In moments of clarity and self-awareness, Cassandra understands that this was just the excuse the other women needed to finally hate her out in the open. She knows she won the marriage Olympics by snagging Andy, and that her appearance and upbringing lent her privilege not many can access. Her past popularity among other PGA wives like Patricia was little more than them keeping a rival close, learning her secrets, trying to get a piece of her. Their unmasked animosity is honestly a relief to Cassandra.

Maybe that is why she went out of her way to be nice to the Farmer girl. Sarah was young, not yet polluted by golf politics. She'd seemed so inno-cent. It was clear, based on Sarah's apparent instinct to run away from cameras and, even in some of Jared's recent interviews, that neither of them was getting any kind of PR training or advice. She would need an ally, probably one less ostracized than Cassandra, but that's what Sarah had right now.

It's apparent that the poor girl is trying to be everything at once: the bombshell, the supportive wife, the semi-public figure. It had been gut instinct to reach out to her in the restroom, offer what little help she could, even if Cassandra's help was tainted these days. Sarah couldn't have known that the "correct" thing to do would be to completely rebuff her and befriend someone else. Hillary Torre may be less of a social pariah than she is these days. And it really, really doesn't matter to her, the games these women play. Andy and her children are all she truly needs to be happy, after all.

Still, it would be nice to have a friend.

Cassandra can't eliminate the possibility that she was included with the other women this morning in the press tent because of her husband's new loyalties. She hadn't lied when she said she was confident he wasn't cheating on her. Entertaining the idea would be a waste of her energy.

It didn't need to be true to damage her family, though. There are plenty of old photos from Andy's party days. Having those resurface, passed off as new, could be devastating, especially since her children would be old enough to understand what was happening.

No, if the note was telling the truth, it was for one of the other three women. Whoever sent it could have just delivered it to the one intended wife, but Cassandra thinks that the uncertainty is part of the torture.

That, and all the women could have been the catalyst for inspiring revenge from a stranger. Cassandra's loyalty to Andy amidst his decision to leave the PGA and her subsequent support for the new league has earned her more than a few fresh enemies. It's her current best guess that she was delivered the note this morning with the other wives to punish her for those transgressions. What better way to sabotage the new league's reputation than by manipulating Cassandra into distracting her husband?

It's a flimsy hypothesis at best, but it's all she has as she shoulders her bag again and follows Andy to the second tee box. While he lines up his next shot, Cassandra thinks that figuring out why Hillary, Sarah, and Whitney received notes might be the key to finding who wrote it.

8

BARTENDER #3

I use my sleeve to stop sweat from dripping into my eyes as I wipe the counter between customers. The air conditioning is on full blast, but it doesn't seem to be helping, especially with how much we move behind the bar. If I don't clean now, it won't get done before the next wave of people come in to sit.

This year, I got promoted to the clubhouse, a vast improvement on my position last year as one of the tent bartenders, both in terms of working conditions and the tips I receive.

Well, it depends on who's tipping, but mostly they're better.

Player's wives and those with the money for a Presidential Pass to the Desert Invitational filter in and out, mingling amidst the tables and chairs of the clubhouse. It's familiar territory for me, even if the crowds take getting used to. I'm regular staff at the country club here, but every year for the tournament our smaller operation gets infiltrated with professional golf corporate types as well as completely untrained volunteers who want a free day pass to watch the men play.

Luckily, in the clubhouse I only have to deal with one outsider, though he is technically our supervisor.

Bryce, my teenage barback, comes through the side door with fresh ice just as I see the man in question burst through the double doors of the clubhouse.

I snatch the bucket from him. "Thanks! Can you take the trash around back?"

"Is it full already? I just took it out, like, an hour ago."

With a tight smile, I dip my head backward toward the dining room. "Greg is coming."

"Oh, shoot," Bryce hurriedly pulls the pathetically empty black contractor bag out of our main trash can and shoves through the side door. "I owe you one," he whispers before making himself scarce.

As I pour the ice on top of a chest with all the bottled beer, Greg approaches the counter and begins drumming his fingers impatiently, as if I'm supposed to read his mind and know exactly what he wants.

He finally clears his throat.

"Did you need something, Greg?"

He stops drumming long enough to cross his arms. "Where's Bryce?"

"He got pulled away to help out with one of the tents. I said it was ok, since we've got a small lull between breakfast and lunch here."

Greg glares at me, as if the standard American dining schedule is my fault. "How are sales?"

"Between nine and ten this morning was our most profitable hour all week," I reply. It's true, but I know he is just testing me to find something to be angry about. Unfortunately, he'll be even more pissed that I didn't offer that reason up to him on a silver platter.

Maybe I should have played along, let him verbally rip into me like he wants. Yet I can't bury the small part of me that is satisfied with winning this interaction, even if it costs me later.

The lecture never comes, though. Greg sees someone or something that distracts him, so his only retort is thrown at me over his shoulder as he leaves. "You're on thin ice, Andrea."

I roll my eyes at his back. My name isn't even Andrea, but I've never corrected him. He uses a different name every time anyway.

Once the ice is evenly covering the beers, I replace the trash bag and wash my hands. Hopefully Bryce will come back soon. I'll actually need his help when people start filtering in for lunch.

While drying my hands, a flurry of brunette hair sits at the bar stool in front of me. Without seeing her face, I know it's one of the player's wives or a groupie. True fans of the game who are women would wear a hat or a ponytail in this kind of heat. Most will have a bare face, or the white, goopy remnants of a strong SPF. They'll have mini water sprayers and portable fans in neon colors attached to lanyards around their necks. Only someone protecting her territory or on the prowl dresses for the male gaze around here.

I look up and see that I'm right. "What can I get you?"

Steven Torre's wife sits in front of me. I frown, trying to calculate where her husband is on the course. He's already teed off, but I don't think it's been long enough for him to have made the turn yet. Maybe he's stuck behind a slow player on a hole near the clubhouse and she has time to stop in for a drink.

Hillary Torre doesn't look up from her phone long enough to address me directly. "Grey Goose martini."

"Dirty?"

"Sure. No olives, though," she replies while scrolling.

That was another change from serving in the tent. The drinks ordered by those who have access to the clubhouse are pricier, and as a pleasant result, my tips are usually larger. Last year I was slinging aluminum bottles of Coors Light and Michelob Ultra for pennies. This year I craft cocktails for women who wear a full face of make-up in the New Mexico summer sun.

I pull a chilled martini glass from the freezer and strain Mrs. Torre's drink in front of her while she passes me her credit card. "Glassware needs to stay in the clubhouse, by the way."

"I know. This isn't my first day here."

She doesn't say it with any vitriol, and I don't respond. I know she's been here this week, I'm just required to say it to all customers who get a drink served in glass.

People tend to forget rules after drink number three, but before drink number five.

When I slide her card back to her with a pen and her receipt, I see she's already finished the martini. "Would you like another one?"

She signs in a hurry. "Nope. I need to get going." Without a single look in my direction, she struts out the door back to the tournament.

After rinsing her glass and putting it in the small dishwasher, I look at the receipt and curse.

She stiffed me for a tip.

9

HILLARY

Hillary is not unaware of her public reputation. She's seen as a conniving gold digger, a woman who hunted down a successful man with an appearance that doesn't quite match hers. This is okay with her, since it makes her look smart and scheming. She likes the idea that the world sees her as a sexy mastermind, a puppeteer and the people around her marionettes.

The truth is, she had no idea who Steven was when she met him.

To be clear, she was husband hunting. At twenty-one, she ran away from Gwen, changing her number, deleting social media, and living frugally with three roommates in a house outside of Scottsdale. She relished being her own person for the first time, away from the shadow of her half-sister. She was finally free.

Hillary did learn very quickly that freedom still came with bills, and she was self-aware enough to understand her own strengths and weaknesses. She would never become a genius entrepreneur or save the world by curing cancer, but she knew she was pretty. And the men of the world who do start businesses and cure cancer happen to like pretty girls.

Where does a woman find men like these? Some single ladies will overthink it, trying to find tickets to charity galas, or infiltrating wealthy groups, or even trying to find employment in proximity to a specific gentleman, but

Hillary's plan was far less complicated. It was so simple most women gloss over it.

In her mind, she wanted a husband who could afford to wear expensive suits most of the time. So, she took a job as a sales associate in a store for extremely high-end menswear. By simply going to work every day, she was meeting dozens of men who fit what she was looking for.

She rejected some obvious duds—married men traveling for work who tried to leave her a hotel room key, men so unattractive she couldn't stomach touching them even for their money and protection—but about twice a week, she would be asked out for drinks or coffee by a respectable man buying pricey clothes like they were just a part of the budget.

One day, Steven Torre came in looking for a blazer.

"I just need something off the rack that fits," he explained. "It's last minute and doesn't have to be the nicest thing you have."

He was built like most men, though on the taller side, so Hillary thought they could accommodate him. "I'll just pull everything in your size," she said as she got his measurements.

Most men didn't talk at all or filled the silence with an explanation for why they were shopping, but Steven was different.

"Are you from here?" he asked over his shoulder.

"Stop moving," she scolded through a smile. Steven obediently turned back to the mirror and waited for her answer.

"I'm from the Southwest, but not Scottsdale."

"How mysterious. I assume you like the heat then, if you stayed?"

Arizona had been the farthest Greyhound ticket she could afford when she ran away from Gwen. "It's alright. I'd like to travel someday, see real snow."

"You've never seen snow?"

"Never."

Hillary finalized the measurements and pulled the three blazers they had stocked in Steven's size. The first two, one a classic navy and the other a respectable charcoal grey, were the ones she assumed he would choose. The third had been in stock for years, an online order that had been returned to store. It was a horrendous red plaid, something that they never would have stocked but had been stuck with in their inventory.

After she slid his arms into the first two options, he shrugged off the second and handed it back to her. "Either of these would work, but is that all?"

She winced, "There's actually one more."

When she pulled the last blazer, Steven's expression turned gleeful, and he hurriedly threw it on. As he stood before the three-paneled mirror, he smiled at her along with his reflection. "Well? What do you think?"

Flattery might win her a sale, but something told Hillary that wouldn't work on him. "You look like Santa Clause about to meet with his board of directors." The harsh red plaid hurt to look at.

After a full-throated laugh, he stepped off the platform and walked to the register. "Then it's perfect."

The price of the unsellable blazer had been reduced so significantly that Steven was able to pay cash for it. "Clearance items are final sale, is that ok?"

He grinned at her as he shrugged it on, electing to wear it out of the store. "What if I come back tomorrow morning wanting to return it?"

"I won't be able to help you with that, I'm sorry."

"What if I come back tomorrow wanting to take you on a date?"

She almost said no, missing the real question. "Oh, I actually don't work tomorrow."

"Even better," he said and wrote his number on the back of his receipt.

The rest of the afternoon passed quickly, and once Hillary texted him to exchange contact information, she set about getting ready to call it a night. A pack of ramen for dinner, followed by a glass of boxed wine on the couch watching whatever local channels they got at the house. None of the girls, Hillary included, wanted to shell out for expensive streaming services, so they stuck to the lower channel network affiliates.

She was painting her nails for her potential date tomorrow with E! News running in the background. It wasn't awards season, but some kind of children's hospital charity event was being covered by a young reporter when a familiar clash of colors moved across the screen.

"Your blazer is brighter red than this carpet! What was the strategy behind this fashion choice?"

Steven appeared to be a natural at interacting with media. "A pretty girl sold it to me," he explained with a wink for the camera.

A few questions into the brief interview, and Hillary gathered that he was a professional golfer. Why hadn't he said anything? If she'd known this would be public, she would have talked him out of the ugly holiday garb.

The interviewer was wrapping up. "Now that you're headed into the off season, what are your plans for relaxing?"

"I was thinking about visiting Jackson Hole and spending Christmas in the snow."

Hillary shakes herself out of the memory as a bead of sweat trickles down the back of her neck. She's made the trek to Steven's tee time and will follow him the rest of the day, though she doesn't see why she should bother. She could be enjoying another martini inside, watching his highlights on the television screen instead. Licking the remainder of the brine from her lips, she soldiers on, trying to recall her first tournaments with Steven, when she enjoyed herself more.

It wasn't always like this, was it?

10

WHITNEY

It's too hot for black, but Whitney has worn little else this past year. It wasn't really on purpose; her wardrobe has always been structured more or less around neutral tones. Too many bright colors tended to clash with her bright red hair. She'd always been told it would darken as she aged, but at almost thirty it was still the same strong red, so she hasn't changed her style much over the years.

The fact that she is a widow in mourning is purely coincidence.

Whitney looks around her at the spectators and volunteers. Staying out of the line of sight of the players, she still had trouble remaining in the moment. She hasn't been to a tournament since Rowan's death and it's far too easy to let herself forget he's gone now that she's surrounded with imagery of how her life used to look. At Desert Invitational any other year, her husband would be somewhere on the leader board.

Every time she must remind herself that he's gone, she feels that sharp pain in her diaphragm, as if her chest is constricting around an empty cavity. It's too hard, so she needs to remember why she's here.

A few familiar wives wave at her as they pass, and she gives a tight smile in return, grateful her sunglasses can hide the rest of her face. She turns to walk on the cart path with no destination in mind. A not insignificant part of her regrets attending at all but arriving for only the award tonight when she had been invited to view the tournament would have seemed unappreciative.

There had to be a way she could keep busy in the meantime.

Whitney didn't even have the benefit of allowing the note from this morning to distract her. Cassandra, Hillary, and Sarah had all behaved predictably. Whitney found herself most surprised at her instinctual reaction to Sarah's worry. Her response had been the most natural one—fear, anxiety, feeling foolish—yet Whitney was angered by it. She should have found Cassandra's confidence irritating, or Hillary's coldness too calculating. But it was Sarah she wanted to slap across the face.

Do you have any idea what I would give to worry about my husband cheating on me now that he's gone?

It seemed a luxury, to believe one had lost their husband to another hole for his dick instead of a grave. Whitney is almost nostalgic for the days she would check Rowan's phone when he was in the shower or track his location when he was out. He hadn't been a perfect husband, but he'd been hers for too short a time. He didn't travel often for tournaments without her; she'd left the Cowboys when they married and they'd never had children, so she was always available to him on tournament weekends.

Still, being married to a high demand professional athlete was a full-time job. With him gone, she had almost too much time. She didn't even need to manage any press like she used to. Death had a way of making even the greediest tabloids and news organizations unwilling to print unflattering portrayals of Rowan. At the one-year anniversary of his death, she wonders how long this media honeymoon will continue for his memory.

This adds a small concern for her about the note she received with Cassandra, Hillary, and Sarah. Could information be released about her late husband, or about her, that would lose her the goodwill of golf fans?

Whitney had perhaps given Rowan a slightly longer leash than the average married man. She didn't mind his occasional wandering eye, an innocent dalliance. He never embarrassed her publicly and they truly loved each other for the duration of their marriage. But she was always fully aware of and prepared for the true threats. She knew how to protect her marriage from destruction in almost every way it could come for her.

But even a woman as crafty as Whitney had no way of out-smarting death.

"Mrs. Silver?"

She looks up at the speaker, a volunteer. She needs to stop getting lost in her own head; it doesn't do any good to be unaware of her surroundings, she thinks. "Yes?"

"I've been sent to see if you need anything," says the kid. Ah. They must have assigned her some kind of visitor status that came with extra attention. "Can I grab you a drink or a lunch? Maybe a folding chair?"

He was so earnest she almost smiled. "No, thank you," she replies. "I believe I may return to my hotel soon and rest up for this evening. Could you organize a shuttle to take me back?"

"Sure thing, ma'am," and he's off before she can thank him. She follows behind him, so as not to lose her transportation. Whitney wasn't lying when she said she needed to rest. She'll be expected to say something tonight, not a lengthy speech or address, but at least an acknowledgement of the award and something sad but dignified about her dead husband. Even thinking about it is exhausting to her.

As she moves toward the exit, she stays focused on her surroundings: the crowds, the cheering, the collective gasp at a missed putt witnessed a few holes away. She lets herself embrace the atmosphere without pretending Rowan is still here, surprised to find that she missed it a little. Maybe she misses not only her husband, but also the glamor of being a golf wife.

The volunteer waves her over to one of the stations and explains that a car is waiting for her outside. There's a small perk to being a VIP, then. She doesn't have to share a bus back to the hotel with a bunch of sweaty drunk strangers.

This is a small consolation to her as she ducks into the back seat, immediately blasted with air conditioning. After pulling her seatbelt into place, Whitney directs her gaze out the window, ignoring the driver's question about the weather.

She hadn't anticipated having so many eyes on her during the actual tournament. No longer a player's wife, she'd assumed she'd get less attention than she had in years past, not more.

Whitney will have to find an inconspicuous way to keep prying eyes off her this weekend.

11

SARAH

When Sarah agreed to get snow cones with the lanky Jared Farmer one summer afternoon at age sixteen, she would have had no way of knowing that she was signing up to be the future wife of a professional athlete. In truth, she hadn't even known she was agreeing to a date. They were supposed to meet a group of friends at the Snow Shack in Ottawa, but when Sarah showed up, only Jared was there.

"Yeah, that's like, super weird," had been Jared's only explanation for why six other teenagers had simultaneously cancelled on them.

Seven years later, she wouldn't change a thing. Her husband, it turns out, was a safe bet when he was passionate about something. His success on the tour wasn't overnight, but he's now a top contender for the Desert Invitational.

His first five holes were pars, played almost textbook, but Sarah knows he wants something better. On the sixth hole, Jared holes out a chip, bringing him into a tie for the lead with Andy Bell. Sarah cheers, caught up in the energy of the crowd. He is playing almost well enough to distract her from this morning.

Almost.

Sarah follows the small crowd dedicated to her husband's tee time and ignores how many seemingly unattached women are in it. When he's actively over the ball, she has no problem focusing on supporting him. Jared is incredible to watch, a true prodigy of the game. She always believed in him, but she thinks now that he might have an actual shot at winning Desert Invitational.

"If we cut to fourteen after the turn, we can watch Carl Sheffield and Steven Torre complete their rounds, then have plenty of time to double back and watch the leaders finish," a man says to his middle school aged son, pointing to a map of the course.

"So, I'll be able to watch Garcia, Bell, and Farmer too?"

"Yep," his dad replies. "Plus, we're here tomorrow, but if you want autographs, I'd fight for them today."

"Why today?"

"After they finish tomorrow, they'll be tired and distracted, wanting to either celebrate or go home. Most of them will still sign for fans, but we don't want to risk missing out on one of your favorites."

"I don't want to miss out on Jared or Andy!"

"I'll make sure you don't," the dad says, patting his son's shoulder.

"Cool. Can I have a hot dog?"

Sarah can't help but smile at the innocence of the interaction. If she had shown any interest in golf prior to dating Jared, her father probably would have loved to take her to an event like this.

Unfortunately, there's too much downtime in between his shots. Sarah has too much room for her mind to spiral. She's successfully set aside the immediate problem of the note, having chosen not to show him. Instead, she finds herself locked in recent memories, memories now shaded with the sharpness of hindsight and regret.

Nothing catastrophic. Sarah is a good wife. She just wonders if there's something she missed, and now all her recollections are being filtered through a paranoid lens.

Only two weeks ago, she had been washing the dishes after dinner. This is another reverse marital trick she learned from her mother, who couldn't clean her way out of a sterile padded room and never kept up with any homemaking. Sarah made sure their home was a place Jared could rest after his long days on the course. He appreciates it, she thinks, though he doesn't say much about it either way.

On this particular night, she was scrubbing away, maybe halfway done with her hands deep in the soapy water. She didn't hear much over the dishes clanging, so when Jared wrapped his arms around her middle she yelped, making him chuckle.

"These will still be here tomorrow," he'd said over her shoulder towards the sink. "Come lay with me for a little while."

Over her dead body was she going to leave dishes for the morning. "I'll only be fifteen more minutes, baby."

He ignored this, leaning his head into her neck from behind. "Please? I just want to hold you."

"Jared…"

"I'll do the dishes later," he insisted. "Just come lay with me. I need to spend some time with you."

"Baby, I said fifteen minutes." Sarah hadn't meant for it to sound so firm, but she was going to get that kitchen clean.

He'd sighed and dropped his arms, not saying anything else. Sarah went to work, making sure the kitchen was spotless, every spoon in its correct spot.

What she thought would take fifteen minutes took closer to thirty thanks to a particularly stubborn and corroded pan and a counter that needed to be wiped three times. Sarah dried off her hands. She was proud of her work. Looking around, she didn't see Jared in the kitchen, or the living room. As she opened her mouth to call his name, she saw a note, scribbled in his handwriting.

Went for a walk.

Sarah walks along, wishing she'd lain with Jared instead of doing the dishes that night.

Post Round Panel Interview with Alex Garcia
July 13, 2022

CBS: What's the atmosphere like this weekend, with the new league players finally competing against PGA members again?

Garcia: I don't feel a difference, to be honest. I show up to win every tournament I play. That doesn't change with location or league membership. Once we tee off, we all have to play the same eighteen holes. That being said, the PGA guys seem more on edge than usual.

CBS: Why do you say that?

Garcia: Now that they're having to face off directly against us again, I think they realized they oversold their value. With a near monopoly on media representation, they can set the narrative without any of us new league guys being able to defend ourselves. They've been talking a lot of <EXPLETIVE> since the new league started poaching the most talented guys.

FOX Sports: Do you think that assessment is accurate?

Garcia: What do you mean?

FOX Sports: The idea that the new league has the strongest players. General consensus among most fans would indicate that most of the younger, up and coming talent stayed with the PGA.

Garcia: Frankly, that's moronic. Anyone watching this weekend can see that's not true.

NBC: Twelve out of the top fifteen on the leader board this weekend are PGA members.

Garcia: Oh, yeah? Well, check their net worth and get back to me. Does anyone have a real question?

12

SARAH

By hole nine, Jared has maintained his progress. There's a three-person tie for the lead between him, Andy Bell, and Alex Garcia, another player who competes with the PGA. From what Sarah could gather on television from her brief reprieve in the clubhouse, the commentators had differing takes on what this would mean for professional golf. PGA loyalists had made their bones talking about how everyone who defected to the new tour was bound to perform poorly at the Desert Invitational. They had been giving very educated sounding excuses for why their claims were still correct, despite two thirds of the leaders proving them wrong.

Sarah obviously wants Jared to win, making her necessarily committed to the PGA's success. However, she always found the commentators' critiques of the new league to be elitist and out of touch. The old league had a lot of tradition and sway with golf fans, but it had failed in many ways to adapt for new generations and demographics, a more diverse viewership. It relied too heavily on the individual players to bring viewers in with their own brands without offering much support.

Luckily, Jared was naturally marketable, and his fan base had grown rapidly as he racked up wins this past year.

Another group of squealing women reminds Sarah that her husband might be too marketable.

"Looks like we have some congestion."

Sarah turns to the voice, recognizing it as Cassandra's. "What?"

"Congestion," she repeats, pointing towards Jared's group waiting on the tenth tee. "A traffic jam? One of the guys in front of Jared is a notoriously slow player, even when he isn't this high up on the leader board. Our guys will be waiting on each tee, probably for the rest of the day."

"Well, that sucks. Jared hates waiting on the tee. Says it throws off his rhythm for the day."

Cassandra smiles. "Andy is the same way. There is such a thing as thinking too much, and it usually reaps a poor harvest."

Her wording is odd, but Sarah understands. Jared is a "feel" player, as he likes to say, and any thoughts on swing mechanics during his round are to be avoided at all costs. Even his caddie had to be coached out of saying too much during competition, his role relegated to carrying the clubs, reading greens, and checking yardage. Jared can stand over the ball and visualize where he wants it. When he's focused, that's all he really needs to make it happen.

"I hope he gets to tee off soon," is all Sarah says back.

They make their way closer to the tenth tee, and she sees Jared throw his head back and laugh at something his caddie said. It might be one of her favorite things about him, how quick he is to smile, how accessible his happiness is. There was a time when she worried that his participation in something as grueling as a professional sport would dim that light in him. What if his drive to win made him too serious, turned him into a stuffy shell of himself?

Sarah's worries had been eradicated after his first tour win, when he'd insisted on watching one of the Shrek movies to celebrate.

It's one of Sarah's favorite memories, one she returns to often when they feel distant. Kind of like right now, when she has insecurities he can't alleviate and she can't even speak to him until he signs his scorecard. He's barely halfway done for the day, and she can only comfort herself with his laughter from afar.

Jared approaches the tee box, finally pulling on his glove. His caddie hands him the driver and he bends over at the waist to tee his ball. Volunteers outlining the cart path hold up signs telling the crowd to be quiet for the shot, and everyone respectfully obeys. According to the stats from the first two days, this is the second hardest hole on the course, the only one causing more trouble for the players this weekend being number eighteen. The driver is a bold choice here; Jared would have to carry both a fairway bunker and a small body of water. Most players trying to reach the par five green in two shots don't make it, and those playing it safe have elected to use a shorter club to lay up and have been the lower scorers for this Desert.

Jared does not like to play it safe.

His back swing arcs, perfectly on plane before his body turns into the ball making contact. Spectators, usually quick to cheer, remain hauntingly silent as they wait for the results. It looks good—really good—in the air but the crowd has no way of knowing if his gamble pays off until it lands.

A few breathless seconds later, Jared's tee shot hits softly on the fairway past the bunker and water, taking several bounces before rolling to a stop exactly where he wants it. Fans erupt into cheers, and Sarah's husband smiles and waves. As his eyes pass over the spectators, his gaze finally catches hers, and his smile grows when Sarah offers him an excited wave and a thumbs up.

Both are distracted from each other when two women on the other side of the tee shriek, "We love you, Jared!" Jared simply waves to the other group of spectators, not giving the women more attention than anyone else before returning his driver to his caddie. It's a small comfort to see his indifference towards them.

"Seriously," a woman's voice from behind Sarah says to someone else she can't see, "he's so hot."

Sarah tenses at this, she hopes imperceptibly. Cassandra's comforting hand on her shoulder let's her know she was unsuccessful.

"Ignore them," the woman instructs. "It's like I said, there is such a thing as thinking too much."

Excerpt from the *All Things Golf* Podcast with Drake Jones
Released on July 12, 2022

Britney: We are two days out from the start of the Desert Invitational and based on what I'm hearing about the practice rounds, I'm still confident about Farmer's chances here but I'd also like to add Henry Bolton and Alex Garcia as some of my favorites. Apparently, they're hot this week.

Drake: You coward.

Britney: What?

Drake: You don't get three favorites, that's not how betting works!

Britney: Wha—yes it does, like, all the time.

Drake: That's not how the *All Things Golf* bet was going to go and you know it.

Britney: Fine, what if I give you three favorites?

Drake: I don't need them! My three favorites are Andy Bell, Andy Bell, Andy Bell.

Britney: Well, that's just being stubborn.

Drake: Not if I'm right. But I digress, we can get back to Vegas favorites later in the show. Today, we have one of the players calling in from New Mexico after his practice round. Friend of the show, Steven Torre. Steve, can you hear us?

Steven: I hear I'm not your favorite to win <laughing>. What the [EXPLETIVE], guys?

Drake: Take it up with Vegas, old friend. What can you tell us from behind the tee this week?

Steven: Besides it being hotter than Satan's butt crack down here?

Drake: <Laughs> Yes, besides that.

Steven: So far, it's a great time. It always is. The Desert is one of my favorite tournaments every year and I think the rest of the guys would agree.

Britney: How are the vibes between PGA guys and the new league players? Any weirdness there?

Steven: Not that I can tell, but I tend to miss that kind of stuff. Look, I've got close friends in both leagues. I'm just glad to have everyone competing again. I don't want any part in the [EXPLETIVE] talk on either side.

Drake: Might not have a choice, bud.

Steven: Hey, I'm a lover, not a fighter <Laughs>.

Britney: With all the tension, it's nice to hear someone remain somewhat neutral.

Steven: That's the goal. I don't like watching my favorite sport crack down the middle. It's like being caught in a bad divorce and having to choose a parent. I'm just grateful I get to make a living doing something I love every day. A lot of men don't get to say that, so I don't take it for granted.

Drake: Was there ever a chance of you joining the new league?

Steven: Not really, no. I'm here for the tradition, the opportunities to play the same courses and tournaments that my heroes did. I grew up watching these great men compete and I wanted to be them, still do. Although, if it were up to my wife, we would have joined the new league.

Britney: Hillary didn't want to stick with the PGA?

Steven: I don't think it mattered either way to her, but there was the potential for a fat payday of course <Laughs>.

Drake: <Laughs> Happy wife, happy life.

Steven: Something like that. She's with me this week, my best cheerleader.

Drake: Don't doubt it. How's the game looking? Should Britney and I throw out our current favorites and add you to the list?

Steven: I mean...I've been better <Laughs>. I tell you what, if you bet on me and I do win I'll donate a good chunk of change to that kid's golf charity you guys like so much.

Drake: Silver Linings Golf Group? Hell yeah, bud. Let's do it.

Steven: You're on. I gotta hit the range, but thanks for having me on.

Drake: Anytime, brother.

13

WHITNEY

Whitney watches the golf coverage halfheartedly from her hotel room while she waits for the evening's festivities. Half the time, she catches herself looking for Rowan's name on the leaderboard. Old habits die hard, and all that. She's avoided professional golf for a year, but she doesn't want to appear ignorant at tonight's dinner if someone asks her about the tournament. It would seem ungrateful.

Still, she finds she's angry with the men leading the tournament.

You people wouldn't stand a chance against my Rowan.

Without the guardrails of reality, Whitney is free to believe that her late husband would have won every single tournament for the rest of his life had he survived the crash. She can fuel her resentment instead of her anguish by pretending that the men who currently grace the leaderboard would lose in a landslide to Rowan.

Anger feels like power when the only alternative is sorrow.

Not really wanting to wallow in either, Whitney turns off the television and begins the process of getting ready for the gala. The routine of doing her hair and make-up is calming, familiar. A practiced habit before something nerve wracking is a blessing, not unlike the routines golfers utilize before each shot. The men have their practice swings, a favorite glove, a tip of the hat. Whitney has her curling iron and lipstick, the motions memorized and soothing.

Rowan used to tease her about how many times she fixed her eyeliner if she didn't get it right the first time. She would blandly reply that one couldn't rush perfection, then turn her music up when he shook his head, giving up and then waiting for her in their living room.

Whitney leaves the music off permanently now, in case Rowan has something to say about how long she takes to get ready.

Whitney pulls her dress out of the dry-cleaning bag on the door. It's a black cocktail dress, probably much too casual for tonight's event, but she couldn't help herself. This event was for Rowan, and she wanted to honor his memory by wearing the same dress she wore when they first met.

Thanks to an almost religious commitment to the gym, she's been able to maintain her dancer physique well after retiring from the NFL. The dress still fits as well as the day she bought it.

As she slides into the sheath, she laughs a little bit under her breath. Shelley, one of her cheer colleagues, had been dating a professional golfer back in the day and Whitney had begged to be set up with one of his friends. The girl had made good on her promise to bring Whitney along on one of her upcoming dinners with the man, saying he would bring someone. In a chance that could only be designed by fate, that friend was Rowan Silver.

When he sat next to her at that hotel bar, she almost panicked, calling Shelley to ditch their double date. This was the man of her dreams—how could she go out with some smelly golfer after meeting this specimen? Luckily, they had cleared up the confusion early in their conversation and had a good laugh about meeting before their blind date.

Unluckily for Shelley, the girl wasn't very smart. Had she possessed the wherewithal of an average woman, she would have done some recon on her own date, whom she'd already spent several nights with, suspiciously, only in hotels. Her mystery man from the grocery store was Alex Garcia. While he hadn't lied about being a professional golfer, he had somehow never brought up the fact that he was already married.

Whitney zips herself into her dress and takes another look in the mirror before reaching for her purse. Inside, she finds the note addressed to her from this morning, and with little fanfare, she rips it to shreds and tosses it in the trash.

It's of no use to her, but perhaps Alex Garcia's wife should have received one.

14

BARTENDER #3

The bar is crowded with happy golf fans talking with each other about their favorite players. Everyone is recounting stories, watching highlights, and bragging about which ones they got to see in person. The two middle-aged gentlemen in front of me are having a second beer while they wait for a third friend, and their tales are as good as I'll hear all day.

"I saw Matthew Price get his hole in one today."

The second man gives his friend side eye before turning back to the screen. "How many beers have you had today, man?"

"Just a few. Why?"

"Because we were together the entire day. You don't have to recount it for me, we saw the same shit."

The first man pouts briefly before drinking more to hide his sullenness. I don't see the big deal. He's excited about his day, wants to keep sharing about it with his friend. He's clearly just grateful to have seen something that people back at the office will be talking about next week. If I was his friend, I would have let it slide.

Unfortunately for the first man, in his mini tantrum, he misses the window of the third friend's arrival, and his buddy beats him to the punch.

"We saw Matthew Price get his hole in one today."

"Dude, no way! The amateur from California? I should have stuck with you guys."

While the first man rolls his eyes, I clear the space in front of them and add some food menus for them to look at. The day isn't over yet, and in my professional opinion, they will need food soon after the day of drinking they've had.

Plus, men who order food usually tip more.

I see my barback sneaking his phone off to the side. "Hey Bryce," I call out. "Can you bus some tables for me? We're low on glassware."

He nods and moves to put away his phone, but before I can warn him, Greg appears out of nowhere behind him and puts his hands on Bryce's shoulders.

Seriously, how does he sneak around like that? It's obscene how quiet his steps are. He's a grown man, shouldn't he be, I don't know, thumping around?

"Now Bryce," Greg's hands are still firmly placed on the boy's shoulders, if not pinching them. "What are the rules about phones?"

To his credit, Bryce appears to be suitably apologetic, if not for the offense, at least for getting caught. "No phones at work?"

"No phones anywhere. It's supposed to be in your locker or your vehicle. The fans can't even bring theirs on the tournament grounds, don't you think if they see you on yours, they'll complain to me?"

Greg's admonishment comes in the form of a creepy whisper in my barback's ear while he continues to rub his upper back.

I cough to break the tension. "Speaking of customers complaining, I've got three gentlemen who need a plate of chicken nachos, ASAP. I think the kitchen dropped the order."

Greg finally releases Bryce, who mouths *thank you* to me as he scurries away to wherever he hides from our temporary manager. The man in question glares at me as if he doesn't quite believe me, but the three men at the end of my bar probably won't remember that they didn't order nachos, and if they do I'll just comp it for them. It's the least we can do for their unwitting help in giving Bryce an escape.

I fulfill more drink orders from the dining area while Greg acquires nachos from the kitchen and probably figures out that I lied to him. Whatever punishment he doles out will be survivable, though.

Like I said, he's only my manager for this week.

"Hey Meghan," he calls out to me from the kitchen.

Meghan is not my name. "Yeah, what's up?"

His smile lets me know I'm caught in my lie, but I don't anticipate his follow-up. "I need you to work a little late."

I check my watch. I'm supposed to get cut in less than an hour. "How late?"

"I need you to cover one of the bars at the gala tonight. We need an extra set of hands for the evening."

After a brief failure to keep my shock off my face, I recover. "The whole thing? I'm supposed to open the bar tomorrow morning. That's, like, a five hour turn around."

Gleeful in his power trip, Greg doesn't bother hiding his pleasure at my clear discontent. "Your work is just oh-so-appreciated around here. We'll need your help, or I'll have to report your insubordination to the club."

"Happy to help," I speak through clenched teeth and continued cleaning areas of the bar that need it. It's not the end of the world, but it's going to take a serious readjustment for me to be of any use the rest of the weekend. I was essentially at the finish line of a half marathon, only to be told it was a full marathon instead and also there's no water yet.

I continue to smile and help the customers, not letting my own bad news ruin their time here. Getting to see their favorite golfers compete is a special occasion for them, one I refuse to ruin just because my temporary boss is an ass.

The rest of the late afternoon passes quickly as I begin to close out tabs for people who have been parked in their seats for a while. The three men from earlier have signed their receipts and left a neat stack of silverware and dirty napkins on their plates, making my bus job easier.

And they all left a 35% tip. Not bad gentlemen, not bad.

15

HILLARY

One of the benefits of being married to a man who isn't winning the Desert Invitational is the early tee time. Is it embarrassing to have your man tee off before almost everyone else? Sure, no denying that. But the early tee time gives Hillary a longer shower later, and she won't be rushed through her getting ready process before the gala this evening.

It's a small consolation as she watches Steven plug it into a greenside bunker from the fairway.

The commiserating oohs from the crowd certainly don't help. Hillary finds herself wishing she could have brought her phone, so she has something to look at that isn't her husband hanging his head. He's not actually playing that badly, but this is a flub he can't afford. He'd been steadily improving up until he landed it in the sand, and this setback will throw him off. He still has a shot at the top thirty if he focuses.

Hillary remembers the text messages from Gwen and rescinds her former wish to have her phone with her. She doesn't need to worry about things she can't control right now, and she needs to focus on being the supportive wife. She has no concerns about too much screentime for herself; most of the cameras are following the winners, but if Steven looks over and sees her not paying attention, it will hurt him. He always had trouble compartmentalizing the issues going on around him when he played. The month after his father passed away, he missed four cuts in a row. It had been a difficult time for him, and Hillary hadn't known how to help. Grief makes her uncomfortable, and she struggled to communicate with him during that time.

"There's a new James Bond movie out," she'd said over dinner one night. "It's supposed to be Daniel Craig's last one. We haven't been to a movie since everything reopened, and I think it would be good for us to get out of the house. What do you say, sweetie?"

It was like he hadn't heard her. He was just staring at his food, moving it around with his fork, taking bites every so often as if it were a chore. His posture was terrible. All these elements together made it hard to look at him, so Hillary just turned back to her own salad, dropping the attempt at conversation.

A few minutes went by before he spoke. "Did you say something?"

"No," she replied. "I didn't say anything."

Hillary walks alone now, within the crowd but not part of it in case Steven needs to seek her out. He mentioned once that he likes to look for her when he plays, that he finds it comforting. If comfort is what he needs to perform, then she'll give it.

Steven and his caddie stop in the fairway parallel to the other man in his group. As his competition palms an iron for his approach shot, Steven turns his head away, eyes scanning the crowd before landing on Hillary. He doesn't react right away, waiting for her. She offers a closed-mouth smile, encouraging but not celebratory. It's a fine line. She doesn't want him to think she isn't taking his poor shot seriously but she also doesn't want to discourage him further.

He smiles back then looks at the ground, shuffling one of his feet. She's given him what he needs, so she continues walking alongside the fairway to stand closer to the bunker where she can see him again. The other player hits a crisp iron shot onto the green, within a makable distance but by no means an easy putt.

"Hillary Torre?"

She turns to the voice, a man in his early twenties walking with two friends. They both gawk at her, while the man who spoke stares as well, but speaks again after confirming it's her without Hillary needing to say anything.

"Holy shit, it is you," he says. "You are by far my favorite Instagram follow. Can I get a picture?"

"You sure can," she says. As she settles into his side under his arm, the young man pulls her closer than necessary and sits his hand on her lower hip. It bothers her but she doesn't do anything besides smile at his friend holding a disposable camera. She understands what her internet presence communicates to the world. Of her six hundred fifty thousand Instagram followers, well over eighty percent are men. It doesn't take long going through her page to see why; there's probably an overemphasis on her time by the pool and at the gym, activities that require minimal clothing.

After the friend clicks through for a small sampling of pictures, the young man next to her thanks her, moves his eyes down her body, then struts on with his friends to the next attraction.

If Hillary could design her life perfectly from the ground up, she wouldn't have chosen for it to be this way. She didn't like being seen as shallow, even if she could admit it's a fair judgement. It would be nice to be seen as more than a pretty face occasionally.

Of course, she would always choose to be beautiful and wealthy. Who in their right mind wouldn't choose that?

She'd just learned early on that she didn't have much going for her besides what was on the outside.

"You better be grateful God made you pretty, because he sure as shit didn't give you any brains," had been Gwen's response to a note from Hillary's teacher at the end of a spring semester. She was being asked to repeat the ninth grade, an unfortunate side effect of her severe dyslexia, only recently diagnosed. It was mortifying on an unfamiliar level for Hillary. She knew the day-to-day embarrassments well enough: reading out loud too slowly in class, the failed tests everyone seemed to take for granted as easy marks. In this instance, she was being publicly told she was dumber than all her classmates. On top of that, she would lose all her friends to their sophomore year, then be forced into classrooms with new kids who would all be shorter than her.

Steven is in the bunker now, digging his feet into the sand over his ball.

He appears to have gained confidence since the last shot and doesn't have the sloped back that typically indicates his discouragement and mental forfeit. Sand wedge face open, he pulls the club back halfway then fires through the sand, splashing the white particles in a flawless wave towards the hole.

The ball thumps onto the green and after a few bounces, rolls directly into the pin.

The spectators erupt with cheers; there's nothing more satisfying than a comeback story, even one that takes place on a single hole of the tournament. Hillary finds herself squealing in excitement as well. It's been a while since her husband's playing has elicited any reaction from her. She's grown used to the ups and downs, has learned to school her features appropriately. It's almost a relief when she finds she's having a little bit of fun watching him again.

From her spot on this hole, the tournament scoreboard is close enough to see. Hillary walks around a few groups to get a better visual. Maybe this unexpected birdie has moved him up in the rankings.

When the names aren't immediately accessible to her, she gives up, frustrated and ashamed, then promises herself she will just ask a volunteer for the information when she finds one next.

As Hillary follows Steven to the seventeenth tee box, she recalls the stranger's entitled hand on her hip for the photo and how gladly she would trade some of her beauty for a stronger mind.

16

SARAH

The last nine holes have been hell on Sarah's nerves. It's not as if Jared isn't playing well, he is, but even tournaments where he's the clear lead make her nervous. In golf, even the best makes mistakes. A highly ranked player once famously said that he'd never played a round in his entire life where he hit every shot perfectly. Jared was good, but he wasn't highly ranked yet, and any missed shot at the Desert Invitational could swing the momentum away from him.

The stakes are particularly high when there are three men still tied for the lead, with two more tied for second only one stroke back.

It appears Sarah's anxiety, at least her anxiety around her husband's performance, is misplaced. He is now leading the other player in his group by four strokes, keeping him in the lead with Andy Bell and Alex Garcia. She can tell he's zeroed in on his goal, especially now that the eighteenth green is in sight.

"Mrs. Farmer?"

She turns towards a man with a clipboard. "Yes?"

"Jared will be approaching the green soon. The Golf Channel broadcast wants to have you waiting for him as he finishes his round. If you wouldn't mind following me, please."

It's not a question, and Sarah doesn't treat it like one. She's relieved to have a small task assigned to her, even if it's standing in a new place. As she walks, she feels eyes follow her, hungry for entertainment in between the men's shots on the course. The attempt to suck in her stomach and hold her head to avoid a double chin for the cameras gives her something new to think about.

As she trails the man with the clipboard, she ignores again how feminine her husband's fan base is. The other man in their group, an older player named Spencer Hannah, had a small following of men around her dad's age. She'd tried to fool herself into believing those were more Jared's demographic, but the girlish voices cheering on her husband disabused her of that notion.

Still, it had been nice to pretend.

Sarah hasn't seen Cassandra since the turn, and it's both a relief and concern. The woman's unshakable confidence is grating to listen to when she doesn't share it. A not insignificant part of Sarah wants to wallow in her fears, feed them. Cassandra doesn't allow such victimhood to proliferate in her presence.

Conversely, Sarah now has no positive voice whispering at her not to worry. There's no one battling her own mental spiraling, no alternate opinion trying to convince her that there's nothing to worry about, that Jared would never do anything to hurt her.

Behind the green, she can still see him from the fairway, taking a leisurely practice swing. Now that Sarah is potentially on camera, she schools her face away from despair and into what she hopes is a stern, driven, but attractive expression. Something that tells the world she knows Jared can win it all, but she's taking his competition seriously. Spencer's shot is already on the green, though it's far enough away that it will require at least two putts to make.

Jared moves over his ball, his hands lifting the club to wiggle before swinging, keeping him from being too tense. Sarah can tell he's in the perfect spot; he sits around 135 yards from the green, his favorite distance for a full swing gap wedge. He hates having to take half swings too close to the green.

It's an out of body experience, hearing the thump of his club making contact with the ground. She doesn't see the ball at first, her gaze distracted by the chunk of grass flying several yards in front of Jared. Briefly, she worries that he caught it fat, hit the ground before the ball too early, and won't make it to the green.

Cheers erupt in the grandstands behind her, and she exhales deeply. Jared's ball landed perfectly, just beyond the hole with enough backspin that it's trickling closer every second. Its final resting place is about three feet away from the pin.

The celebration of the crowds continues as the two players and their caddies walk up the fairway towards the eighteenth green. Both men graciously wave to spectators, though there's no doubt that most of the cheering is for Jared. His shot was stellar, and the cheering is, again, too feminine for Sarah's comfort.

The next hour passes in a blur. Sarah knows she is caught on camera hugging Jared after his round, watching him walk to the scoring booth. He made the putt, giving him a birdie and a one-shot lead in the tournament for now. She wanders around while he gives post round interviews. When it's time to go back to the hotel, he'll find her.

When a hand lands on her shoulder, she moves to follow it without greeting, assuming it's time to leave.

"Are you ok?"

Oh. It's Cassandra.

"Better than ok," Sarah insists. "Jared just took the lead. We're ecstatic."

The other woman appears skeptical. Perhaps Sarah should have sold her enthusiasm better, but it's been a long day, and holy cow, she must do it again tomorrow, not to mention the gala tonight. There's not enough energy to waste on lying to Cassandra.

"If this morning is still bothering you," she says, "then you need to talk to him about it. It will only get worse if you're not honest."

If she'd spent any less time with the woman than she had today, Sarah would assume Cassandra was trying to sabotage her husband. Why would she share something so upsetting when he's in the lead? It would be understandable, the temptation to help take out Andy's main competition.

But while Sarah might not be the best at reading people's intentions, and with a tendency to trust too easily, she can't even find it within her newfound paranoia to think that Cassandra would do something like that. She thinks back to this morning in the bathroom and decides to trust her.

"Are you going to tell your husband?"

She shrugs in reply. "Sure," she continues, "Andy and I will have a good laugh about it before bed or something."

Well, that makes sense. Cassandra will share the note with Andy because she has nothing to worry about.

"You should go find Jared," she says, then squeezes Sarah's hand affectionately. "I'll make sure to look for you at the gala tonight."

Cassandra moves away without waiting for a reply. Eventually, Sarah gets up the nerve to seek Jared out amongst a small crowd of women begging for his autograph. When he sees her, he cuts away politely, leaving girlish cries of disappointment behind him.

It doesn't comfort Sarah like it should.

Jared is on cloud nine, talking about his favorite holes of the day.

"Did you see me on thirteen? It wasn't as exciting as some of the other shots I made today, but holing out that eight-foot putt really upped the momentum for me," he says, taking off his socks from a decorative chair in the corner of their hotel suite. They've got a couple hours to get ready before dinner, and after arguing lightly about who got the first shower, Jared has finally acquiesced and is going to get cleaned up first. He did all the hard work today, after all.

"I did," she replies. Sarah usually has more to say about his round, memorizing its ups and downs, just like he does. She scrambles for something to say so he doesn't worry. "Did you hit every fairway from the tee today? I don't think I saw you miss any."

He shakes his head. "I missed seven and sixteen, but only by a little. Still parred both holes," he says as he reaches a hand behind his neck to pull the collar of his shirt over his head. Sarah is leaning on the dresser as he walks towards her. His tan lines are ridiculous, severe after his hours practicing in the sun, but the sight of him still makes her giddy.

When she recognizes his intentions, she tries to stave him off. "Jared, we're both disgusting from today. I probably smell terrible."

"Come on," he says, grinning down at her. "One big, salty kiss before I shower?"

"I can't say no to that," she replies before giving him a light peck, which was unbelievably salty, as promised.

"You know, you can always join me," Jared calls from the bathroom as she works on removing some of her jewelry.

"Next time," she says back. As soon as she hears the water turn on, she steps quietly across the carpet to their small patio. Having some winning purses this past year has meant that they can afford to stay on site for tournaments these days, and Sarah enjoys the luxury even if she misses some of the intimacy of the motels from their earlier days on tour. Their view is over the hotel's pool area, and the sounds of music and children playing give her an additional sound cover outside as she pulls out her phone.

She hears two rings before her mother picks up the line.

"I wasn't expecting to hear from you this weekend," she says. Her mom must be in a good mood. Usually, it would be a comment about how she doesn't call enough, but Sarah has just graciously been given an excuse.

"Hi mom," she says back. "How are you?"

"Good, good. I've been keeping an eye on the tournament. I know you think I didn't support Jared's career choice at first, but I must say, I'm happy to be wrong here. If he's as good as he looks on screen, then he'll be just fine doing this for years to come."

Sarah chokes on her quick reply. This, on any other day, would be a celebratory concession from her mother. She was used to passive-aggressive nitpicking, a subtle disapproval coating any words that came across the phone. Her mother didn't live in Kansas anymore, so luckily, Sarah doesn't have to take the digs in person.

It was almost as if the older woman could sense there was a reason for her call and was cushioning the blow.

"Thanks, mom. I'm super proud of him," she says. "I think he has a real shot at it."

"That he does. I got to see a shot of you as well, dear. You looked nice for having walked eighteen holes, if not a little sweaty."

The familiar critical terrain almost makes this conversation easier for Sarah, but not by much.

"There's actually something else. I need a little advice, mom."

17

BARTENDER #3

After a thirty-minute nap in my Honda Civic with the vents blowing cold air on me, I run into the staff locker room. I keep an extra set of work clothes on hand in case of spills mid-shift, so at least I didn't have to worry about that aspect of my unexpected overtime. Last thing before dressing, I engage in the humiliating ritual I once heard an old coworker call a European Shower—splashing water from the bathroom sink under your arm pits—and I am ready for a night of bartending at the hotel event.

Well, I'm as ready as I can be. I'm still ignoring the fact that I have to open the clubhouse bar again tomorrow morning.

My co-bartender tonight is Pete, a competent teammate even if we don't work together all that often. Tonight's pseudo charity gala takes place at the resort where most players are staying, and it's not technically connected to the golf course hosting the tournament and where I'm currently employed. But we need all hands on deck for events like these, so the blended staff of hotel, golf course, and USGA employees is necessary.

Right now, Pete is giving all the glassware a last wipe down, getting rid of dust and fingerprints I already know aren't there. Though I'm loathe to admit it, I'm kind of sulking and not much help to him right now.

"That sucks about your double shift," he offers as a conversation starter.

"Yeah, it does," I say. I almost laugh at the absurdity of it all, but I don't want Pete to think I'm making fun of him.

He keeps working, facing the door in case someone walks in early, he continues, "How did you get stuck working tonight?"

"Just some staffing issues," I lie.

"Weird," he shrugs. "I liked your idea about the tap to pay options for tips, though. It would have made a huge difference for us."

I liked my idea, too. Ask any bartender what they think of staffing open bar events, and you'll get almost universally negative feedback. The vast majority of people attending won't know how to handle their alcohol, making the entire night a slop fest. Then when you cut them off, you're the bad guy and not someone trying to avoid liability in a lawsuit later when the drunk person hurts themselves or others. They're an absolute nightmare, though I'm hoping that the fact that most attending tonight are also competing tomorrow, and we won't have to worry as much about drunkenness.

The other main complaint about working at an open bar, and what Pete is referencing specifically, is the tipping situation. Most won't bother tipping at all, as if their drink magically stirred itself because it's free. Of the people who do care to tip, half of those folks don't carry cash and can't leave anything in the pathetic glass jar we sit on the counter announcing its purpose on an index card in huge bubble letters. Those customers will ask for a card option, and when we don't have it, they sheepishly walk away with their drinks and make a small apology. It hurts them too, since golfers specifically love to be seen as good tippers. A lot of men still carry cash though, so we might get five or so dollars for every ten drinks we make. Not terrible, but not ideal either when your hourly pay is below minimum wage.

My idea was to have a small iPad with a tap to pay option and an easy question: "Tip your server $2?" It's not greedy, and people usually tap their cards without thinking anyway.

"I liked my idea, too," I say to Pete and pick up a rag so I can pretend to work.

Unfortunately, when I pitched the idea earlier to the hotel bar manager, Greg walked in and completely shut down my idea, saying it was tacky. He's probably right, but his main motivation was to continue punishing me for earlier.

I'd do it again in a heartbeat, though. Slaving away for a weekend is worth it if it means keeping our nasty temporary boss away from my under-aged coworkers.

When Bryce first complained to me, I was skeptical. The guy had only been around our staff for a couple weeks. What did it even mean that he made Bryce and some of the other kids uncomfortable?

"I don't know how to explain it," he'd said. "It's just this gross vibe I get from him, like he takes any opportunity to touch me. I'm never alone with him, so nothing has happened, but it's not just me who feels it. Cassie complained to me this week, too."

Cassie was the fifteen-year-old hostess at the clubhouse restaurant who, like Bryce, was only able to work in four hour increments due to her age.

"Ok," I said. "Let me handle it."

Essentially, this entailed me warning the teenagers of Greg's arrival and keeping him busy in areas where they weren't typically needed. I thought I'd gotten fairly adept at juggling all the moving parts and conflicting motivations, but I fear my blatant lie had revealed our strategy.

But what could he really do? Complain to the country club that he didn't get enough one-on-one time with the teenagers he temporarily managed? No, he wouldn't be able to tell anyone what I was doing, but he could definitely punish me for it himself.

"Sam!" I hear called at me from across the room.

Speak of the devil. "Yes, Greg?"

Sam is not my name.

"We need you to move a back-up keg from the main bar to the travel cooler for tonight."

Pete sets his rag down, confident in his chivalry. "I'll get that for her," he says.

"Nope," Greg says, sounding too triumphant. "Sam can handle it. Hurry though, guests should be arriving soon."

As I toss my rag to the side, Pete whispers to me before I go, "Does he still not know your name?"

"I stopped correcting him two weeks ago," I say. It's true. Continuing to correct him would only make him think that I care if he gets it right, which I kind of do, but I won't give him the satisfaction.

As I leave to follow Greg on whatever pointless tasks he deigns to assign me, I see Hillary Torre enter and make her way towards Pete's bar.

I take small wins as they come, and not having to deal with her again will have to suffice.

18

WHITNEY

Whitney's hand is steady as she applies her final coat of lipstick. Maybe she should be nervous, but years of performing in front of NFL crowds has made her immune to anxious reactions anyone else would experience in her place.

Giving a short thank you speech in front of about one hundred people should be simple. She's gone over her speech plenty of times. At one time, she thought about involving a speech writer, someone who could give her something clean and focused. Nobody liked an emotional or meandering public speaker, especially when they needed rest for Sunday's competition. Eventually, she decided that she could come up with something herself, and that's what Rowan would have wanted. He'd been a very tactful and socially aware man, but he abhorred inauthenticity.

Standing up and giving a focus group tested, heartless, corporate sermon would have gone against his legacy.

Tonight is still about him, after all.

It's still sweltering outside, and the sun setting later won't be enough to cool the temperatures. Despite this, Whitney is still in black, her dress sleeveless with a classic Hepburn cut. Having a set uniform is comforting, her memories of the frock acting as more armor for the night. She's grateful the event is in one of the resort ballrooms, and she won't have to deal with the climate at all.

She wants to get to the gala early as she's a stickler for punctuality, and arriving with other people or, God forbid, late, is unacceptable. Rowan had been the same way, and it suited them well.

"Early is on time, on time is late, and late is in trouble," he'd say. Rowan had expected the same from others and was a strict enforcer of this rule. As a Ryder Cup captain for the United States in 2019, he led seriously, with demanding practice hours and intense reminders to be at the range two hours before teeing off. Grumbling among the other players was minimal, though. Everyone there wanted to beat Europe just as much as Rowan did.

The controversy started when one of the younger players slept late on Saturday morning. He hadn't done anything untoward the night before, but a faulty alarm was just as devastating as a public hangover. With only forty-five minutes until the tee time, the recent college graduate hurried to the practice range apologizing profusely. He said he was still ready to play, and he was so sorry, would Rowan please give him another chance?

The answer, shocking the world, was no. Rowan sent the kid home early for disrespecting his teammates and ultimately his country. Whitney personally had felt bad for the kid, especially since he seemed to be telling the truth. However, she always sided with Rowan, even in the privacy of her own mind. The United States went on to lose the Ryder Cup that year, with half the media blaming the young man and half blaming Rowan. The empty place on the team resulted in a one-point advantage for Europe every remaining day of the tournament.

"Mr. Silver," a reporter had called out during the post round press conference on Saturday evening. "What would you say to the people arguing that your decision to cut Bobby Winslow is going to cost America the Ryder Cup?"

"Does a police officer cost a man his license when he arrests him for a DUI? Or did the man who drove drunk do that to himself?"

Rowan's statement was followed by affirmative murmurs from the press tent, and he continued, "Look, I really like Bobby. I think he's a great player with a bright future and I didn't relish having to send him home. Rules are rules. I can't make exceptions for him without losing the respect of the other players who did show up on time. This wasn't an arbitrary boundary made so I could boss everyone around—the team gets together at the same time every morning to form cohesion. Golf is an extremely individual sport, and these guys are competitors for most of the year, so I need to do what I can to encourage trust between the men. When someone shows up late, like Bobby did, it breaks that trust."

His press conference statements went viral, earning him notoriety in certain corners of the internet. Fans of golf specifically resonated with firm commitment to principles, and when the time came to select captains for the 2021 Ryder Cup, the committee voted for him unanimously.

He didn't live long enough to see it.

Whitney closes her hotel door and makes her way to the elevator. Other guests won't arrive for another hour, but she'll get there early, find her seat, grab a drink. This way, she won't have to be the only woman arriving alone. Everyone else will be here for their husbands, and being inundated with her old life all day has made her sensitive.

The elevator chimes and the door opens, revealing Jared and Sarah Farmer. His arm is around her waist as he speaks excitedly about his pairing with Andy Bell tomorrow. She looks decidedly less enthusiastic, her face tense as she nods along with his voice.

"We've been close in tournaments with our scores, but I've never been in the same pairing as him before. He joined the new league before I started winning, you know."

"Hmmm," is Sarah's thoughtful response.

Whitney enters and turns to face the door before it closes, then speaks over her shoulder, "Aren't you both adorable together?"

This quiets them and she smiles, her comment having the intended effect.

As they descend to the main level, everyone remains silent. Less than a minute later, they arrive and Whitney leaves first, hoping they aren't planning to be early to the ballroom like she is.

Based on what she heard, she thinks Sarah probably has not told Jared about the note from this morning. All things considered, Whitney thinks it's a bad idea for Sarah to keep hiding it, but she's not going to insert herself. It's not her marriage, so she doesn't judge. Plus, she remembers her own decisions as a married woman when confronted with turbulence between her and Rowan. She didn't always do the wise thing, either, especially when emotions were high.

Stepping into the ballroom, she sees caterers setting up the buffet line while a man standing at the sound board tests music levels. Thankfully, the bar is already operating.

Whitney approaches, choosing the empty side of the bar. A man and a woman are at the other end, whispering. She orders her gin and soda from the guy behind the counter, then eyes the couple to her left. Almost laughing at her luck, she drops a dollar in the tip jar and brings her drink and walks over to the other two.

Hillary Torre lifts her head as Whitney stands next to her, her expression wide and guilty. "Hi, Hillary," Whitney says before looking at the man. "Where's Steven?"

19

HILLARY

The steam still pouring out of the bathroom is making Hillary sweat through her make up despite the AC being on full blast. She fans herself as she waits for Steven to come back to the room. At this rate, he might even be late for dinner if he doesn't hurry back.

She hopes he is working on the range but knows it's unlikely.

Steven didn't play as poorly today as he did yesterday, but it might not be enough. He seems to be content to practice when his coach demands it and play a few rounds a week for fun without taking his career too seriously. Steven loves the game, but he doesn't love hard work. It's frustrating, watching someone who could be great settle for just okay.

This attitude would have been fine with her if he'd signed up for the new league like so many other men. His lower finishes could have been larger purses than even winning first place in the PGA. In her mind, it was a horrible idea to turn it down, but Steven had insisted that while he wanted to make a living playing golf, he wanted the PGA more than being rich.

This conversation reverberates in Hillary's mind as her phone buzzes on the nightstand, and she winces at Gwen's name. Even as she pretends to contemplate not answering, she knows she has no choice.

"Hello?" She answers as she holds up two different earrings to each ear, trying to decide which one she wants. One is a chandelier style and flashier, one a diamond stud. They both had the same price, but sometimes Hillary needs a little extra sparkle. It's not like anyone would confuse her for being old money anyway. She puts her sister on speaker while she slides the chandelier's hook through her left earlobe.

"I hope your husband is practicing," Gwen replies. "His showing is less than formidable this weekend."

"Of course he is," she lies.

Gwen scoffs. "I suppose it doesn't matter. You're due for the same amount no matter how he plays."

"So, it would seem," Hillary says. Her tone holds confidence she doesn't have, but letting Gwen know how much power she had over her is always a mistake. She doesn't get a discount for begging for mercy, for letting her sister gloat. Maybe if she did, she'd bother being nicer to Gwen.

"I really should have been billing you earlier. I housed you all those years and you're not even my kid."

"Sorry for being born," she answers. Gwen had wisely left their mother's household as soon as she could at eighteen, but two short years later Hillary came along. In her case, she was pulled from the house by CPS before she started kindergarten when a neighbor called the police because her mother was drunk and passed out in the driver's seat of her car with Hillary buckled in the backseat. It could have been much worse, with the revolving door of boyfriends, the drug deals she handled in house with Hillary upstairs sleeping. All things considered, she feels pretty lucky, even with the hindsight of knowing Gwen could also be a headache to live with. Their mom is out of jail now, but hasn't contacted either of them.

Neither Hillary nor Gwen have ever met their fathers.

As Hillary's only living relation, Gwen took on the responsibility of raising her, though she didn't do so without complaining.

"Yeah, well, me too." Gwen hangs up without saying goodbye.

If there was ever a time when Hillary had hoped for her sister's affection, she doesn't remember it. The resentment around having to raise her only grew when it became clear to Gwen that Hillary was becoming more and more beautiful with every passing year, while she, who had never been more than plain, was rapidly aging.

"Go up to the front with our check," Gwen had said one night after dinner at a local diner. When she turned fifteen, her older sister had started demanding Hillary be the one who delivered the check after they ate in restaurants. It didn't take long to figure out why.

"You didn't give me enough money," Hillary said. "I can't cover the bill with this." She had a hard time reading, but even she could tell that the twenty-dollar bill Gwen had handed her was not enough to cover all the food she ordered. This had also become a habit of hers, asking Hillary to underpay and leaving her with the consequences. She was usually lucky if she got chased out or forced to wash dishes, while some managers required other even less appealing means of payment.

"Kurt likes you," Gwen stated, tipping her head backwards towards the middle-aged man standing behind the register. "Just smile and apologize, then he'll let you get away with it. I'll be waiting in the car."

After Gwen left, a fifteen-year-old Hillary had stood on shaking legs and made her way up to the register. When Kurt noticed, he waved her over, punching a few keys to begin the process for her.

"How'd everything taste today?"

"It was great," she said, then handed him the check and the twenty. When he saw it, he looked at her with an eyebrow raised.

"I'm sorry," she whispered. "It's all I have."

He sighed and opened the register, placing the twenty in its spot and closing the drawer. "I know it's not your fault."

After he stamped the check with a false paid in full notice, he handed it back to her but held her wrist before she could turn away.

"I hate to do this to you, but I can't serve you guys anymore," he explained. "Gwen's done this too many times and I can't afford to give away food."

Hillary held back tears but nodded. "I understand," then she walked out the door to tell Gwen the news.

Her older sister would only be mildly upset, but Hillary was devastated. None of the other restaurant managers were as nice and forgiving towards her as Kurt had been.

Hillary learned at least one valuable lesson from those experiences: men are fools with their livelihoods around pretty girls.

Steven barrels into the room, a tall can of Budweiser in hand. Hillary doesn't think he's drunk, but only because he hasn't had the time to get there yet. She tries to smile at him. "How was the practice range?"

He grins at her and leans in for a kiss, one she receives but isn't happy about since she's already dressed, and he still smells like he spent twelve hours in the sun. Steven notices and laughs, keeping their bodies from touching as a courtesy. "It was fine. I didn't stay long."

Of course he didn't. "We have an hour and a half until dinner. I may head down and say hi to some of my friends if they happen to be out and about."

Steven frowns at this, rudely implying that he doesn't think she has friends, and technically he's right but she needs to get out of the suite. "Sure, babe," he replies. "I'll just get showered and meet you down there."

Hillary finishes packing her purse and walks toward the door before Steven turns on the shower. She could use a drink, or a muscle relaxer, or a strong punch to the temple just to knock her out for a little while. But as stressful as these public tournaments could be, as bad as it was to have Gwen breathing down her neck, it was still mostly better than being alone in their house.

On days when Steven practiced or had work that didn't include her, she used to go absolutely nuts before she learned to fill those days with spa treatments or extensive workouts.

Sitting alone with her thoughts did not suit her.

Two steps into the hallway of the resort and Hillary's foot kicks something across the carpet. Odd, this place is usually spotless. The item's smooth roll across the carpet is confusing to her, until she looks closer.

A tiny model car painted to look like a police cruiser sits in front of her, its back bumper attached to a piece of paper. The short note doesn't reveal any sender, nor does it clarify anything for Hillary, but its message leaves little room for misinterpretation.

They're going to catch you.

Steven's room is on the first floor, so Hillary doesn't have to wait for an elevator, but she begins picking at a tassel on her purse as she walks through the mostly empty halls. As sweat beads along the back of her neck, she finds a restroom and rushes toward it.

At the sink, she tears the note from the model car then soaks it under the sink, destroying its message and her own fingerprints. She then runs the car under the water in the same manner, wiping it down with a paper towel before throwing both in the trash bin.

There are only a few people who could have left that message, and Hillary has nothing to gain by reporting it, or even acknowledging that she received it. If Gwen is the one who placed it, then she has to deal with the fact that she's here, and she doesn't want to do that. She wants to have a drink, stand next to her husband, then sleep for twelve hours.

After burying the offensive toy under other damp paper towels, she checks her reflection in the mirror. Everything is still in place, hair, make-up, and clothes. Her eyes are too bright, a little bit crazed if she's honest, but there's nothing to be done about that now. She consoles herself with the fact that nobody is going to look that closely at her, that all her conversations for the night are going to be surface level anyway. That's how these events always go.

Time to put on a brave face.

As she exits the bathroom, she starts to become self-conscious. She's dressed for a gala by herself. Is she supposed to just post up at the bar and drink until everyone else arrives? Maybe she and her husband aren't so ill suited after all. He'd probably be thrilled if she planned a date for them just like this—dolled up and boozing at a bar somewhere like when they used to date. Instead of going back to find him, she heads closer to the gala.

She didn't plan this far ahead, trying to get away from Steven and Gwen and all the pressure. Hillary follows the signs directing her to the event room, avoiding any paths that take her outside in the heat. When she passes the open lobby bar and social area, she sees it's surrounded by a few players and caddies having a drink after just finishing their rounds. These must be the later tee times, and she recognizes some of the tournament leaders. Better to go to the gala bar then, rather than be the only dressed up woman surrounded by sweaty men.

One of said men catches her eye as she passes, but she shifts her gaze forward toward her destination.

The resort is large, so a same floor trek from her room to the gala takes almost fifteen minutes and by the time she arrives, she's relieved to find stools already set up in front of what looks like a fully stocked bar. Her feet don't care for the shoes she's chosen, but Hillary learned once from Marilyn Monroe to never complain about sore feet.

Two familiar looking workers leave as she enters, but she doesn't waste time identifying them. She really needs to sit down, and a friendly looking young man stands behind the bar dressed in a standard white button down. She sits at the left side of the bar, not caring who sits next to her. Secretly, she hopes Steven will get here soon so she won't look so conspicuous.

"Vodka martini, dirty but no olives, please," she says to the man. As she waits for the beverage, she rubs her temples, more to give herself something to do than to relieve any pain.

As the bartender sets her drink down, Hillary feels someone approach her from behind. She hopes it's someone who will be nice to her. It's a waste of energy to have that hope, but she nurses it alive in her chest all the same.

When Alex Garcia, one of the tournament leaders and the man who'd been looking at her from the bar grabs the stool next to hers, she changes her mind. She'd rather have someone bitchy.

"Hillary," he says by way of greeting. "You look good."

She uses a cocktail straw to grind into the ice chunks at the bottom of her glass while she responds. "Thanks. How's your wife?"

"Can I get the hazy IPA?" He ignores her to order from the young man, tosses a pathetic couple of coins in the tip jar, then sits down next to her. "She's at home with Jake. Can't believe I've been a dad for six months."

"Congratulations," Hillary says. She means it, silently wishes that becoming a father has made him a better husband, but doesn't want this conversation prolonged. She checks the entrance to the ballroom but doesn't see any new guests.

Unaware or uncaring, Alex drags his seat closer to Hillary, beer in hand. "What about you and Steven? I doubt we can expect any kids out of you guys anytime soon," he says, then winks at her, as if they share a secret.

Her grip on her drink tightens but betrays nothing in her face. "I wouldn't be so sure. Steven and I are working on it."

Alex just grins at her over his glass as if he doesn't believe her. He's not wrong, but Hillary doesn't care for his assurance where she is concerned. She knows what he's doing, testing the waters. The fact that he thinks her an easy mark is offensive. What does he think? That she would swoon over his mostly unimpressive tournament finishes and follow him to his hotel room?

Oh Alex, I love how you got a triple bogie on the last hole of the Milwaukee Classic. Do me again, Big Man.

She barely keeps herself from scoffing out loud. As if.

And where would it go? Affairs leave people in an iron-clad sexual prisoner's dilemma. In one quadrant, they pinky promise to both tell their spouses, and end up together. Technically, according to game theory, this is the best case scenario, but in Hillary's mind connecting herself to Alex Garcia in matrimony would be a living hell.

On the opposite side, the quadrant that is diagonal from the first, neither tells their spouses, and they stay married to other people. Technically, the second-best scenario, and the same result if one avoids the affair all together.

Actually, that would be Hillary's winner quadrant.

Last, there are the loser quadrants, where one party tells their spouse and ends up alone, while the other party gets to remain married with the tiniest bit of plausible deniability surrounding their fidelity or lack thereof. All they would need to save their own marriage is to double-down on the gaslighting.

She's insane and lying! I can't believe you don't trust me.

No, no, she's making it up. Their marriage ended for other reasons. I had nothing to do with it.

What are you talking about? I've never even met her!

All this paranoia makes me think you're the one hiding something.

It's a mind game Hillary has no intention of playing with Alex if she ever plays it with anyone again.

Having been distracted, she didn't notice anyone else approaching the bar, but Hillary is pleased to see someone else coming over. Her relief is short lived when she sees who it is.

"Hi, Hillary," Whitney Silver stands before them, looking smugger than she usually does, which is admittedly impressive. For all the time they've known each other peripherally, Hillary has felt that the widow sees her as trash. It's not even like Whitney came from a wealthier background than she had. They both grew up without financial security, without fathers, then married professional golfers. There's no legitimate reason that the other woman should act all high and mighty around her. Yet here she is, raising a judgmental eyebrow at Hillary. Even Alex seems less sure of himself now, as if her presence has sucked the flirtatious energy out of him.

Whitney continues, "Where's Steven?"

Hillary finishes her drink, then smiles. "He should be almost here. If you'll excuse me, I need to find a restroom." Not the cleanest getaway strategy, but she's able to extricate herself from both parties without much hassle.

As she walks back into the vast hallways of the resort, passing the greedy eyes of staff, guests, and media personalities, she thinks that she probably should have just stayed with her husband until the event started.

**Interview with Whitney Silver on *Late Night with Marty Simpson*
Filmed February 1, 2022**

Marty: Our next guest is someone very special, someone whose charitable efforts have even impacted members of my extended family. Sadly, she lost her husband last year in a tragic car accident. Widowed far too young, she didn't let her pain make her a victim. Instead, she decided to honor her husband's memory by starting Silver Linings Golf Group, a nonprofit dedicated to bringing the sport of golf to youth communities that wouldn't typically have access. In these efforts, she has memorialized her late husband while changing the lives of children all over the country. Please welcome Whitney Silver!

Whitney: Thank you for having me, Marty.

Marty: The pleasure is all mine. Before we brought you out, the viewers got to watch a short testimonial video about how positive an impact Silver Linings had on their lives and communities. When you had the idea for this charity, did you ever believe it would get so big so quickly?

Whitney: I suppose in a lot of ways the organization has already outgrown my initial plans, so no, I didn't know it could be this big. When I started recruiting sponsors back in September, my only goal was to do something positive with Rowan's memory. He loved everything about golf and would have wanted as many people to have access as possible.

Marty: I bet he'd be pretty proud of what you've built here.

Whitney: I appreciate you saying that. I miss him every day, but my work with Silver Linings has helped me feel close to him.

Marty: It's truly impressive what you've done. In less than six months, you've managed to gather funding for dozens of children to attend golf camps over the summer and have even begun the process of backing college scholarships. What's next for your organization?

Whitney: The plan right now is to scale what we're currently doing across a few more states, maybe into Canada. We've expanded our staff to accommodate, and now it's just a matter of getting through all the red tape. Someday, I'd like to open our own camps and clinics, but that would take a different strategic mind than my own <Laughs>.

Marty: I don't know about that. It's been fascinating to watch this come together so quickly. Are you sure you didn't have experience in the nonprofit sector before this?

Whitney: Not an ounce.

Marty: I just can't believe it. You must have some kind of background in corralling people to a cause. Perhaps you're an older sister to some rowdy siblings?

<Audience Laughter>

Whitney: <Laughs> No siblings, though I always wanted some. I think any experience I have that helps me today was developed as Rowan's wife. He relied on me for certain organizational things, travel bookings and schedules. We both wanted his focus to be on golf, so I took on the other things for him. Charity work is new to me, something I have only started doing since he's gone.

Marty: Well, I guess there's a silver lining in itself.

Whitney: <Pauses> What do you mean?

Marty: I just mean that you've made something positive out of his passing.

Whitney: I don't think there's anything positive at all about my husband's death, Marty.

Marty: I didn't mean that. I was just thinking that if he was still here, you wouldn't be free—

Whitney: Free? My grief is a prison.

Marty: It's just that—

Whitney: If putting a bullet between your eyes right now on live television could bring Rowan back to me, I would do it without blinking.

<CUT TO COMMERCIAL>

20

SARAH

"I hope we're at the same table as Andy and Cassandra," Jared says as he pushes the elevator button for the lobby level. Sarah nods, still distracted by the conversation with her mother.

She shouldn't be surprised by the advice she received. To a certain extent, she anticipated it, even sought it out. Part of her had desperately wanted some confirmation for a decision she had essentially already made. She doesn't feel any better about it, but at least she found one person to agree with her.

"Obviously," her mother had said after Sarah explained the note from this morning. She had avoided going into too much detail, simply asking the older woman whether or not she should bring it to Jared. "You don't tell him. If I'd had that kind of ammo going into my divorce with your father, it would have been a game changer. I barely walked away with anything from him, remember?"

"I don't want a divorce, mom," Sarah said. "I just don't know if I should ignore it or ask about it."

"Would it matter? Whether he lies or tells the truth, it will probably be the same answer. He's going to deny it."

"I don't think he's been with anyone else," she explained further. The longer she thought about it, the more she believed that to be true. The note had to be some kind of sabotage, meant to poison her marriage with distrust or to distract Jared during the tournament. She just couldn't believe her husband, the love of her life, would do something so callous. "I just don't feel confident bringing it between us until I understand the intentions behind it, you know?"

Her mother had huffed before saying, "Whoever she is, she sounds like a Good Samaritan."

Well, Sarah almost can't believe Jared would cheat. A small part of her is still worried. She had been his first girlfriend, and now he was surrounded by temptation anytime he traveled without her. Men aren't made of steel, and if he got lonely one night, why should he hold out for Sarah back at home?

"Never mind what you think, Sarah," her mom continued. "There is no reason to tell him. It's ok not to share every little thing within a marriage, you know."

Sarah didn't know that, and how should she? Her parents had separated young, seemingly assisted by the secrets her mom insisted were a good thing and up until this morning she thought she and Jared had shared everything with each other. She wishes she could go back to boldly ignoring her mother's marriage advice.

The elevator doors open early, stopping for another passenger. Whitney Silver enters, and Jared shifts over to make room. Her presence dims the atmosphere considerably. Even Jared, ever positive and social, has tempered his excitement, though he continues to speak, attempting to stay upbeat.

"Aren't you both adorable together?" Whitney voice cuts through Sarah's anxiety enough to give her a more empowering emotional alternative: anger.

At least Whitney's bitchiness means that Sarah won't have to talk to her.

Sarah wonders, not for the first time, why the widow was included in the group this morning. It's possible her husband had an affair before his death, but why twist the knife? He's gone, and she's clearly still grieving openly. There was no marriage to break up, no leader in the tournament to impair. It would only serve to drag an already broken woman further into her own misery.

She must have done something very, very bad to be on the receiving end of such a hateful note.

The elevator dings, announcing its arrival on the lobby level. Sarah and her husband give Whitney a chance to move ahead of them before Jared grabs her hand for a squeeze and pulls her behind him.

A loud, masculine laugh draws her attention to the lobby bar where caddies have collected to unwind. As crowded as it is, the reception desk remains relatively unused. Everyone staying in the hotel is here for the Desert Invitational and would have checked in days ago.

As they round the corner to a new hallway, a different chattering noise begins to rise in volume. Closer to the ballroom, other couples are arriving, hand in hand, smiling eagerly at their surroundings. It's still early, and most are still mingling outside, not wanting to be the first people to enter the ballroom, but the energy is high. Apparently, no one is too established or too famous to get excited the night before Sunday of a major tournament.

Sarah's palm slips from Jared's grip slightly, perspiration gathering where they are connected.

I can't do this, she thinks. *I can't pretend to be happy for these people.*

"I have to pee," she blurts out. Not her most eloquent statement, and Jared notices.

"No one is stopping you," he laughs and gives her hand a firm squeeze before letting her go. "I'll meet you inside. I need to check our table assignment and say hi to few guys."

Without responding, Sarah darts into the first women's room she sees, then quickly looks underneath each stall. Giving a relieved sigh when she finds it empty, she walks to the last sink and drops her bag onto the counter.

In other circumstances, she would be thrilled at what she sees in the mirror tonight. Her diet appears to be working, her face having lost some baby fat around the jaw. Her make-up hasn't budged yet. Her dress is a deep emerald green, a color that never ceases to make her feel beautiful and grown-up. The hotel did a fabulous job steaming it, ensuring no wrinkles from travel survived their superior care. This is as pretty as she'll ever look, she thinks, even compared to her own wedding day, and her husband is tied for the lead in a major tournament. She should be happy, ecstatic even.

"We have to stop meeting this way."

Sarah whips her head to the right, seeing Cassandra has entered the restroom without her hearing the door open.

Of course, any confidence Sarah had in her appearance evaporates at the sight of the other blonde. Cassandra is wearing a tight red dress with an appropriate split up one leg. She must be close to six feet tall with the heels she's wearing.

Sarah offers a courtesy laugh at her joke. "Andy played well today," she says. "Jared is so excited to be playing with him tomorrow."

"I'm excited too. It means I have a friend to walk with me tomorrow. I think we're all at the same table tonight too."

What a relief. As intimidating as the other woman is, she seems genuinely kind. Sarah doesn't think she'd survive having to sit next to someone catty like Hillary or some of the other wives. She's minutes away from a nervous breakdown as is.

"That's good," Sarah replies with a tight smile.

Cassandra clicks closer to Sarah in her heels, turning to look at her in the long, unseparated mirror hanging behind the sinks. Her eyes wrinkle slightly at the corners as she looks closer at Sarah with some solemnity. "Is everything alright?"

"Sure! Just nervous, I think. This is all such a big deal."

Cassandra nods. "It is. But it can also be a lot of fun, if you let it be."

"I don't think I'm there yet," Sarah says.

The other woman pauses, digging in her purse. Catching Sarah's eye again, she pulls a lipstick out of the bag. Without removing her gaze from the task of reapplying, she speaks. "You're worried about the note."

It's not a question, not really. "Aren't you?"

"No," Cassandra doesn't hesitate. "Not like you are." She puts the lipstick back into her purse and turns to face Sarah, her face sterner than before.

"There's something else happening," she explains. "The note isn't what you think it is."

Sarah frowns. "How do you know?"

"I don't. Not yet, at least," she admits. Cassandra stands up straighter, ready to return to the growing mayhem outside the bathroom door. "Listen, if you need someone to talk to, I'm here. We might have just met, but I like you," she smiles. "But you should really talk to Jared. Have you told him about the note?" When Sarah shakes her head, she continues, "I thought so. If it's really bothering you, you need to discuss it with him. It's not fair to keep something like that from your husband when you could easily eliminate your worries with a discussion."

"I don't want to distract him from the tournament," Sarah says, mostly telling the truth.

"You being upset and him not knowing how to fix it will be more distracting. Trust me."

With that, the other woman turns and leaves Sarah alone with the mirror once more. She rinses her hands quickly to remove any lasting sweat and gathers her small bag. What could the note possibly mean besides what it said? More importantly, who wrote it?

Just as she begins to ponder the absurdity of such a note, she exits the bathroom to a camera flash. It distracts her long enough to wonder if its aimed at her, so she fakes a smile, and returns to the safety of her paranoia.

I can't tell Jared about this.

~

TMZ Archives: World's Top Ranked Golfer Arrested in Second DUI
June 14, 2012

Andy Bell was arrested early Monday morning by San Diego police after crashing his rental vehicle into a covered bus stop. The professional golfer, aged thirty, is currently ranked fourth internationally in PGA rankings. The crash comes off his win last weekend at Torrey Pines golf course after he and some friends were seen drinking heavily at multiple clubs in the area. Witnesses at the clubs say illicit drugs were being used casually by the group, but this is not confirmed in the police report.

The arrest comes hot off the heels of another DUI earlier this year near his condo in Tampa. He was pulled over after police reported seeing his truck struggling to stay in the lanes on a residential street. He was arrested after failing a field sobriety test but later pled no contest to the charge and was not given a suspended license.

This second DUI brings up concerns surrounding his career.

"He's obviously still winning," said one source close to the golfer. "But it's more than that. If he doesn't clean up his image, he risks losing sponsorship and advertising opportunities. At his age, the partying isn't cute anymore."

Bell currently awaits bail hearings in San Diego County after his charge. No one was harmed in the wreck, including two unnamed female passengers who were with him at the time.

<This is a breaking news story: Please refresh the page for updates.>

21

CASSANDRA

The ballroom is filling quickly with players, wives, and certain big names in the media with allies in the right places. Whoever prepared for the event made an economic use of the space, making the room seem far more crowded than the guest list would imply. Cassandra finds Andy at the entrance, waiting for her as promised.

She's no closer to figuring out who left the note for her and the other wives, though she has a few educated guesses on why each woman might be involved.

Cassandra still firmly believes that she was given the note as a punishment for Andy leaving the PGA. It was likely meant to distract her husband and sabotage a potential win so the media could continue to spin lies about the new league players being uncompetitive. If taken further, the note's author could still go to the media and harm her family publicly. Andy was less than a decade removed from his youthful party days, and it would only take a few lies to unravel the goodwill of his fan base. It was petty and gross, but all's fair in war, and everyone here plays to win. She's honestly a bit impressed by the ingenuity of the tactic.

Sarah is a tougher case. There's a slim possibility that if there's any truth to the note, Jared might be the husband who was unfaithful, but Cassandra doubts it. She saw the young man walking with his wife earlier and couldn't imagine that kind of affection being faked, not to mention his spotless reputation.

Sarah's insecurities make her a larger threat to herself than the note, in Cassandra's opinion.

Hillary is another category all together. Plenty of women hate Steven's wife, some with more motive than others. The list of people wanting to hurt her is so long it's unhelpful.

Even women as magnanimous as Cassandra tire easily around the woman.

Whitney makes the least amount of sense, with her husband already gone. Someone must really want to destroy the widow if they bothered dragging her into this whole nightmare. After the last year, Cassandra can't really blame whoever it is.

None of this is as urgent as the man in front of her, though. "Have I ever told you," he whispers in her ear as they walk further into the room, "how utterly breathtaking you are?"

"Not today," Cassandra smiles back. As natural to them as breathing, they share a mostly appropriate kiss. Over Andy's shoulder, she sees Whitney sitting at the bar by herself.

A perfect opportunity.

"Do you want something to drink? I can bring you something if you want to mingle."

After agreeing, Andy sees one of the men he was paired with for Thursday's round and walks over to greet him. Cassandra makes her way to the bar in one straight, continuous line as guests and wait staff move to make room for her.

The line waiting for drinks is short. While no one in attendance could be accused of puritanism, it is Saturday, and tomorrow is not a day when players or wives want to be nursing a hangover. Some men, mostly casual golfers, claim to play better after a night of drinking, but Cassandra has never believed it. They probably just use the mental fog to distract themselves from how terrible they are at the game. The subdued nature of this event lets her know that most in attendance agree with her. The real party will have to wait for when the golf world has a winner for the Desert Invitational.

She hears one of the analysts discussing the new league loosely with someone she doesn't recognize, and she's able to pick up a small snippet of their conversation before they see her.

"They're getting desperate," the analyst says.

"They should be," the other man sputters. "The PGA sank how many millions into marketing against the new league only for some of the defectors to be in contention? Even if a PGA member wins tomorrow, this has been deeply embarrassing."

"What would you have them do? Without dramatically increasing the purse for every single tournament, they can't compete with the new league's signing bonuses. The only way to fight against that kind of money is a public smear campaign."

"Or, and call me radical here, the PGA could put the money they blew on ineffectual marketing into the purses so their players will want to stay?"

The two men turn away from the bar before Cassandra must embarrass them by letting them know they've been overheard. They were talking about Andy, a co-leader this weekend and proud defender of the new league. Contrary to what most people believed, her husband hadn't made the decision lightly. Most assumed that everyone who joined the new league just wanted an easy paycheck, but Andy had agonized over the decision.

In the end, he chose his family.

"The travel is too hard on us now that the kids are in school, and I don't want to miss out on seeing them grow up because I'm away every weekend," he'd explained. The new league offered shorter tournaments, less travel, and more financial security. Even players as strong as Andy could lose money on tournaments if he didn't place well after all the travel and training expenses.

Cassandra never voiced her own opinion when he was debating with himself, but she had been thrilled when she heard his decision. She missed her husband when he was gone, and she missed her children when she went with him.

She stands behind Whitney now, and the widow turns on her stool as if she'd been waiting for her. "Cassandra," she says in greeting.

"Two Arnold Palmers," she says to the bartender.

Whitney scoffs into her glass at being ignored. "This kind of pettiness is beneath you."

Cassandra turns toward her while the bartender pours lemonade into the bottom half of two tall glasses filled with ice. "I'm not being petty. I just don't have anything to say to you."

Before Rowan's death, she wouldn't have considered Whitney a friend, but they certainly had more in common than they do today. They would be pleasant toward each other, interact kindly around their husbands. Rowan and Whitney were even a staple invite at Andy and Cassandra's annual party before each Desert Invitational, at least until the disaster that was last year's event.

"I don't know what you're talking about," Whitney says.

"Really," Cassandra deadpans. She waits for the man behind the bar to move farther away toward the pitcher of iced tea before continuing. "Because I could swear you dragging my husband's name through the mud on public television gave me the right to ignore you whenever I want."

Andy's decision to leave the PGA had not been made lightly, and both of them knew one of the drawbacks would be negative press from the legacy golf media. What neither of them anticipated was the vitriol coming from someone they had hosted in their own home multiple times.

In her press tour after establishing Silver Linings Golf Group, Whitney Silver had become one of the loudest voices in opposition to the new league, telling anyone who would listen to her what she thought of the players who left the PGA. She called them sellouts, has-beens, washed-up traitors to the game of golf. She said Rowan would never have left the PGA, and anyone who did would have been no friend to her late husband.

She mentioned Andy by name in these tirades on more than one occasion.

The redhead raised a sharp eyebrow and set her glass down. "What do you mean?"

"Your gall actually impresses me," she replies. Cassandra sits down on the bar stool next to Whitney, pretense gone now.

"It's not personal," the widow doesn't try to defend herself. There is enough shared history between them to be cordial, and despite the widow's public betrayal of her family to the media, Cassandra can't help but feel immense sympathy for Whitney.

If she, God forbid, lost Andy tomorrow, she would be utterly devastated, but she would have her children to think about. Her life would become even more dedicated to them, making sure they had what they needed. It would be difficult, and she would never be able to fill the aching chasm their father would leave, but they would be her purpose.

If she lost Andy before they had children? Cassandra can't even contemplate what she would turn into if she were to be so untethered in her grief. Creating a media fire storm around former friends would be the least of her capabilities.

But the empathy she feels for Whitney still isn't enough to let her off the hook.

The man returns with the mixed tea drinks and moves away to serve patrons on the other side of his bar. "What are you trying to accomplish here, Whitney?"

"You wouldn't believe me if I told you."

"You're right, I wouldn't," she admitted. They sat in silence before Whitney spoke up again.

"What if I told you," the widow lowers her voice as more people walk up for drinks. "I don't believe Rowan's death was an accident?"

Cassandra rears back, appalled. "How could you possibly know that?" She's spent the last year cooperating with police alongside Whitney and everyone else who had been with Rowan the night he died in the accident. She'd sat in front of cops, had to drag her children to the police station's waiting rooms, and participated in repetitive interviews. Like everyone else, she'd had no information to offer. If this woman knew something that could break the case all this time, Cassandra was going to lose her mind and take the other woman with her.

Whitney ignores her to finish her drink.

Cassandra is done with the conversation and stands with her two glasses. "Whitney," she begins, waiting for the other woman to give her full attention. "My heart breaks for what you've been through, truly. I cannot imagine what the past year has been like for you."

Whitney stiffens at this, but Cassandra doesn't pause for a response.

"But whatever you're planning won't bring him back. If you want someone to talk to, go get a therapist. I hope you find the strength to heal and move on." She leans closer and allows her voice to drop in volume.

"But if you ever pull shit like this again, if you ever come near me and my family, my marriage, I will kill you myself."

Her point made, Cassandra takes the Arnold Palmers and returns to her husband's side.

22

SARAH

"Jared, good to see you again. Have a seat," Andy Bell stands to shake Jared's hand as Sarah stands next to him, slightly relaxed by the glass of wine she's just swallowed. This might be the key to surviving: stay tipsy enough to be unbothered but not drunk enough to embarrass herself.

Jared's firm hand around her waist means that he can tell the drink went to her head, but he's not upset about it. He's one day away from a possible huge victory and likely assumes that Sarah is just celebrating a little early. He has no reason to wonder if it's anything else.

"Thanks, man," Jared says to Andy. "Have you met my wife, Sarah?"

"Not had the pleasure yet, though Cassandra speaks highly of you. Nice to meet you, Sarah," Andy responds to her husband but looks at Sarah, hand stretched out waiting for her to take it.

His grip warm and firm, she begins to understand why Jared is so starstruck by this man. Everything about him should be intimidating: his height and build, his traditionally handsome features, the light sprinkling of grey throughout his hair. It was like standing before some kind of wise supermodel, if such a thing exists.

Contrary to his otherworldliness, Andy has kind eyes and an open smile, the only things making it possible for Sarah to respond simply with, "Nice to meet you, too."

As he redirects his attention to Jared, asking about Kansas and where to golf there if he ever visits, she tries to reconcile the man in front of her with the man who graced the covers of tabloids when she was growing up. He is attractive enough to get away with murder, no doubt, but the Andy Bell here tonight is no loose cannon. There's seemingly nothing being restrained under the surface, no wild streak being held back on a leash. This guy oozes wholesome family man.

"There she is," Andy pauses his conversation with Jared to kiss his wife on the cheek. Cassandra hands him a glass of iced tea, gazing back at him.

It's almost gross to look at.

Sarah wishes she had another drink.

"Why don't we have a seat, and Baby, I'll grab us a couple refills before this thing gets started," Jared says to the group, as if reading his wife's mind.

Andy pulls out his wife's seat and Sarah moves toward a chair two spaces over at their eight-seater round banquet table before she's interrupted. "Oh no, Sarah, you should sit by me," Cassandra insists. "Andy will sit on the other side of Jared for dinner." The arrangement separates Andy and Cassandra, though Sarah doesn't understand why she would suggest this.

Cassandra's smile has something cunning behind it that Sarah doesn't quite understand, but she knows she's being protected from something. In this arrangement, she's buffered by her husband and a woman she trusts, and Jared is guarded on the other side by Andy.

It occurs to Sarah that maybe Cassandra planned this with her husband ahead of time, but she knows not to ask.

"Thank you," is all she says back after she sits.

"I love your hair's highlights," Cassandra redirects. "Do you get it done at home?"

"Thank you, but I don't color it," Sarah admits, catching on to what the other woman is doing. "I suppose I just spend a lot of time outside."

"I envy you. Blonde is so expensive to maintain. Plus with all the chemicals, I run the constant risk of it falling out any day now."

And thus begins the inane female filler talk. Anyone passing by would not double-back for more information, and the topics will remain surface level to not be upsetting but engaging enough that Sarah won't be able to spiral in her own mind.

Jared returns with the drinks and excitedly jumps back into conversation with Andy. Sarah has relaxed so thoroughly she almost misses Cassandra's next comment.

"Andy knows all my tricks," she says, as if in reference to the pros and cons of Botox injections they'd just been discussing.

"He does?"

The other woman nods. "I keep him updated, especially of big changes, so he knows."

Dread seeps into Sarah's veins. They aren't talking about beautification procedures. "I see," she whispers. "Does he have any reason to inform Jared?"

"No, I told him not to," Cassandra replies easily. "But I stand by my earlier advice."

Sarah nods and takes a deep swig of her wine, "I'll think on the micro-needling you suggested."

With a friendly smirk, Cassandra raises one eyebrow along with her glass and clinks it against Sarah's to seal their discussion as the lights in the ballroom dim.

23

HILLARY

Hillary doesn't feel much better with Steven on her arm. She thought that his presence would be a comfort, but he's just drinking more beer and laughing way too loud with the other people at the table. The other couples seated with them are familiar to her, but she doesn't know any of the players well and the women are giving her an obvious cold shoulder.

At least Alex Garcia is at a table far away from her.

This pointless gala shouldn't run too late; everyone here must be up early and competing, after all. Hillary can only pray for a quiet exit, though the rate Steven is drinking won't allow for that luxury. At least the wait staff are beginning to guide everyone away from the bar and toward their tables. Starter salads have already been placed at each setting, but Hillary won't be able to get anything solid past the knot in her stomach.

When they were first married, Hillary loved the public events, getting dolled-up and shown off on Steven's arm. New to the scene, she'd been open to meeting people. She pictured friendships with other wives, someday hosting other couples in their home like Cassandra and Andy. She made grand plans for her future as a golf wife.

It hadn't taken long to become disillusioned with that dream. Hillary was an outsider, not from an approved background. She was too young, too sexual, too new money to be considered a matriarch amongst the other women. Her presence was a threat to the wives who married before their husbands became famous. Why should she get to reap all the benefits of being a professional athlete's wife when she hadn't put the time in before Steven started winning? After repeatedly receiving the cold shoulder from almost every other wife, Hillary decided to lean into the reputation they assigned her of being the gold-digging whore. They wanted to alienate her as competition, as a threat? She could show them what a threat really looked like.

Watch out for your husbands...

A gentle clinking of silverware against glass comes from the speakers throughout the room, moving everyone's attention to the stage.

"Thank you, everyone," the speaker says. "It is an honor to have you all here, the best in the game all in one room. I find that I'm a little starstruck myself," he jokes to polite laughter.

He continues, "For over fifty years, the Desert Invitational has hosted the champions of golf in a competition unparalleled in its intensity. The harsh weather conditions and mental acuity required by the players means that only someone truly talented walks away with a win. There are no accidental champions in the Desert.

"This year is no different, and tomorrow we are in for an exciting Sunday. That being said, we want to go ahead and get started with dinner before we end the night with a brief word from a special guest. I know everyone here probably wants to focus on rest tonight," he finishes to a smattering of polite laughter followed by the clinking of china filtering around the tables.

Steven doesn't appear to have listened to the speech, having already finished his salad and two rolls from the breadbasket. On a normal night, Hillary might have said something about it, but she doesn't have the energy. Too much has happened today for her to care that her husband is overeating the night before his final day of play in the tournament.

The fact that she is continually ignored by the women at her table doesn't ease her paranoia. It's like everyone around her, the wives, the other players, the stranger with the note from this morning, and whoever left her the tiny police cruiser knows something she doesn't. Or worse, knows something she knows she did and just hasn't been caught yet.

"Oh, Patricia," she says to the woman next to her, interrupting a quiet, giggly conversation between her and another wife on the other side of her. They can get away with not initiating a conversation with Hillary, but they can't rebuff her completely without drawing the ire of their husbands.

"Yes, Hillary?"

"Gordon's tie," she begins, alluding to Patricia's husband, "is fantastic. That color really works for him. I've never seen him look this good." She punctuates her statement with a drawn-out gaze at the man in question, not bothering to respond to Patricia's sputtering and insincere thanks. Hillary knows how the other wives see her, how the media has branded her throughout the years. Might as well weaponize it whenever she can. The other woman takes a long drink from her glass and pouts, not laughing again with her friend for the rest of the night.

Good. Now someone else at the table is as miserable as Hillary is.

How satisfying.

A tingling sensation settles across the back of her neck as she scans the room. She's used to having eyes on her in public, and she's accustomed enough to know the difference between being seen and being *watched*. The latter is what's causing her blood pressure to rise currently.

Her eyes catch one of the supervising waiters a few tables behind her, and she recognizes him. After he removes some glasses and plates, he turns to leave. His back and shoulders, though outfitted differently now, are the same ones she followed this morning.

This waiter is the man who delivered the note.

Hillary darts her gaze to Cassandra and Sarah's table. Neither of them has noticed him, nor can she locate Whitney in the crowd right now.

"Excuse me," she mumbles to the table as she stands. He's already at the door but if she hurries maybe she can catch him.

It's difficult to appear nonchalant when chasing a service worker.

Hillary is moving in the opposite direction of the halls leading toward the bathroom, so it looks like she is run-walking to the bar. Maybe she should have caused a scene; it's not like Hillary Torre has the best reputation with service workers as it stands. A tabloid headline about her yelling at a waiter would be a small price to pay for knowing who wrote the note.

As she loses sight of him behind the door, she picks up her pace. With a palm on the double swinging door, she pushes, only to be stopped by a hand on her wrist.

"Ma'am," the bartender says, "that's employees only. We can't have outside contaminants in the kitchen."

Had a man grabbed her wrist like that, she could have justifiably gone off the handle, but yelling at a woman both younger and shorter than her would do Hillary no favors. She also refrained from commenting on the fact that if they were so afraid of contamination, the wait staff shouldn't be interacting with the guests so much. Instead, she settled on a tight smile. "Of course," she offered, and stepped toward the bar with the younger woman not far behind her.

From here, she could plausibly wait for drinks for her and Steven while waiting out the man in the kitchen. He hadn't seemed like he noticed her following him, but he also wasn't in the standard uniform, wearing something more managerial. If he didn't have an assigned table, he might not come back out. Plus, he could easily sit in the kitchen or make some back door escape.

What was his role in this? Hillary couldn't get a grasp on what purpose the note served. Maybe he was an errand boy, but that meant someone had hired him. If this was all a silly and mean-spirited prank, then hired help would be overkill. People engaging in pranks enlisted free assistance, like friends with twisted senses of humor.

A hired hand meant this was something else, the realization causing Hillary's blood to chill.

I've had an affair with one of your husbands.

The idea of Steven having an affair gives her a feeling akin to acid reflux, but it is so unlikely that Hillary wastes little time thinking about it. Unless the note was meant to draw someone out—

"Ma'am?"

"What?" Hillary snaps at the bartender.

"Last call," the young woman responds. "We've been instructed to close the bar during the speeches, but we'll be open again for dessert and after dinner coffee. Can I get you something?"

Though she's loath to be seen walking with it, she orders a tall can of beer for her husband. He is most likely to complain that the bar is closing at all, so she may as well keep him stocked up. As she watches the bartender crack open the can, she sees the woman's eyes wander to a glass tip jar, almost as if hinting toward an action from Hillary.

Hillary glares back at her, eyes narrowing. *What? I'm not tipping you for opening a free beer can you greedy little shit.*

Just in time, she returns to her seat as the lights above them dim and the dinner plates are either removed or left empty on runners in front of each guest. Steven sees what she brought him and looks so grateful it's almost pathetic. When he leans over to kiss her cheek, Hillary accepts it, beer breath and all. "Thanks, Hil," he says.

When was the last time she did something small and thoughtful for her husband?

"Ladies and gentlemen," the announcer is back, too soon in her opinion. "I spoke earlier about all the talent in this room, the excitement we feel rolling into Sunday morning. But there is also some sadness here tonight. One of our top PGA players, a man lost to us too soon, should be here with us this weekend. He was a leader among his peers, and a pillar of the golf community. The world lost him when he was at the top of his game, and we can only speculate, heartbroken, at what he would have been capable of had he been given more time. As a community, we all lost Rowan Silver last year in a tragic accident."

Hillary clenches a single fist under the table, where no one can see it.

"And we mourn that loss every day, but his wife, Whitney Silver, mourns that loss most acutely. In her grief, she has worked hard to preserve Rowan's memory through her charitable foundation, Silver Linings Golf Group. In less than a year, she has already generated scholarship opportunities for dozens of kids nationally and the group is only growing in its charitable influence.

"Because of this selflessness on Mrs. Silver's part, and in memory of

Rowan's great legacy, the PGA board wanted to do something new. As of the Desert Invitational 2022, we are officially instating an annual award to be given to an outstanding player every year. This award will not only represent strength and excellence on the course, but also humility and commitment to charity in their daily lives."

The announcer pauses to indicate the small statue on the table behind him. "We will be awarding the first annual Rowan Silver Commemorative Award at tonight's dinner, but for the first and last time, this award won't be going to a player in the tournament. Please join me in giving a round of applause to Whitney Silver, this year's award winner."

Politely enthusiastic applause follows the announcement, as Whitney carefully steps up to the stage and walks toward the podium. After a handshake in which words were shared privately between Mrs. Silver and the announcer, the widow approaches the podium while she clings to the trophy. Hillary can see the tight grip from her seat in the middle of the crowd.

After using her free hand to adjust the height of the microphone, Whitney begins speaking. "Wow, thank you everyone, and thank you to the PGA for this award. This is truly a surprise."

Hillary almost gives herself a brain aneurism trying not to roll her eyes.

"When I lost Rowan last year, I was tempted to think that my life was over," the widow continues. "I loved my husband. When the car wreck took him from me, all I could feel was disbelief or despair. It was like giant parts of myself had been torn out and buried with him."

The audience is quiet, unsettled. They were prepared to clap respectfully but weren't expecting such a public display of grief.

"In the days after his death, I let myself wallow until I felt a tug. It was like I could sense Rowan pulling me up, telling me that he didn't want this for me even though he was gone. I realized that all I could do was move forward. So instead of allowing parts of me to die with him, I chose to continue his legacy.

"Rowan loved golf. He loved the strategy, the tradition, even his unlikely friendships with competitors. He lived for the game, and I know he always lamented that not everyone was able to give it a shot. He often privately paid for lessons or fees of children who wanted to play but couldn't afford it.

"These actions when he was alive became my inspiration for Silver Linings Golf Group. It was the best way I could think of to continue his dreams and his legacy after he was gone. I think if he could see what his name was accomplishing today, he'd be as proud of these kids as he was with any of his tour wins."

Light clapping emits from the tables, emphasizing Whitney's sentiment without cutting her speech short. "When I started Silver Linings, I didn't anticipate the success we'd have. I thought we might get some donations from Rowan's old friends and colleagues, but I had no idea that the national response would be so resounding and supportive. It heals my heart to see so many people resonate with my late husband's dreams for the game of golf.

"Because of this unexpected growth, I fear that the foundation has outgrown me. In the next few weeks, I will be stepping down as CEO so someone with more business savvy can take the reins." A soft chuckle comes from the crowd at Whitney's self-deprecation. "Though I will still participate on the board, freeing up the top position will allow me to be more hands on with children involved with Silver Linings. With no children of my own, I very much look forward to that change in pace.

"All that being said, I don't want to take up too much more of your time. I just want to reiterate how grateful I am for this honor, and for the honor you've bestowed on my late husband by instituting this award. I can't thank you all enough for helping make Silver Linings the success it is today."

Whitney smiles softly, sadly, as the audience erupts into its obligatory end-of-speech applause. The announcer from earlier is making his way back up the stairs to presumably usher in the dessert course, but Hillary sees the widow's fist around her trophy whiten further.

Before the woman speaks again, Hillary holds her breath. This won't be good.

"One more thing," Whitney says into the microphone, surprising everyone except Hillary. The clapping stops, as does the announcer on the steps. He wasn't expecting this either.

"Rowan was not the one driving that night. Whoever was in the car with him, the one in the driver's seat, just know that I haven't stopped searching for you. Eventually, I will find you, and I will get retribution for the death of my husband."

Whitney pauses for a breath before walking herself off the stage without an escort. There's no clapping this time, the small crowd stunned silent. No one knows how to respond to the scene she just caused, and it seems like the widow knows she made everyone uncomfortable and is proud of it. She leaves the stage, finds a door to the hallway, and exits without saying goodbye to anyone.

The announcer makes a valiant attempt to lift the crowd's spirits by reopening the bar and pointing out the dessert buffet to one side of the room, making a lame joke about taking the edge off before bed. Hillary doesn't hear much of it though. She's too busy reading the text message from Gwen on her phone.

One day left.

≈

BREAKING: Professional Golfer Found Dead in Car Accident
July 6, 2021

Early this morning, emergency services discovered Rowan Silver, aged 41, dead in an apparent car accident in the woods outside Andy Bell's, aged 39, Sante Fe mountain home. The golfers were joined by their wives and several other couples in what appeared to be a casual dinner party before practice rounds for the Desert Invitational began. No witnesses at the party saw Silver leave that night.

The police arrived after park security saw the car in a ditch off the road during a nightly surveillance drive. Silver was pulled from the passenger seat of the wreckage shortly after by EMTs and declared dead due to traumatic head injury by the same workers at 1:15 a.m. No driver was found in or around the vehicle at the time.

The car was a rental registered to Steven Torre, though both he and his wife were witnessed staying at the party until its conclusion and are not being treated as persons of interest.

Silver's widow, Whitney Silver, was unavailable for comment. Local law enforcement is asking for anyone with information regarding the wreck or the missing driver to please contact them immediately.

<This is a breaking news story; Please refresh the page for updates.>

24

CASSANDRA

Cassandra walks out of the ballroom on Andy's arm and scans the crowd. Its size wasn't overwhelming, but all the players who made the cut were invited. No one knew what to make of Whitney's speech. If her goal had been to completely alter the mood of the tournament, she very well might have succeeded.

Cassandra is glad that Andy was able to catch up with some old friends he didn't get paired with this weekend. Everyone loves her husband, and she doesn't mind sharing him at events like this. Even with the unpleasant conversation with Whitney, Sarah's very clear distress, and the continued shunning she received from some of the PGA wives, these tournament dinners were a breath of fresh air compared to what she grew up dealing with in her own family.

Formal dinners and charity galas remind her of when she met her husband. Her father, in an effort to bolster donations before election season, had hosted a dinner with some of his wealthier supporters. Cassandra had just graduated from the University of Montana and was home for the summer before work in her father's senate offices commenced for her. She didn't care about politics, but it was supposed to be an easy job. According to her father, nepotism was only bad if someone truly incompetent benefited, and incompetent she was not.

However, Cassandra had started realizing shortly after being seated that her job had less to do with political office work and more to do with the young man she'd been assigned to sit beside at dinner. The son and heir of a major oil processor in the state, William Harris, Jr—Harry—was directing most of his attention her way. Too much attention.

It wasn't difficult to speak blandly with him about safe topics. She was raised in that world, and she could navigate it with the best of them. In politics, one learned early to converse in a way that made the listener believe they heard what they wanted to hear without actually promising anything or picking a side. Cassandra had spent thirty minutes nodding along and saying "that's nice" to most of what he'd been saying, while poor Harry probably believed they were one step away from an engagement.

"Do you play?" Harry asked.

Cassandra hadn't been following the conversation, and unfortunately didn't know what Harry was talking about. She began with a reluctant smile before replying, "It's just so hard to find time with Daddy's election coming up."

"I understand," he said, empathy coating his expression, and he reached an arm around the back of her chair. "I find it hard to find time to get out to the courts since graduating from Harvard. Their student center was unmatched. Next week I have a spot reserved to practice here locally with a buddy, but he ended up cancelling on me. Maybe we could go together?"

It was courts, so probably tennis. Or racquetball, or basketball, or handball.

Shoot.

"I'm sorry," she mustered with the full artillery of apologetic posturing in her arsenal, "but I'm actually out of town next week."

"Really? I thought your dad said you were available for me while I was in town."

"He must have been mistaken," Cassandra replied before fisting the napkin in her lap. It was then that she began to fantasize about murdering Harry and her father in earnest.

A girl had to entertain herself somehow.

Long-term strategic donors weren't the only ones in attendance that night. Her father had also recruited a few Montana-based celebrities to keep excitement high among the guests while he made deals quietly throughout the night. One of them was a nationally ranked bull rider and was currently surrounded by the bored older wives of Cassandra's father's team. He appeared in his element, happily indulging their innocent attraction with exaggerated tales of taming wild beasts. They oohed and gasped appropriately when his stories required it. One of the bolder ladies was fondly rubbing her hand up and down his left bicep hypnotically, possibly experiencing an overdose of testosterone exposure.

The other celebrity guest had been Andy Bell.

Perhaps less inclined to carry on for attention like his counterpart, or maybe just more jaded by fame, Andy had kept to speaking with men he already knew. He was open and laughing but didn't appear to desire to play the role her father assigned him. More likely, Cassandra's father needed Andy more than Andy needed him.

After a fifth mention of Harvard came from Harry during their short discussion, Cassandra's façade broke, a small eye roll sneaking out even as she fought it. She was good, but she wasn't that good. Luckily, Harry didn't notice, but a strong, compelling laugh from across the room attracted her attention. If something was funny, she wanted to be a part of it, even if it meant abandoning her station.

When she looked for the laughter, she didn't find any ongoing conversations or spilled drinks that could explain it. She only saw Andy, two tables away, still shaking in the shoulders but grinning directly at her.

While she tried her best to return her attention to Harry, she couldn't shake her awareness of the other man, especially when she saw him stand in her peripheral vision and make his way closer. The moments of his casual stroll towards her table took forever and no time at all. In the meantime, Harvard was brought up a sixth time.

Soon, Andy had been standing right next to Cassandra and looked directly at her. Holding his drink, all he said was, "Come with me." No permission asked, no excuses given. She didn't need to be told twice.

When she moved to stand up, Harry tried to get out of his seat as well but was stopped by Andy's firm hand on his shoulder. "Not you," he'd said, still looking at her.

Trying not to laugh, Cassandra had taken the hand he held out to her and followed Andy to the balcony, where an early summer Montana breeze kept the air balmy. The sun was already behind the tree line, leaving them with only the light pouring out from the dinner room while they walked deeper into the night where the quid pro quo discussions couldn't reach them.

Normally, she was extremely comfortable with high profile strangers, but alone with Andy she recognized this was not going to be a standard interaction with one of her father's donors.

"I'm Cassandra." She started with the basics when his elbows met the railing of the balcony, not bothering to ask who he was. It would have been a silly question.

"I know," he smiled back at her, his expression relaxed. His lean put them close to the same height, and Cassandra's pulse elevated being in the proximity of someone so good looking. She thought that if an injury ever took him away from golf, he would do well in Hollywood. Well, only if he ended up being full of shit, as most people from that town are, but she would give him the benefit of the doubt.

"And I'm sure you can take care of yourself, but I could tell you wanted out of that conversation," he continued, humor in his voice.

"Harry is nice enough."

"How diplomatic of you."

She gave him a sardonic lifted eyebrow. "I was raised by the best," she only halfway joked.

"I see that," he responded. His face was more serious after that, as if he'd heard what she hadn't said aloud.

"Are you at least having fun?" Cassandra redirected.

"This isn't my usual scene," he admitted. "My agent thinks that participating in more serious extracurriculars would be good for my image."

"Smart guy," she said. She wasn't wrong. Andy had been on what she estimated to be month eighteen of a PR rehab tour. He hadn't been photographed at strip clubs or casinos or with women in general for over a year, instead establishing himself as a wholesome man of the people, with children's charities and stopping to autograph for kids and not groupies.

Family-focused, Republican politics appeared to be the next step of his agent's plan.

Not that she'd been following him that closely.

Andy gave her a knowing look then turned to face her. "I think I'm starting to have fun, though."

Over the next month, they met in secret, with Cassandra hiding the relationship from her father and Andy protecting her from the media. It was new and exciting, but fragile, as all new relationships can be. Part of her thought it was somehow meant to be. They laughed together often, sharing a similar sense of humor. Andy also had her awareness and distrust of the media, both of them having been coached in managing the public eye. Every time he kissed her it felt like a first kiss, and she could gaze at someone as beautiful as him for hours.

Cassandra had concerns though. He was ten years her senior, and they came from different, albeit parallel worlds. She was also hesitant to bring the relationship up to her father until she was sure about Andy. The senator was still pushing Harvard Harry at her, and she could only dodge questions about her unwillingness for so long.

After two months of secrecy, Andy took her to a formal dinner where he had rented out the back half of the restaurant for privacy. Orders placed, he leaned into the table on his forearms and began speaking.

"I want to keep doing this," he said. If he was nervous, it didn't show. "I care about you, deeply, but I need to make sure we're on the same page. Continuing means eventually telling people, specifically your father and the public. I don't want to do that unless we're both serious here."

"I agree," she responded. "What would you call serious?" It's a question she'd been wanting to ask, and he gave her the perfect opening. She hadn't wanted to seem desperate or clingy, asking him "what are we" like an insecure teenager.

He broke his tight-lipped smile as the waiter approached with their wine. Cassandra held her breath as Andy tested then subsequently approved of the wine he'd chosen. She hated the waiter for interrupting such an important moment for her, and she hoped that Andy would come back to their discussion quickly.

She wasn't disappointed.

He set his glass down and looked directly into her eyes. "What I mean by serious is that I want a wife. I want a partner that I love, and who supports me, who will be the mother of my children. When I look at you, I can see those things for us. I want it to be you.

"However, my life is not a normal one, as you know. I'm going to ask a lot of my wife. The travel, the media, all of it. I need someone who is not only committed to me, but to supporting my profession. Now, I'm fairly sure we want the same things, but I need to hear you say it. If you have any kind of aspirations outside of family, maybe a desire to follow in your father's path with a political career, then I need to know now, because we won't work. It will break my heart, but it would be better to end it now.

"But if you want the same things that I do," he continued, looking vulnerable suddenly in the midst of his speech. "Then I'm all in."

Cassandra had stood up from her seat and moved toward Andy as he pushed his chair away from the table. As she curled into his lap, she held his face and kissed him, attempting to communicate before she spoke. He responded by pulling her close, and the shaking she felt told her he had been far more nervous about this conversation than he'd let on. She almost wanted to tease him; how could he think she'd give this up for anything?

"I choose you," she whispered in his ear, followed by a giggle when she saw an extremely uncomfortable looking waiter standing in the corner with their food.

That night had been bliss, but reality followed shortly after. Cassandra knew she needed to get the news of her relationship to her father before he found out from someone else and decided to confront him the next day.

It did not go well. The senator had ranted and raved about her lack of gratitude for all he'd done for her, how she owed him this and that. She'd heard it all before and had to stop herself from mouthing the lecture back to him mockingly. When he finally hit her with what he thought was the trump card, she was prepared.

"If you continue seeing Mr. Bell, I'll disown you."

It would hurt. Cassandra had always been close with her father, closer than she had been with her mother or siblings. They complemented each other well, and he often engaged her in debate surrounding whatever vote was coming up on the senate floor.

"Why did you vote 'no'?" She asked once while sitting next to him on the porch when she was in the eighth grade. "I thought we wanted more national park funding?"

"We do want it. But we need Senator Corbin to vote yes on the foreign aid to one of our key allies and he won't do it unless we release that funding to his home state for migrant aid. We made a deal."

Cassandra frowned. "Why can't we just vote 'yes' on the good stuff and 'no' on the bad stuff?"

"It doesn't always work that way," he smiled down at his daughter. "Someday you'll understand."

She did eventually understand, but that understanding came with resentment toward the political order rather than affection. If her father thought the machinations of an over-bloated federal machine appealed to her at all, he must have been blind.

But in spite of their differences, Cassandra had a deep well of affection for the old senator, and choosing Andy over him would cause an irreparable fissure between them. "I don't care," she smiled back sweetly. Before he could bluster further, she explained calmly that she was more than happy to move in with a roommate and work a regular job if that's what it took. She didn't mention that she felt a proposal was coming from Andy soon and it would be a moot point anyway. Cassandra just emphasized her willingness to be financially independent.

"What happens when he's done with you? I won't have you crawling back to me."

She had stood up and approached the senator's desk while he remained seated. "I would hate to see all the press surrounding this if you publicly disown me," she continued. "You've spent your entire career branding yourself as a family first politician, the loving father and husband. What do you think the New York Times or CNN or Fox News for that matter will have to say about you disowning your beloved daughter because she refused to marry into Big Oil?"

As redness flooded her father's face, she knew she'd won, but not without cost. He wouldn't disown her, but their relationship would never return to the tenuous affection they'd had before. Cassandra had chosen Andy, and they both knew it.

Andy guides her towards the elevator now. He pulls her through the entrance and slams his thumb on the button requesting a closed door, ensuring they're alone.

"Finally," he whispers, his hand on her lower back.

"You read my mind," she says back, thinking she would rather die than let any anonymous threat come between them.

She needs to find the note's author before the tournament ends tomorrow.

25

WHITNEY

Lying in a hotel bed alone holds no appeal for Whitney, so she's trying to sleep on the small couch in her suite. She learned quickly that having too much space around her at night means she won't get any sleep, but having the sides of the sofa press into her is a comfort. Rowan had always held her at night and the vastness of a king-sized bed is too much for her these days. Even at home, she gave up their bed months ago, sleeping on couches and once in the bathtub, though a sore neck the next day meant it was the only time she did that. She wonders what this must look like to the house-keepers who haven't had to make the bed since last September.

If Rowan could see her, what would he think? Would he be proud of her? Would he understand that she's trying, in her own way, to keep him alive in everything she's doing?

When he was here, his charitable spending had been a point of contention. Sure, she loved his generosity, but he would often go overboard, paying for entire semesters of college and even cancer treatments of children who took golf lessons with any of his swing coaches. It was all very inspiring, but Whitney did not understand his need to remain completely anonymous.

"You could start a foundation or a 501c3, at least," she'd argued.

"That's not why I do it, Whitney. I do it because it's the right thing to do, and these kids need help."

"But keeping it hidden this way doesn't make any sense. Your work should be known by everyone, maybe not for the thanks, but at least to inspire others."

"Sweetheart," he'd said, motioning for her to sit on his lap. She moved towards him eagerly, always hungry for his touch, any connection to him. As he held her, he continued, "I don't want anyone to know. It's important to me to remain anonymous."

"But why?" Whitney didn't understand. Plenty of professional golfers had charities and donated publicly. No one condemned them for not being private about it.

"It's not even really about charity or where the money is going," he sighed, pulling her closer and placing a hand on her stomach. "I'm doing it to heal. I'm still processing the fact that we won't be able to have our own."

Whitney turns on the couch and rests a hand on her lower abdomen. Rowan had been devastated by the news, but sensitive enough not to blame her. Giving away vast amounts of his wealth had been his way of dealing with the pain of never becoming a father. While he wasn't practicing as an adult, his Catholic upbringing meant he was resistant to surrogacy and before his death they had talked about adopting, but the process promised to be long and arduous.

She wishes his Catholic background had kept him from his other, more inappropriate ways of coping with his grief, but she loved him enough to ignore certain indiscretions. As long as he came home to her, she could be happy.

At the time of their struggles, a small and deeply selfish part of Whitney had been relieved that she couldn't have kids. This way, she wouldn't have to share Rowan. They could exist in a honeymoon forever, a world of their own. If the adoption updates were "lost" under stacks of Whitney's shoeboxes in the closet, well then that was just an unfortunate accident. They had other things to focus on, like Rowan's practice schedule and their time together.

Whitney winces with guilt as she thinks back on her husband. In many ways, Silver Linings Golf Group went against much of how he operated when he was alive. Having his name slapped across every charitable dona-tion he made would have been anathema to him.

Do you understand, Rowan, what I am trying to do?

Giving up on sleep, Whitney rises and pulls the blanket around herself. The dry night air has cooled, not enough to turn on any heat but enough that the extra layer is a welcome comfort to her. Maybe after this weekend, she can make some of the changes she's been planning in her head. They would be necessary this time. She's been punishing herself, staying in the house they shared, keeping his side of the closet full of his old things. Instead of moving on, as everyone seems to think she should, she spends every morning reopening the wound, smelling his old shirts.

She leaves his favorite coffee mug next to the espresso machine, and his loafers by the door. It's a punishment, a reminder of who she lost.

Sliding the balcony door open, she walks into the night. For being a populated area and a well-visited vacation destination, the resort has done a good job of limiting light pollution, and the stars are bright overhead. Whitney has never been a stargazer, but even she can appreciate this view.

For a brief moment, she turns to mention how lovely it is, to share the spectacle with someone.

But there is no one behind her. She's utterly alone, Rowan is gone forever, and she'll never be able to share this night sky with him.

After a sigh, she returns inside and admits to herself that it's time to put her husband's loafers away when she gets home.

26

SARAH

I'm in over my head, Sarah thinks as she washes her face. The whole weekend is a nightmare. She should be focusing on the fact that Jared has a shot at winning tomorrow. This should be a time of excitement and celebration, but Sarah has only added confusion to her laundry list of concerns today. She's surprised Jared hasn't said more to her about her attitude, but he has more important things to think about.

"Weird speech," she hears Jared call from their room.

"Yeah, for sure," is all she says back. After rinsing the suds away, she pulls her hair out of her bun and begins brushing it. She brushes through her strands fifty times before bed every evening, outdated advice perhaps, but a habit she can't seem to break, and which now gives her comfort. She uses the countdown in her mind to catalogue her thoughts. One pass of the brush, Jared has a chance to win. Two passes of the brush, someone wrote her a note this morning accusing her husband of possible infidelity. Three passes of the brush, Sarah hasn't decided if she believes it.

"Maybe she just cracked," Jared replied. "She's had a hard year and stuff. I can't imagine." Sarah hears him rustling around in their luggage through the door.

Four passes of the brush, there are other wives involved who know more than she does.

"Babe, did you pack any Aleve? I don't want to be sore tomorrow." He always keeps a bottle in his golf bag but must have forgotten to bring extra in his luggage.

"I think there's some in my purse," she calls back. She's at eighteen brush strokes now.

The movement outside stops, Jared having found the pain relievers. Sarah counts diligently through her final brush strokes, listing out her other worries about her mother and what to wear tomorrow before moisturizing her face and brushing her teeth. It's a routine she commits to every night, even at the occasional complaint of her husband, but she needs her routine now more than ever. Sometimes she finds he's already fallen asleep before she's done. It happens more often than not, and she assumes that's the case tonight. He's still quiet in their room, and he's probably exhausted from a week of practice and three days of playing.

Sarah exits the bathroom, quietly tiptoeing into their suite when she stops at the fully made and still empty bed. Frowning, she scans the room and sees Jared hasn't even gotten undressed yet. He's sitting, dress shirt unbuttoned, hunched over something on the desk. Whatever he's reading, it bothers him.

"Jared?"

He doesn't hear her, or maybe he's ignoring her. She doesn't have to take more than a few steps before she recognizes what he's reading.

Sarah left the anonymous note from this morning in her purse. Jared is reading about a woman claiming to have had an affair with someone's husband and she has no idea what to say to him. Keeping this a secret from him now feels amazingly foolish. How does this look to him? It occurs to her briefly that he may believe she wrote it, but then she dismisses this. It's not her handwriting, and Jared is used to little notes from Sarah throughout the house.

"What is this?" he asks.

"A note." Brilliant, Sarah. Absolutely brilliant.

"Yeah, I got that," he says. "Where did it come from? How did you get it?"

Sarah swallows, then tries to explain, "They called a few of the wives to the press tent this morning. Cassandra Bell, Whitney Silver, Hillary

Torre, and me. They said they had a communication for us or something."

Jared doesn't say anything. Simply giving her a flat look that tells her to keep going.

"One of the volunteers collected us into a corner and said there was a note for each of us. When we opened them, they all said the same thing."

"Are you sure they found the right people? Maybe they called your name by mistake."

She shakes her head. "My name was on the envelope."

"Why didn't you tell me?" Jared's eyes aren't focused anywhere when he speaks, not on the note, and certainly not on his wife. He looks sick, or maybe just confused.

"Cassandra thought it might be a prank or a distraction. Something meant to pull your attention away from winning, so I didn't want to tell you," she says.

"I can handle distractions, Sarah," Jared responds, his knuckles whitened with his grip on the chair. "You could and should have brought this to me. Some freak is sending my wife notes, apparently trying to get me off my game," he stands now and takes her face in his hands. "You can't just keep something like this from me. I should have been able to help handle this for you."

He stands up, tossing the note behind him. Seeking to comfort her and perhaps further understand how this all came to be, Jared holds both sides of her face. She can feel his desperate imploring, his attempts to make a connection with her, but she needs time. She isn't ready for him to see her yet.

When Sarah finally looks back into his eyes, she fails to hide something unnameable, yet vital, from her face. When Jared sees it, he drops his hands, and the tenderness behind his gaze shatters.

"Unless you thought it might be true."

He runs his hand through his hair, and it stays mussed, still heavy with product from earlier in the night. He steps away from her as if she's a physical manifestation of what she just revealed. Every move he makes farther away from her is like a jagged ice pick tearing through her soul.

"Fuck, Sarah. Are you serious? You really thought it would be possible?

That I was capable of doing that to you? To us? You cannot possibly be that insecure." The harsh way he speaks only confirms that she's made a huge mistake. They are isolated from one another now, all because she didn't trust him. This isn't the first time her lack of confidence has created problems for them, but it's about the worst example she can think of right now.

"I was going to tell you after the tournament," Sarah lies, a desperate attempt to bring him closer. In truth, she hadn't thought that far ahead when it came to the note and its implications. It's possible she would have kept it from him forever if she could, especially if it meant keeping that broken hearted note from his voice.

Jared releases a humorless laugh. "I don't think I believe you. I think you were just going to let this fester."

He glances back at the note, then at Sarah, then the single bed in their one-room suite. Shaking his head, he continues, "I need space."

"What?"

"I...I'm going for a walk or something. I can't be here right now," he says.

Without looking back at her or waiting for a reply, Jared picks up his phone and wallet, pocketing them in a jerky manner. When he leaves, the door doesn't slam, like Sarah thinks it should, instead it slowly closes.

The sobbing begins in earnest when it finally clicks shut.

27

CASSANDRA

Back in the room, Cassandra kicks off her heels with a soft sigh and she digs her feet into the carpet. She tosses her purse on the desk in their suite and rolls her neck, worn out from the day. There is a lot going on, even for her, and the volume on the drama feels like it's been turned up to eleven. Dealing with other wives, the media in everyone's ear poisoning public opinion surrounding the new league, not to mention the competition itself all weigh heavily on Cassandra as she gets ready for bed.

She makes a mental note to send flowers to her mother-in-law next week as a thank you gift for her babysitting this weekend.

She'd never doubted Andy's loyalty for a moment, but the note came as a reminder that caring for her husband as a man in many ways came before their required roles as parents. Plus, any false rumors started about his infidelity could be quashed easily when they were seen sharing a room together for the whole tournament.

No need to tempt fate when she could have him alone with her for another night.

Another sigh escapes her as she thinks on her conversations from earlier.

"What if I told you I don't believe Rowan's death was an accident?"

Cassandra can't judge. She'd go insane, too, if anything ever happened to her husband, but Whitney appeared to be clinging to news of her husband's death as if it would bring him back. If she had any doubts about Whitney's sincerity about her beliefs surrounding Rowan's death, the bizarre turn of her speech eliminated them. The widow was a true believer in the conspiracy of her husband's fatal end. The police had never found the driver of the car Rowan Silver had died in, but there was no second car, no witnesses to interview. There was nothing about the scene of the wreck that implied anything other than what it seemed: an accident.

A tragic, heartbreaking accident.

Shaking off the thoughts, Cassandra removes her wedding band and sets it on the desk. Even the idea of that happening to Andy hints at a pain so unbearable she might not survive it. Perhaps she should have more grace toward what Whitney is going through.

Then she remembers the countless negative interviews Whitney gave about Andy and changes her mind.

As she walks into the bathroom for help with the zipper on her dress, Andy spits some toothpaste in the sink and grins at her, waving the note she received that morning.

"'I've had an affair with one of your husbands.' What kind of middle school bullshit is this?"

She'd told him about the note while they were getting ready for dinner. Cassandra had explained her suspicions, not about his defecting to the new league specifically, but about someone just trying to stir up trouble for the tournament leaders. They'd had a good laugh before the charity gala, and Andy had agreed not to say anything about it to the other husbands. His interaction with the note in any way would give its author exactly what he or she wanted.

The best revenge on the note's author would be for him to win tomorrow.

If he had concerns about the other husbands being unfaithful to their wives, he hadn't voiced them. Men didn't share like that with each other, so it was one hundred percent possible he didn't have any relevant information that would help her anyhow.

Sure, there were the players with reputations, men who embraced the scoundrel image. Andy himself had engaged in many of them in his youth before he met Cassandra and was not one to pass judgement. However, the men who are known for their wandering eye, who see a weekend alone as a chance to stray, are men that Andy avoids. He wants no part in that, and if asked about it, he would say something clichéd about how playing near a pigsty makes everyone around them dirty.

Better to be nowhere near the pigs, as they say.

"Maybe we should have your agent loop in his PR guy," Cassandra says. "If there's any validity to the threat, it would be best to have a response if something comes out."

"Easy enough," he replies. "PR should be easy when you're telling the truth."

She raises an eyebrow at him.

Andy throws his head back and laughs. "Point taken, Mrs. Cynical. Do we even care who wrote this thing?"

She shrugs. "Probably someone looking to distract you," she says, and presents her back to him. He works her zipper downward without hesitation, and his practiced fingers moving down her spine give her a little thrill. After ten years, she thought it would be different, but she finds she still can't get enough of Andy.

"The only thing powerful enough to distract me is you," he responds, moving his hands under her dress to cup her breasts from behind. As his mouth moves into the dip between her shoulder and neck, Cassandra looks up into the mirror, seeing the image they present.

She takes a mental snapshot, hoping to keep it forever, and thinks to herself that anyone who would imply infidelity between them doesn't know a goddamned thing about her marriage or her family.

28

BARTENDER #3

We finished cleaning up after the gala around 11:30 and, mercifully, a different crew is going to go in tomorrow to break down tables and bars. I have no idea if this is standard practice for the hotel staff, but I'm grateful, nonetheless. As I drag my feet to my car, I negotiate with myself on whether I go home for the night or sleep in my vehicle.

Sleeping in my bed would be better for me, and I could shower privately, but I live thirty minutes away from the course. If I sleep in my car, I get an extra hour of rest but risk extreme soreness tomorrow. I'd also have to bathe on site, which would be annoying, but the country club does have better shampoo than I can afford for myself. On the other hand, then I also have to re-wear whichever of my uniforms is less grimy since I don't have a clean one.

The fact that I have to make choices like this pisses me off. I'm a bartender. I'm not saving lives or making millions, so why am I subjected to this kind of workload? One of the perks of being lower-middle class is that I'm supposed to be free from stressing about a career in exchange for being stressed about bills. Now, I'm having to do both? Jesus.

Well, pouting won't change anything. Taking a deep breath, I remind myself that it's a major golf tournament, and most of my work weeks don't resemble this one even remotely. I tell myself I have a lot to be grateful for, even if I can't list anything right now. The engine revs to life after I turn the key and my phone pings at the same time. A quick glance at the screen tells me the decision on where to sleep has been made for me.

"Mother Fucker," I whisper, livid.

Greg Yeager: the pos system at the clubhouse bar needs to be updated before anyone can clock-in tomorrow btw

Greg Yeager: need you to do it

You cannot be serious, I type, faster than I can rationalize. This could get snippy. *It takes over an hour for that system to update. I'll have to get there at four am, so it's done before our kitchen staff arrives.*

I wish I had a pillow to scream in. I want to hurt something. This is utterly infuriating, and I need to yell into the void, but I settle for banging my head on the steering wheel three times before letting it rest with my eyes closed. After I gather myself, I sigh and roll down my windows then shut my car off. At least my driver's seat can be reclined, unlike the passenger one, which has been stuck for years.

I have almost relaxed enough to let my anger go and finally get some sleep when my phone pings one more time.

Greg Yeager: What's done is done. We can only move forward.

What the hell does that mean? The asshole can't even feign an apology. It sounds like therapy talk for not taking any responsibility for your actions. The text reminds me of my high school boyfriend that I caught making out with another girl at homecoming my junior year. He'd tried to reason with me that it was in the past, and why couldn't I be more chill about it?

Because "the past" is still sitting on your lap, Josh.

Now I'm mad at Greg, and a relationship that has been dead for over five years. Great.

I cross my arms and lean back, trying to calm my breathing. Unless I get some rest, I'm almost guaranteed to have a worse day tomorrow.

❧

Sunday

The Golf Channel: Final Round Coverage for the Desert Invitational
July 17, 2022

Barbara Knoll: In all my years of covering USGA events, I think this Sunday of the 2022 Desert Invitational is going to be one of the most exciting days of golf I'll ever see.

Curtis Sheffield: I couldn't agree more, Barbara. This weekend is all coming to a head in today's pairings and with no clear leader running away with it, we're in for an entertaining competition. First, let's go over some of the younger guys on the leaderboard.

Barbara: Jared Farmer is a clear standout for the newer guys in professional golf right now. Tied for the lead, he's had a strong and consistent showing this entire weekend. If he can keep his head on straight, he has a real shot at being named the winner by the end of the day.

Curtis: That's right, Farmer has been really steady competition for the more veteran players this weekend, alongside Matthew Price. Only an amateur, Price's consistency leaves something to be desired, but he had that fabulous hole-in-one yesterday morning and with the right score today, is very likely to leave the Desert Invitational with a top twenty finish.

Barbara: What are your thoughts on the other leaders, Curtis?

Curtis: Andy Bell and Alex Garcia are causing quite the upset this weekend. Their absence from PGA events this past year has made them dark horses coming into one of the largest majors in professional golf and nobody could have guessed at their performances.

Barbara: It really could have gone either way. Both men were strong competitors when they joined the new league, and the online betting markets were split over whether or not the lack of young players in the new league was going to make them soft, or if they could maintain their legacies coming back into the fold.

Curtis: Which of them do you think is going to pull ahead?

Barbara: I wouldn't bet a cent on this tournament, Curtis. There's too many variables.

Curtis: You always were smarter than me, Barbara. <Shuffles papers>

Now, we have a quick commercial break before we start getting coverage from the practice range, but first we have some tragic news.

Barbara: Yes, unfortunately we don't have very much information for you guys watching at home yet, but we just received breaking news that one of the USGA volunteers for this week's tournament was found dead outside the resort early this morning. The identity of the volunteer and the cause of death have not been released to the press yet to give time to locate next of kin, but as soon as we have any updates we will share them with those of you tuning in.

Curtis: In the meantime, please keep the deceased, as well as their friends and loved ones, in your thoughts and prayers today. I know Barbara and I will.

29

BARTENDER #3

SUNDAY

My neck hurts, badly, and my eyes have an exhausted grittiness to them that makes them tender enough that I can't even rub them clean. And yet, I got just enough sleep to not be a horrible person to everyone around me. After a cold shower and some coffee, I think my attitude is just neutral enough that I can make it to 1:00 p.m. when my shift ends and I never have to see Greg ever again.

"Bryce, I need detergent from the kitchen for our glassware," I yell over my shoulder.

After dumping the last load of ice into our cooler, my barback nods in my direction. "Sure thing. How long until people start filtering in?"

"Pretty soon, I imagine," I answer. The first tee time is at eight this morning, but plenty of people will come through for drinks and breakfast before that. It's still before seven, but the summer daylight hours offer plenty of natural light even this early. Bryce and I have our opening duties squared away sooner than usual with no distractions, so now we're just fine-tuning the bar area. We won't have a chance to clean it again when the crowds start rolling through.

"It's weird, isn't it? Like, he's usually here by now, interrupting things."

Greg is late. Bryce isn't wrong, it is weird that he isn't here yet, but I can't argue with the results. His supervising mostly added to our workload.

Balancing my own duties, all while covering for my teenage coworkers when I told them to get scarce, meant that Greg's presence dragged down our efficiency dramatically. We were done with our opening duties far faster than the other days now that he had decided to skip out this morning.

Nope, no one here misses Greg very much.

"No doubt, but don't get too comfortable. I'll keep an eye on when he arrives and let you know." It would be like him, to sneak up on us like that. I wouldn't put it past him, a mean prank of some kind, but it's more likely he's letting himself sleep in. He must be tired from torturing me all night.

"Yeah," Bryce says back, lost in thought. "Thank you, by the way. I don't think Cassie and I say it enough."

"Hey." I set the glass I'm shining down and look at him. "Don't even think about it. I'm happy to help." Instead of responding, he gives me a small smile and leaves the bar area.

Thankfully, players and spectators have started filtering in to distract me from the fact that we technically have no supervisor this morning. I take breakfast orders from players and begin pouring Bloody Mary's and mimosas for excited fans. The routine lulls me into my comfort zone, and once I hit my rhythm, I can observe the patrons in my clubhouse.

Adrenaline and excitement cut through any exhaustion felt by competitors as they place orders at my bar. I recognize a few of the men but think I won't be able to name any of them until the later tee times when I see Jared Farmer approach the bar. I wasn't expecting him until way later, if he came in at all. Not even Sunday nerves can keep someone alert for as long as he'll need it if he gets started this early.

His hat covers the top half of his face, but there is no disguising the dark circles under his eyes. He must be exceedingly tense to have gotten so little rest.

I can't keep myself from commenting. "You're here before expected. I thought you had the last tee time?"

Jared tries to smile, but it doesn't move anything in his face above his nose. "Just making sure everything is dialed in. Can I get a sausage biscuit and blue Powerade to go, please?"

"Of course. Just try not to wear yourself out before the day really gets started," I reply. God, I must be as tired as he is. What a stupid thing to say to a professional golfer.

Hey, you know that thing you do, that makes you millions of dollars a year that you're really good at? I've got some tips on that, you know, if you want them!

If anyone knows their own practice stamina, it'll be the guy in the final tee time competing to win, that's for sure.

I get back into my duties, keeping my mouth shut this time. No more friendly interactions with patrons, it's time to focus on feeding everyone.

After another hour, things really start to pick up. I'm relying more heavily on Bryce and Cassie than I usually do, but they've risen to the challenge, bussing tables, picking up slack where needed. They're good kids, and I trust them to handle everything except run alcohol, which I'm legally required to do as the only adult in the room. It's hectic, but we're having fun, too. Coverage of the tournament plays loudly over the television sets, along with an advisory in red along the bottom of the screen reminding everyone to hydrate in the desert climate to avoid any heat stroke injuries.

My last open seat at the bar suddenly gets taken by a short, somewhat dumpy older woman. I don't want to be mean, but she really is unfortunate looking. It's not an unnatural ugliness, per se, it just appears to be a culmination of many decades of ignoring one's appearance weighed down by bitterness that never went addressed or corrected. As she struggles into the tall chair, I wince at the fact that I'm about to kick her out of the clubhouse.

This space is reserved for players, VIPs, and people who can afford the purple wristband. This woman only has a yellow one, meaning she should be getting food and snacks from the outside vendors.

I apologize, ma'am. Poor people aren't allowed to have air conditioning.

She speaks before I can address the situation. "Can I have a Coke and a breakfast burrito?"

Sighing, I reply, "Actually, ma'am, the clubhouse is reserved for players and spectators with the purple wristband. Unless you have one, I'm going to have to ask you to leave."

"Well, you're wrong," the woman bites back, her jowls alive with anger. "I was told this was for family of the players, too."

"Yes, but family of the players either purchase or are gifted the purple wristband."

"This is outrageous. I'm related to Steven Torre by marriage, you know."

How this woman thinks I would know or care about that is beyond me. If she's so close to Steven, he or his wife should have gotten her a purple wristband.

"I'm sorry, ma'am. I'll have to redirect you to the customer service tent at the entrance of the tournament grounds. If there's been some confusion, they can get your wristband updated, but until then, I'll have to ask you to leave."

I seriously worry she won't leave, but eventually she grumbles under her breath while wriggling herself out of the tall top. I keep an eye on her as she moves toward the exit, making sure she doesn't make any pit stops at a new table or try to hide in the restroom.

Once she leaves, I exhale, wondering why the situation stressed me out so much. In fact, this would have been one time we actually needed Greg to do his job. He is an expert at letting people know they aren't good enough to be here and getting them to leave. It was the only part of his role that he did well.

So, where the hell is he?

30

SARAH

"She's clear. No phone."

The déjà vu of this week might kill Sarah before her own nerves do. After the security guard waves the metal detecting wand across her body, followed by a brief search of her purse, she finds herself back at the entrance of the Desert Invitational. The location, the unbearable heat, and the crowds could all be a simulated replay of her last three days here for how much has changed.

Except this morning, she woke up alone.

Sarah had rolled over, reached out next to her looking for Jared only to find his side of the bed cold. Even with how little sleep she got, she was still disoriented enough upon waking that she'd forgotten their fight and his leaving. When she finally recognized her situation, despair and dread seeped in.

Jared never came back to their room last night.

As Sarah scrambled out of bed, she tried to formulate some kind of strategy, but everything in her mind was jumbled with pain and a lack of direction. She rushed through a shower and decided that she didn't have a plan. It was impossible to prepare one not even knowing what her plan was supposed to accomplish, but she knew one thing. She needed to see her husband as soon as possible.

She threw on her outfit for the day, skipping the shapewear. In the bathroom, Sarah stared at the vanity covered in her own make-up products. This would take far too long. Cameras be damned, Sarah slapped on some concealer and mascara, shoved her hair into a hat, and ran out the door.

If she was lucky, she might run into Jared before he was at the practice range with his caddie. He was in the last tee time with Andy, so her chances were decent.

But what she really fears is that Jared won't want to speak to her at all.

Moving quickly without breaking into a run, Sarah tries to make her way toward the practice area, but the crowds are dense. It's shoulder to shoulder this morning, and the relentless moisture coming off the bodies of the people around her is staggering. Instead of fighting her way through, she doubles back. If she had a volunteer escort, she might be able to move through the crowds quicker.

"I don't care if it's your day off, we're down three men this morning," she hears a volunteer coordinator bite into a walkie-talkie before slinging it back on his hip. Perhaps not the best person to interrupt, but Sarah doesn't care.

"Excuse me?"

The man's face is bathed in anger before he recognizes her as a VIP. "Mrs. Farmer," he says, all smiles now. His glad handing would normally bother her, but she needs someone willing to kiss her ass right now. "What can I do for you?"

"I'm looking for my husband. Have you seen him? And if so, could you get me there quickly?"

The coordinator's smile tightens as he replies. "Mr. Farmer is already on the practice green," he responds, and Sarah's heart drops into her stomach. He is avoiding her, then. It's too early for him to warm up.

"And even if we could get you to him, I can't spare the manpower this morning. We've had several volunteer no-shows, and another shot himself last night, the selfish bastard."

"What?"

"I can't have any of my guys wasting time showing VIPs around when you've been here all week. I need them as standard bearers."

"Not that," Sarah replies, her disgust at the man's callousness momentarily distracting her from her worries about Jared. "Did you say one of the volunteers killed himself?"

"Sure did. It was last night, some of the news stations have already reported on it. He got into his car after the gala last night and shot himself in the head. We barely got law enforcement to clear everything up in time for the tournament to get started this morning. A dead body might scare away spectators, and we need today's revenue."

Who kills themselves out in the open like that? It was sad, to be sure, but the young man was already gone, and Sarah had her own life to worry about. "Well, I'm sorry to hear that. I'll let you get on with your duties then."

The coordinator doesn't respond, just turns away and yells into his walkie-talkie. Sarah is moved more by the flow of the crowd than her own volition toward the clubhouse. With no way to apologize to Jared before his tee time, she doesn't have anywhere else to go.

After the blast of frosty air welcomes her inside, she looks around for a seat. The tables are all occupied with other wives and some of the players getting breakfast, so she opts for a single seat at the bar, the only one open.

"Ice water with lemon, please."

Sarah keeps her eyes in front of her, and as the woman behind the bar sets her glass before her, she presents a posture that would be unwelcoming to someone trying to socialize. She just wants to drink her water and then follow Jared today. No new friends, press, or any distractions.

"This may be one of the more exciting leader boards I've gotten to commentate on in my career," a voice from the television overhead pulls her gaze.

The presenters are speaking about some of the men competing, including her husband. Despite their fight last night, she finds herself glowing with pride for Jared. He works so hard, and to see him get the recognition he deserves makes her want to scream his success to anyone who passes by.

You see that? See how good he is? That's my man!

Sarah is lulled into a comfortable solitude by the compliments toward her husband coming from the screen when the tone changes.

"Before we begin coverage, there is a local tragedy that we addressed this morning and we finally have new information to share with you," the woman begins. "One of the volunteers for the Desert Invitational this year, Greg Yeager, was found deceased outside the resort last night due to an apparent self-inflicted gunshot wound. This comes as a shock to the community as well as the players who got to know him during his work for this tournament. We just want to say that our thoughts and prayers go out to his family and loved ones for their devastating loss. The organizers on the ground have arranged for a moment of silence in remembrance of Greg before the first tee time this morning."

At first, none of it registers for Sarah. It was sad, suicide always is, but did she even know the man?

"Shit," she hears from down the bar. Several seats away is Hillary Torre, staring at the television still showing the photo of the dead volunteer. A busboy and the hostess stand behind her, staring slack-jawed at the screen as well. They must know him. When she turns back to the screen, a head-shot of the dead man is being revealed to audiences all over the country.

It clicks for Sarah now; Greg, the man who killed himself, is the same man who delivered the notes to all four wives yesterday morning.

31

HILLARY

"Shit," Hillary thinks to herself, or perhaps she says it out loud based on the flinch from the bartender. Talk about derailed plans. Before, she just wanted answers: who gave him the note, what they were trying to do, why they are annoying her, and some other stuff she can no longer remember.

It had all felt very high school, some drama to distract her from Steven's lack of conviction and Gwen's ominous threats. She'd planned to corner the guy and give him a piece of her mind, maybe throw around some threats of complaining to his manager, which is more effective than people think. Everyone hates a bossy woman until they need a refund or a flight upgrade.

Now, though, he is dead. The only lead she had over whoever started this is gone.

Does this mean the note's threat of going to the press is eliminated? Not unless he wrote it, which she doubts. It's possible the author will still leak extremely private information about her.

While it's true Hillary hasn't been overly empathetic since childhood, normally she would feel...something for a man's suicide. It's tragic, and she's never handled death well. Even obituaries of people she didn't know well would trigger some kind of dry throat at the least. The articles of celebrities passing away, young and old, would make her tear up as a young girl. Death announcements in the news make her nervous.

She can't seem to muster any grief for the waiter. Most recently, he was involved in a plot that dragged her into something annoying and stressful. After the note and chasing him down last night, she's been thinking harder about where she recognized him from when it finally came to her this morning.

"Hey. Where the fuck is my next drink?"

He'd been a waiter at a party she'd attended last year. Hillary never let herself think about that night, so she didn't make the connection soon enough. She remembers seeing him, what he had been doing...

It may have been an artless request, but it was loud enough to get the waiter moving and execute what she'd wanted to do.

Hillary may be materialistic and egocentric, but she's effective when she needs to be.

Well, the waiter is dead. It's different. Her mind back in the present, she finds herself trying to reevaluate her situation. Hillary would have previously ranked Gwen's emotional and financial extortion as her biggest issue. For a reason she's unable to pinpoint, the note now has a bigger meaning. The man (Gary? Garfield?) is dead, maybe by his own hand, maybe not. She doesn't think it matters to her either way.

Hillary chugs her water before standing to go outside. Steven's tee time is one of the early ones, of course, yet it doesn't bother her anymore. Her concerns about money that consumed her focus for most of her adult life pale in comparison to this new thing happening that she doesn't understand.

As she walks away, she sees Sarah Farmer on down the line looking back at her. If the bags under her eyes are any indication, she'd gotten less sleep than Hillary. Out of the four women, Sarah seems to have taken the note the most personally. It might be smart to connect with her, to combine information, but she can't shake the anger she feels toward the other woman. Her wholesome, girl-next-door persona is so foreign to Hillary, in no small part because she never had access to that life. There'd been no one to dote on and protect her, no wholesome high school boyfriend to marry her. Hillary had gotten hard, fast. She resents the fact that Sarah got to stay soft and naïve well into her twenties.

The instinct to say something demeaning to Sarah to make herself feel better is strong.

Your natural look for today is quite brave.

I've never seen someone your height attempt that style of skirt before.

Guess you can't ask that guy if the note was about Jared.

Instead, she walks away without saying anything. Even at her most charitable, Hillary has no desire to befriend the woman.

A blast of heat from outside sweeps across her body as a superfluous reminder from an automated speaker tells her of the heat advisory for the day. The line for the hydration tent wraps around the pavement filled with sweaty looking people in overpriced Desert Invitational merchandise. Ridiculous, if you asked her. They should just spend the money on fresh water from the concessions tent and buy discounted merchandise later. No one would know the difference when they wear it to the office later and they wouldn't have to waste away in the sun.

For Hillary, all she brought is a debit card and an ID. Normally she'd complain about the outdated ban on phones within tournament grounds, but it's making her lighter now, able to ignore unpleasant notifications. She only wishes she could Google search the dead waiter, but even that can wait.

Earlier tee times are usually less crowded, and this is no exception. While the grounds are already packed, it appears that most spectators are wisely saving their energy to walk with the winners. Steven will not have a huge group following him. He has a small number of loyal fans, typically new to golf and who enjoy getting day drunk when they're playing with their friends, loud music blasting out of Bluetooth speakers as they go. They're the weekend warrior types.

Hillary doesn't care about the demographic, as long as they spend money on Steven's brand. She sees him on the first tee and heads in that direction, swiping a map from a volunteer with which to fan herself throughout the day.

"Aren't you going to get me one, too?"

At first, she thinks she's dreaming. Or rather, having a terrible nightmare.

"Nope," she says over her shoulder to Gwen, saving face while in public at least. Her half-sister is here, making her day immeasurably worse. "You can get your own fucking map."

32

CASSANDRA

The first time Cassandra followed Andy for a tournament, she underestimated how much it would take out of her. *It's just walking,* she thought. She competed in half marathons and took spin classes. She played intramural basketball in college on a competitive team. A couple days of sauntering around in the grass would be nothing—she might even gain weight on concessions and libations if she wasn't careful.

"Might want to slow down," Andy had joked at dinner. Cassandra was on her third cocktail the Wednesday night before a minor tournament in Wisconsin. He'd flown her in as a gift, and she was excited to see him compete in person, having only so far caught him in glimpses on television whenever the media deigned to cover him. She was excited enough to overindulge. "You've got a couple of long days ahead of you if you want to the see the whole thing."

"You're the one playing all the golf. I'll just be tanning on the cart paths."

With a knowing smile, Andy only shook his head and sipped his water, letting her think she won the discussion.

She regretted her flippancy the next day around hole thirteen and apologized out loud to Andy on Saturday evening. "Just walking" turned out to be exhausting when it's eighteen holes, four days in a row, with not a cloud in sight. She was sore for almost an entire week afterwards with nothing to boast about besides some fresh blisters on her feet.

Today in the clubhouse, Sarah Farmer's appearance reminds Cassandra of how she felt that last Sunday morning, though she knows the other woman has different reasons for her fatigue.

Passing full tables of families and bachelors alike, she moves to stand near the younger wife. There are no more spots at the bar, but enough standing room behind her tall chair allows Cassandra to stand close enough to place a comforting hand on Sarah's shoulders, but she decides against it at the last minute. Instead, she introduces herself with what she hopes are reassuring words.

"One more day," she says.

When she doesn't get a response, she looks closer. Sarah's eyes are glued to the screen, pulling Cassandra's attention there as well.

It appears to be standard coverage. Early players have teed off and commentators are discussing the possibility of a large swing in favor of one of the PGA loyal players. They insist that there's still time, that anything can happen on the Sunday of the Desert Invitational. She's too well trained to roll her eyes, but Cassandra knows there's a huge commentator bias against the new league. No one in corporate golf is cheering for her husband to win. That is solely her job these days.

She looks closer. Sarah wouldn't care about that kind of coverage any more than she would, so Cassandra reads the banner below.

A clenching of her jaw is her only tell that something upset her, but she releases it before anyone around her can notice.

"Sarah," she says, pulling the young woman's attention.

"Oh, hi. Sorry, I didn't see you there."

"We'll walk together today," she smiles. "Andy and Jared are in the last tee time, so it'll be easy for us to stick together. I'll come find you in an hour or so."

Sarah nods, but Cassandra doesn't see it because she's already out the door. Perhaps she could save time by asking a volunteer for help, but she doesn't want anyone else involved. Scanning across the concessions and merchandise tents, she stays diligent in her search. The crowds don't make it easy, but the person she's looking for is easy to find. It takes her mere minutes to find an out-of-season black outfit attached to a meticulously styled mass of red curls.

Whitney doesn't make any move to avoid her, staying in her place alone under a shady tree. "Cassandra. I hadn't thought you'd have anything more to say to me after last night."

"It won't become a habit." Cassandra stands next to her under the tree, their bodies facing the same direction overlooking hole two. Any passersby would assume they're friendly colleagues. Two golf wives who have been cordial for years, catching up at events when they have time. The stiffness in both their stances would go unnoticed by anyone not looking for it.

"I certainly hope not."

Cassandra unclenches her jaw before speaking. "What have you done?"

"Besides mourn my dead husband?"

"Really," Cassandra deadpans, trying to keep her tone cool, her emotions under control. She waits for a small group of teenage boys to move farther away toward the first hole tee box before continuing. "Because I could swear yesterday morning's note was all your doing."

The redhead raises a sharp eyebrow above her sunglasses. "What gave me away?"

Whitney speaks firmly but evenly, allowing only Cassandra to hear her words. The tone could be a statement made about dry cleaning for all the emotion she releases with them.

"You did, just now," she replies. Cassandra leans her hip against the same tree as Whitney, pretense gone now. "I wasn't sure until you confirmed it."

"Hmm," the widow doesn't try to defend herself. She was hoping for some kind of confrontation, and a place to expel some energy. Cassandra had geared up for a fight with Whitney and now she feels as though the wind has been pulled out of her sails. Single sided wars are simply not as satisfying.

"This needs to stop," Cassandra cuts, her sympathy for the other woman's loss evaporated. "Whatever you're doing here isn't worth it. What happened to the man who delivered the note?"

Whitney doesn't answer with words, only a sly smile, which is its own answer.

"I would understand why you tortured Hillary with the note," Cassandra continues as Whitney's smile drops. "But why me?"

"Cassandra," Whitney shakes her head now, as if disappointed in her denseness. "Rowan died at your party. You didn't think I could just forgive that?"

Technically, Rowan died after leaving Andy and Cassandra's party, but she knows the widow isn't in the mood for rationality and nuance. She probably hasn't been capable of either in a long time.

"And why the girl? Sarah hasn't been a part of this world long enough to be dragged into your mess."

Whitney lifts a shoulder, as if the younger wife's panic didn't phase her. "Her husband ought to be more careful about how he speaks about my husband in public."

"Seriously? You pulled her into all of this because of a fucking interview?"

"Maybe I did her a favor. She's too soft for this life."

Cassandra straightens her back. "You should leave her out of this. What do you think you're going to gain here?"

"Trust me, I'm only trying to bring the truth out. You'll see."

"I don't trust you. I don't even like you," Cassandra says without venom, only resignation. "Whatever it is, leave the rest of us out of it. No more notes, no bringing stories to the press. Let it be done."

Whitney only smiles, but there's no humor in it. Only bitterness. "I don't need you to trust me in all things. Just trust that my motives are, in their entirety, to bring about justice for Rowan. If that goal doesn't cross any of yours, and you've done nothing to earn bad press, then we'll be fine. I only want to tell the truth."

Cassandra knows she should push harder—the widow dragged them all into the scheme for seemingly no other reason than to make them as miserable as she was. She could think of no plausible reason that upsetting them would get Whitney any information about Rowan's death. The police had investigated her and Andy's party heavily last year, clearing everyone present including her and Hillary. Sarah and Jared hadn't even been there.

Well, they'd investigated everyone except the driver.

There's also the dead waiter to consider, and she doesn't understand why he died, just that he was involved after he delivered the note. She'd recognized him at the time as Greg, a man her and Andy had fired from their employ after some inappropriate incidents, but she'd said nothing yesterday to the other women. She hadn't wanted the other three wives to connect her to him.

She doubts anyone will really miss Greg.

"I hope you find what you really need," is all she says to Whitney. "Because I don't think it lines up with what you think you're looking for."

33

HILLARY

"You're being a bit cavalier for someone in your situation," Gwen says to Hillary as she follows her to hole one. In her own opinion, Hillary is handling this far better than she expected. She hasn't allowed Gwen to crack her stony demeanor for one moment.

Yet.

Her half-sister is doing this on purpose, speaking too loudly for everyone to hear. "Plenty of sunshine. What do I have to complain about?"

"Less than you should," is Gwen's bitter reply.

It took years for Hillary to realize that the older woman's hatred of her wasn't resentment at having raised her, but simple jealousy. She wishes she'd seen it sooner; it would have altered her approach to Gwen. She could have spent more time trying to be her own person and separating herself rather than begging for love she'd never receive. Throughout the years, she repeatedly attempted to win affection from her sister. Every drawing made in art class, every poem written, every popsicle stick log cabin built had been a misguided attempt to win affection from the loveless woman. Hillary had even gone as far as to make her a Mother's Day card one year, thinking that a changed variable in their relationship would somehow alter it.

It did not work.

Later in life, Hillary tried to send money early on in her marriage to Steven. Her attempt to make up for her childhood only led to Gwen asking for more, and what she sent was never enough. It had been clear what her half-sister's real motivations were, and it wasn't a tearful reunion. Eventually, she'd stopped sending anything.

That was no longer an option.

Steven is on the tee taking a few casual practice swings. He's looser than the other players, seemingly about to tee off for a casual weekend round instead of beginning the final day of a major tournament. He leans on his club with his elbow like it's a countertop and laughs at something his caddie says. Hillary's diaphragm tightens at the sight; if only she'd been more grateful for him before she went and ruined everything. He was simple, but he loved her, and she almost loved him back.

"He's teeing off pretty early, isn't he?"

"I said you'll get your money."

"Hmm," her tone gleeful in anticipation. "How much until he notices? How much can you pass to me before he starts to ask where it's going?"

"Steven doesn't police my spending like I'm a child."

"It was never this much before."

Before.

Hillary ignores her in favor of Steven. In contrast to his practice swings, his arc over the ball always has a precision that reminds her why he's competitive professionally. It's almost like he doesn't want to waste the perfect shot, so he saves it for when it really matters. As he throws his weight behind the ball, it launches toward the fairway. Even from where she's standing, she can tell the ball's flight is exactly where he wanted it. The cheers erupting around them confirm her suspicions.

After clapping along with them she follows the crowd. She's just foolish enough to hope Gwen doesn't follow her, but she is quickly disappointed.

"Maybe I'll ask for more next time."

"And what if I say no?"

"Easy. I go to the police."

"They won't believe you," she says. "It's been too long and it's my word against yours. You were there too." This is something Hillary should have factored into her plans a long time ago, but long-term strategy is not her strong suit. She isn't as conniving as she pretends to be.

Perhaps feigning this confidence is a waste of her energy. She has no idea what the police would or wouldn't believe. All she knows is that Gwen will escalate if she isn't put in her place.

"You think I didn't keep evidence? You really are stupid."

Despite the heat, Hillary feels her skin prickle, the goose flesh breaking out across her arms a summer anomaly. "Why?"

Gwen shrugs, as if blackmail is just a regular Tuesday for her. "Because I thought you might start to get uppity about the whole thing. I needed insurance to make sure you gave me what I'm owed."

The crowd around them groans, and for a moment Hillary thinks it's a reaction to her own personal conversation. Upon further inspection, she realizes that the other man in Steven's group, Jeff Swanson, has launched his ball into some desert weeds. The man tears off his glove while he trades clubs with his caddie, tossing both iron and accessory at the man in his employ. As they walk towards the green, she can see his caddie shake his head in resignation.

She had missed Steven's second shot, one that made it on the green but nowhere near the pin. Hillary wishes she'd paid better attention, that she could clap for her husband instead of arguing with Gwen.

Acquiescing to her sister won't work long term, a fact that Hilary should have seen sooner. "And what if something were to happen to you, Gwen? What if I decide I really don't care for your conditions?"

In for a penny, in for a pound, it would seem.

"Well, it's simple," Gwen is too smug. Hillary immediately knows she took a misstep. "If anything were to happen to me, a package with all the evidence gets sent directly to the Sante Fe police department. I have pre-ordered shipping for random upcoming days that I have to manually cancel only if you do what you're supposed to. If anything happens to me," her smile widens, "then there's no one around to cancel the shipment."

Hillary stares back at her in silence, the crowd moving around them to the green. The current of people is strong, but she stands against it, refusing to be pushed around by strangers, even if she can't protect herself from being pushed around by Gwen.

There's something comforting about despair. Knowing that all your choices are gone is freeing, in a way. It's sort of like being able to pretend nothing is one's fault or responsibility anymore. Hillary is now just along for the ride, her die cast a while ago.

"I don't really care what you do today. I'll be following Steven if you need me."

34

SARAH

Sarah passes another hour or so in her seat, probably angering the bartender. Other patrons are filling seats rapidly and she isn't spending any money on the water refills. The irritated glances thrown at her from both the workers and people waiting for her seat are irrelevant.

Sarah doesn't care.

There's been no new mention of Greg from the commentators. It's a relief not to hear more, pretend it isn't there, and yet her glass of water shakes continuously as she brings it to her lips.

"Sarah?"

Cassandra is back. As put together as ever, she has a comforting smile for Sarah but being around this other woman the past two days has given her more insight into her expressions. She's trying to coax Sarah into relaxing, but there is something worrying her as well.

"What's wrong?"

"Nothing," Cassandra says too quickly. "It's almost time for Jared and Andy to tee off."

Sarah looks at her watch as she jumps off the bar stool. She'd been sitting staring at the television without seeing for almost three hours. No wonder everyone around her has an attitude. She probably cost the bartender over one hundred dollars in tips. She slips her a fifty dollar bill apologetically but she's already serving the new user of her spot.

"Have I missed anything?" Jared hasn't started but it's possible he had an interview or signed autographs. She could have had a moment with him, apologized, or something. Without further explaining, Cassandra understands the question.

"No. The men like to lock themselves away Sunday morning. I haven't spoken to Andy since he left our suite."

"He seemed in good spirits?"

The other woman raises an eyebrow, causing Sarah's face to redden. Hoping it's hidden by the heat, Sarah remembers that their husbands are in direct competition today.

It appears there is a boundary to Cassandra's friendship after all.

"He did," is the simple reply she gets.

They walk among the masses, anonymous in the crush. The speed of the crowd's movement is always, unfortunately, set by the slowest movers, and Sarah has often felt that the slow walkers do it deliberately to annoy those around them. It's as if they don't get enough attention otherwise, and they need to impose their sluggishness on everyone around them.

Today, like the other days this week, it's too hot to move quickly. Cassandra stays at her side, navigating them through the crowds. Their husbands have the final tee time and thus will attract the most viewers.

"Stick with me," Cassandra says. "I've mapped out the best places for us to stand on each hole. It'll get us good views without landing us elbow to elbow with a bunch of strangers."

"Why are you helping me?"

"Well, there's no sense making you find your own places to sit."

"No," Sarah says, then repeats herself, this time with more fortitude. "Why are you helping me?"

Cassandra stops walking, then looks at Sarah. Her focus is uncomfortable, but the younger woman keeps as much eye contact as she can muster.

It could be that Sarah is no threat to Cassandra, so far from being competitive against her in looks and money that the natural feminine infighting isn't useful. It's not like Victoria's Secret models concern themselves with the winner of the Miss Mobile, Alabama, Pageant.

Or maybe Sarah is the pet project, a little sister figure for Cassandra to groom into her image and have follow her around at events, an accessory to make her appear charitable and help her public persona. Humiliation burns in Sarah's veins at the thought of being so pitiful.

But it's not pity she sees in Cassandra's face. It's more like blank determination.

"I'm helping you because you need it." Then she turns and moves toward a spot under some cloud cover halfway down the first fairway.

Sarah keeps up, hoping that the answer to her questions is as easy as Cassandra made it sound. She wouldn't bet money on it, though. People's intentions are rarely so pure.

"One more thing," the woman says when they arrive at their destination. The men are with their caddies on the tee, Andy first off and standing over his ball.

He stands tall and still, no nervous wiggle of the club before his back swing. The arc is smooth, stopping behind his head, and he almost appears to be moving in slow motion.

After a crack of the driver making contact, the ball flies into the sun and Sarah loses its trajectory entirely. Nothing about Andy's body language reveals what he feels about it; for all he was disclosing, it could be out of bounds or exactly where he wants it.

A soft thump right across from the women brings her attention to the fairway, the small white ball rolling to a stop just in front of them. Cassandra really knew what she was doing when she mapped out where they would be standing on each hole. That, or perhaps Andy is so good she's already seen these shots every day, his game just that consistent.

"You should consider," Cassandra pulls Sarah back to their conversation, "staying far away from Whitney and Hillary."

This surprises Sarah. For all her generosity of spirit towards her, Cassandra's friendly attitude apparently didn't extend to the other women with them yesterday morning. Not that she'd planned on being friends with them, Whitney with her unapproachable iciness and Hillary with her mean girl personality, but she is curious about Cassandra's reasons.

"Why?"

The other woman doesn't answer, and Sarah doesn't think she will. She turns her attention to Jared. It's his turn to tee off now, the crowds silent with anticipation. He's not smiling and engaging with the fans like he usually is, no jokes for his caddie. He isn't looking around for her, a fact that breaks Sarah's heart a little, though she knows it's entirely her fault. She caused this rift between them by not trusting him, by keeping a stupid and hurtful secret.

The sternness in his composure makes her nervous for him. Jared never played well when he took it too seriously.

A steady back swing, and Jared rips his body toward the target. The crack of contacting the ball could have been identical to Andy's shot, the sounds interchangeable, except Jared doesn't bother masking his emotions. He almost immediately looks disgusted with himself, angrily tossing his club at his caddie without bothering to watch the ball's trajectory.

A tree snaps on the other side of the fairway, causing some girlish squeals from fans who chose to sit there. It's not out of bounds, and it's probably not lost, but it's an extremely out of character first shot for Jared. The crowds on that side of the fairway rush to where it landed, all of them competing to have the closest place next to Jared. They aren't allowed to rush the fairway, so spectators get as close as possible to the balls that find themselves in the trees. It goes without saying that Jared does not care to have fans this close to him under these circumstances.

Sarah swallows back bile.

Cassandra claps politely with the crowds. "If it makes you feel any better," she says while not moving her attention from the men at the tee box, "my money is still on us getting a good show today."

35

BARTENDER #3

With the busyness of my morning, I hadn't been able to catch any of the television coverage of the tournament, never moving far from my station. The flow of customers during the early tee times had been consistent and kept me in a constant state of motion. We had only the bare minimum of staff in the clubhouse, but we were keeping everyone happy.

I didn't give Greg's absence a second thought, assuming he was reassigned or sleeping in, when Bryce moved behind the bar. I continued my work, waiting for him to announce himself. When Bryce didn't ask for anything, I almost made a snippy comment asking why he was standing around. We were clearly too busy for him to sneak his phone behind the bar.

Looking in his direction with a rebuke ready, I saw something was wrong.

His face was tired, maybe even fearful. My first assumption was that Greg had come in late today and I didn't see him, didn't stop him in time. He must have gotten Bryce or Cassie alone. What did he say that made Bryce so scared?

Or, more terrifying, *what did he do?*

"What's wrong, Bryce? We're busy, but if you need help, you know where to find me," I said, keeping my tone casual but ensuring he knew he could come to me with anything.

"You haven't heard?"

I checked the bar, made sure everyone sitting there wouldn't need a refill in the next few minutes, and moved closer to Bryce. "Heard what?"

Looking at the patrons, then the television sets, he motioned for me to follow him. At this point, I was spiraling. When was the last time I laid eyes on Cassie? What could be so bad that it needed to be discussed privately?

Bryce pulled me around a corner, so we were standing near the supply closet and away from any customer traffic. He pulled his phone out of his pocket, and a small part of me was proud of him for learning, for not bringing it out in front of customers who couldn't have theirs on site at all. He was still breaking a major rule that could get both of us in trouble, no doubt about it. But I decided to celebrate the baby steps.

My celebration was cut short when he showed me the article open in the browser of his phone.

"What is this?" A stupid question. I could obviously see what it was, a headline announcing the sudden death of a tournament worker last night, the byline offering up his name.

Greg Yeager. I guess that explains his absence. For a moment, I felt relief that he wasn't near the kids anymore, then guilt for being relieved at his death, followed by anger for Greg making me feel guilty. He didn't deserve those emotions from me.

"They're saying he killed himself last night," Bryce said.

"God. I guess you can't always tell what people are going through. I never would have expected that from him."

"Yeah, I'm not sure I really believe it either," Bryce replied. "You were with him for a double shift last night, right? Did you see anything that would make sense of this?"

I shook my head. Greg had seemed perfectly normal. He was vindictive, punishing me for my actions yesterday and avoiding troublesome guests at the event. At one point, I'd had to stop Hillary Torre from following him into the employee only area of the gala. Lord only knows what he did to piss her off.

Then there were the text messages. Maybe when he said he had to move forward, he was saying goodbye? Though Greg had never been that subtle.

"Well, whatever," Bryce said, tucking his phone away.

"How are you feeling about this?" There would be no love lost for Greg from any of us, but I sometimes forget how young some of my colleagues are. I had a classmate die in a car wreck when I was sixteen, and while we weren't close, the suddenness of it had shaken me as a teenager. It was my first taste of death that wasn't a grandparent or someone who had been old and fragile.

At Bryce's age, this might have been his first taste of death in that same way. Greg was in his mid-thirties, presumably healthy. He should have shown up today, like he was scheduled.

Watching my coworker, I felt myself grow angry with Greg again. How dare he, in more ways than one, shatter the innocence of sweet Bryce and Cassie? It was selfish of him to do that to himself, to force the kids to grow up a little quicker today than they deserved.

"I'm okay," Bryce said. "I mean, I obviously didn't like him all that much, but it's weird. I think I feel guilty."

"For what?"

"For not feeling bad that he's gone."

I nodded, understanding. "None of this had anything to do with you, but I want you to embrace that guilty feeling," I explained. "It keeps you human."

I didn't say anything else about death or human nature. I don't think I knew how to explain that letting him feel bad about Greg's suicide was another attempt to help him hold onto innocence, that he was much too young to be jaded and unfeeling toward it like I was. There would be time for that later, as he grew up more.

"By the way," I amended, "if you need to take the rest of the day, I can find someone to cover for you."

"No way," Bryce said. "We wouldn't do that to you, not with everything you've done. Cassie and I will work the full shift."

I smiled, relieved. I'd been bluffing. There was no way I could cover the entire clubhouse by myself.

Now that I'm lost in the rhythm of work again, I think on Greg's death, and why he did it. I have no good hypothesis for why he killed himself, only that I doubt it. He was far too narcissistic for the act in my opinion, but he's gone, and while I dry glassware, I let myself pretend that it makes sense, mostly so I don't go crazy.

A flash of red hair pulls me from my task. Whitney Silver stands in front of my bar, somehow the only person not sweating today despite her horribly macabre clothing choices.

Seriously, wearing all black in the New Mexico summer sun is practically self-harm.

"What can I get you?"

"Four Diet Cokes, please."

"For here or to go?"

"To go, please."

I move to the cooler and begin pulling out the sealed bottles of cola when she stops me.

"Oh, would you mind pouring from the fountain? And I'd like a drink carrier as well, please."

"Of course, ma'am," I say while replacing the bottles. The fountain drinks will take me longer to prepare, but who am I to judge? Everyone knows fountain Diet Coke is way better than the bottle.

I gather four cups, each branded proudly with the logo of the club. Along with the purple wrist bands, these cups are a status symbol outside on the course. All other vendors have cups with Desert Invitational logos on them, or none at all. Only the cups purchased from my station have the golf course's coat of arms branding it.

Though, Whitney Silver does not seem like the type to need an additional status symbol out in public. Perhaps she just prefers fountain cola to bottled.

After scooping four Styrofoam cups of ice, I double check that I have the correct button on my soda spout and fill them to the top. Four lids, four straws, and one drink carrier later, I place the drinks in front of Whitney. I slide her the check and move on to another person already in line behind her. As I swing in the direction of the new customer, I push a half-full glass of water over, spilling the liquid in Mrs. Silver's direction.

"Jesus, I'm so sorry," I immediately pick up the glass and grab a rag. I'm lucky enough that none of the water hit her, but I'm still rushing to keep it from spreading.

"That's quite all right," she responds. "You just have to move forward after these things." She smiles and replaces her sunglasses before opening the receipt folder and placing some cash inside.

"No change for me. Thank you," the widow says and leaves out the front door. I make a round of margaritas for the man behind the bar, watch as he tips me a measly dollar per drink, then plaster a fake smile on my face as he walks away. I finally have a moment to process the cash Mrs. Silver left me but I double take when I see it.

Looking around, unfortunately I see that she's long gone, out the door several minutes ago. I have no way of chasing her down to see if she made a mistake.

The widow left me three hundred dollars for her fountain Diet Cokes.

36

HILLARY

Gwen's presence is like a wasp that follows her around the yard but never actually gets around to stinging Hillary. It keeps her anxiety high, but adrenaline can only stay elevated for so long before apathy and exhaustion win the battle.

She wishes Gwen would hurry up and sting her. Metaphorically, of course.

It's hole seven, and Steven is two under par for the day. In any other circumstances, Hillary would be thrilled to see him compete so well. He typically stays towards the middle of the leaderboard so this surge in performance is out of character, especially this late in a tournament when his position is all but solidified.

He's standing on the green now, squatting behind his ball as his caddie points toward a target, reading the breaks across the green. When they agree, his caddie pulls the pin and gives Steven space to make a few practice strokes while looking at the hole. It's not a lag putt by any means, but it's not a free one either.

Surrounding the green, men and women—mostly men—are eerily silent, waiting for the results as Steven finally makes his pass at the ball.

It rolls steadily along the line they chose, so smoothly that if she saw it on television, Hillary might accuse it of being computer generated. There is no doubt the entire time; the ball rolls directly in the hole, exactly as her husband intended.

The crowds around the green applaud the birdie, excited to get such a great performance during this early tee time. She's always known that her husband knows how to put on a good show, though she's usually relieved when that show includes excellent golf and not a drunken display after the round.

Hillary is no exception from the enthusiastic crowd as she claps for Steven and begins her trek to the next tee box without waiting for his playing partner to finish the hole.

"Where was that the past four days?"

Hillary rolls her eyes at the voice behind her. "Oh. I forgot you were here."

"Liar," is Gwen's response. She's been uncharacteristically quiet for a few holes, likely due to the bombshell she dropped when Steven was first teeing off this morning. She knows she holds all the cards here, and there's nothing Hillary can do about it.

Not that it's stopped her from trying. She's worked through a few angles in her head: finding the postal service that has the evidence and destroying it, counterfeiting evidence that incriminates Gwen instead, simply calling her bluff and hoping there's not enough in her half-sister's possession to fully convict her of what she did.

It occurs to her as well that withholding evidence from the police during an open investigation is also a crime.

A cold smile crawls across Hillary's face. If she goes down, she can drag Gwen with her.

Even with their highly fractured relationship, she's still sad it ended up this way. She must not have fully given up on obtaining her sister's affection until the total exposure of her blackmail efforts. It's the final bead that breaks the strand, their relationship now unrepairable.

Spectators are starting to file onto hole eight, just ahead of Steven and the other player. The flow of people moves in one direction, headed for the back nine. Anyone moving in opposition to the crowds is an outlier or a volunteer, making the familiar face walking toward them a definite outlier.

"Well, this is fun!"

"Shut up, Gwen," Hillary hisses in response.

Whitney is walking their direction, hands carrying a cardboard beverage holder. People give her a wide berth, seemingly without thinking about it. Spectators part without looking at her, as if she demanded it out loud.

"Good afternoon, ladies," Whitney greets. Hillary nods back, attempting in vain to keep her attention on Steven. She doesn't think Whitney has any idea who Gwen is, but it's in her best interest to keep them apart. Gwen is causing enough trouble as it is.

"You, too," she says finally, when its clear the widow was waiting for a response.

Hillary is grateful her sunglasses give her some cover, though Whitney is also wearing them so she can't get a read on what the woman wants. They're not friends, never will be. She has no family here, no husband to cheer for, and honestly, who would stay willingly in this heat otherwise? Why is she still here? She got her consolation prize last night, being here without Rowan is just self-flagellation at this point.

"I'll be heading out soon," she says, almost answering Hillary's unasked question. "I was in line for refreshments when I saw you walking with Steven. I thought I'd grab a few extra Diet Cokes in case you wanted something too."

"Perfect timing, I'm parched," Gwen interrupts, pulling the fountain soda out of the holder.

"You're pretty far from the VIP area," Hillary replies. She hasn't taken the offering yet.

Whitney lets a small, sad smile escape before answering. "I wanted to walk the whole course before leaving. I don't think I'll be around professional golf again for a long time."

Hillary swallows her guilt and takes the last soda. "Thanks for the drink."

With a final nod, the widow leaves and passes them without saying goodbye, taking the two leftover beverages with her. Hillary doesn't bother looking back; they'll never be friends, and the less she sees of Whitney the better. It's a relief that the widow is gone, shrinking Hillary's problems back down to Gwen. She can't wait for this stupid weekend to be over.

As she watches Steven walk across the fairway with his caddie, she takes a swig from her straw.

An overly sweet flavor hits her tongue, and she immediately spits it out on the ground next to her. Some of the spray ricochets onto someone's shoe next to her, but she ignores their complaints.

"Hey! Watch it!"

Hillary spits again, just for good measure. "Maybe don't stand so close to me, then."

"You almost spit on my kid!"

Huh. There was a kid there, standing behind his dad, that she hadn't seen before.

Oops. Instead of apologizing, she walks faster, trying to keep up with Steven and somehow leave Gwen behind simultaneously. Meanwhile, any goodwill she had toward Whitney two minutes ago has evaporated faster than her Coke spit on the sidewalk in the desert summer.

That bitch.

It wasn't Diet Coke, it was a regular, full sugar cola. As if Hillary would waste liquid calories on something that wasn't getting her buzzed.

This kind of underhanded move was so high school, she's surprised Whitney lowered herself to do it. She'd executed that trick before, understood the mean girl motivations. Hillary briefly worked at a small coffee shop when she was sixteen, one her classmate Alexis Henry frequented. Alexis had cut Hillary from the cheerleading squad, for reasons officially unstated, but Hillary suspected it was because there was only room for one girl at the top of the pyramid. To maintain her place at the top, Alexis only ordered skinny, sugar-free, nonfat lattes from the local coffee shop every morning.

Hillary always served her the full sugar, full fat lattes instead. Just to be mean.

"Here," she passes her beverage to Gwen. "You can have mine."

Her half-sister has already chugged her own coke and happily takes Hillary's from her hand.

"Don't mind if I do."

When will this day be over?

37

SARAH

For the most part, public reputations are earned or at least have some truth to them. It's hard in the modern age to hide one's true self from the masses, so most celebrities and politicians are unable to hide negative character traits for very long if they are seen in public often. Rich and famous people who are bad tippers, rude to service workers, or unfaithful to their spouses get found out pretty quickly these days. In the age of social media, everyone is an investigative reporter.

On occasion, Sarah will learn of a reputation or characteristic assigned to one of the players that she sees as unfair. For example, a man last year walked off hole eighteen with a double bogey, ruining his chances of making the cut for the weekend. He was understandably upset. His goal was likely to sign his scorecard as soon as possible and get out of there with limited time wasted on the press. As he walked into the scoring tent, single destination in mind, a young teenage boy ran towards him with a hat, a pen, and the obvious desire for an autograph. The player either ignored him or didn't see him, but the very brief interaction was caught on tape, eventually going viral on all the golf Reddit boards and popular meme pages, earning him a reputation for being uncharitable to fans. Never mind the truth, the internet thought he was a diva, so he was a diva.

Never mind that he participated regularly in Make a Wish Foundation events and had signed tens of thousands of autographs for fans of all ages. That single clip of a crestfallen eleven-year-old boy had taken the golf world a long time to forget, and Sarah found the reaction to one bad day ironically uncharitable.

Conversely, Alex Garcia has earned his reputation as a slow player, and then some.

Garcia is in the pair that teed off just before Jared and Andy, yet he and Ted Swanson are a full hole and a half behind the group in front of them. Sarah can tell it isn't helping Jared, who hangs on by a thread. After hole one, where he was able to save bogey after his tee shot, he's maintained par scores on every hole since, but not without struggle. He sank a few lucky putts after missing greens and has missed more than one fairway. A favorite saying of his coach is that "the scorecard doesn't know how ugly your shot was," meaning that a par is a par. But there is a significant momentum difference between missing a birdie putt and the fight against a bogey.

The slow play isn't helping.

Sarah has yet to make eye contact with Jared. The longer it takes, the more worried she becomes. She knows it's egocentric to be so concerned with their issues when he has more immediate stresses. There's certainly no permanent damage, she reasons, but her own actions this weekend have caused her husband additional distractions that he doesn't need. Andy has pulled ahead by two strokes, an insurmountable lead if Jared continues to play as he is. But Sarah is a woman, and her fears are more esoteric than his score on the next hole.

Alex and Ted have started their walk onto the fairway, yet Jared and Andy are already on the tee box, waiting. It's painful for the final tee time, sure, but also the crowd. They're antsy, the pile up of tee times causing two large groups of spectators to take up each other's space. Cassandra stands her ground, but even she can't ward off every shoulder bump from a dehydrated fan.

The climate is almost unbearable. In Kansas, their summers get very hot, but then there's the additional problem of humidity. The desert is supposed to be a dry heat, a sauna rather than a steam room. Perhaps the air is dry, but it feels humid, and Sarah thinks it is coming off the people, rather than the air itself. The hordes of spectators have created their own sauna with just their sweat, most of them probably not drinking enough water to keep up.

Speaking of dehydration, Sarah is on her last leg. For all the water she drank earlier, it seems to have done her no good even a couple hours into the round. She hasn't had to use the restroom once. She can barely manage to keep her mouth from fully drying, and it's only a matter of time before she becomes the next heat stroke warning.

That's the last thing she needs, to pass out publicly and become the next viral golf meme.

"Do you think I have time to refill my water bottle somewhere?"

"With Alex in front of us," Cassandra replies, "you have time to get water from a mountain stream in Colorado."

Sarah looks for the closest water station and sees a line that would make a solid case against the other woman's assertion. "Are you sure? I don't want to miss anything."

Two creases form between Cassandra's eyebrows, her expression agreeing with Sarah as she looks at the lines of thirsty people. "If you hurry," she says, "the first five holes should be empty now. Any one of those water stations will have a shorter line."

Smiling in thanks, Sarah darts between sweaty onlookers before finally breaking out into more open space. She can cut directly across hole three now to the closest water station. Urgency drives her, not because she thinks she'll miss Jared's next shot, but because she doesn't want to miss the moment he finally searches for her in the crowd. What if he seeks her, needs her, and she isn't there?

She doesn't want to fail him in this, after failing him so catastrophically yesterday.

Sarah ignores all distractions except the water fountain, cursing its lazy trickle. It's the slowest one she's used all week, and though she isn't superstitious, she ponders the existence of cosmic punishment, or an example of Murphy's Law at work. She fills up halfway before abandoning the fountain to run back.

Thirst slightly quenched now, she's unable to block out distractions like she had been on her way to the fountain. Every bug buzzing around her head is a new obstacle. Every tent she must walk around is an impediment to the straight line back to her husband, the shortest distance available. If it weren't for the heat and the fact that she's not wearing a sports bra, she might even start running.

As she passes one of the empty grandstands returning to Jared, she hears noises from behind the white panel. Normally, she'd continue, but these are not the sounds of someone breaking down equipment or moving cameras. Sarah hears distress: hacking and sputtering, she thinks maybe the warning signs of a heat stroke. With no cell phones, if this person is alone, they could be in grave danger should she ignore them. When she figures out what is happening, she can bring them to a medical tent for help.

Convinced of her own heroism, Sarah rips open the white Velcro panel leading her under the stands before halting at the scene.

"Oh, crap."

38

HILLARY

Unfortunately, Gwen shows no signs of tiring out. In fact, she may be more energetic than when they started walking this morning.

She's been following Hillary for fourteen holes now. Her own energy flagging, Hillary wonders if maybe she should have given in and drank some corn syrup earlier. It appears to have done wonders for Gwen's mood.

"I think I'd like a nicer car. Something flashy and foreign, like a Mustang."

Hillary fights not to react. If she wasn't enraged with the extortion, she'd find Gwen's misunderstanding of both money and luxury goods to be pathetic. The amount of cash her half-sister was trying to pry away from her wouldn't even buy her a Camry off the lot. It would feel like a fortune to Gwen, as well as teenage Hillary, but she knows better now. Poor people think that there's only poor and rich, maybe with a small middle class. She certainly used to have this over simplified understanding of wealth. But then she married a man with some money, more than most, placing them safely above middle class, and she finally understood the difference between *some* money and *real* money.

Real money doesn't buy flashy cars. They don't have to brag, let the world know about their finances. In fact, real money hides its wealth for a multitude of reasons.

Hillary and Steven have good money, rich people money, but not *real* money, not that she could ever explain this to her perpetually impoverished half-sister.

"Sure, Gwen. You can get a Mustang."

Applause patters amongst the crowds for Steven's short par putt. He's finishing a Sunday low on the leaderboard without spacing out and going through the motions. It's out of character, and Hillary wonders what changed this week. She certainly didn't. If there was a way for her to activate her husband's competitive nature, she would have found it. If there was a fun new trick in bed, or a favorite snack, or even a form of meditation that would trigger this fight in Steven she wanted to know what it was, pocket it for later. As it was, getting him to practice when he wasn't in the mood was like trying to separate a wad of gum from one's own hair. An irritating, painful, yet somehow delicate chore.

Steven nods to the crowd, offers a polite wave, and pauses when he makes eye contact with Hillary. He gives her a small but earnest smile, a smile just for her alone. These times are rare, when they get to be in public but have a connection that's just between Hillary and Steven.

They used to be more frequent than they are now.

After a moment just for them, he flips his hat backwards and gives her a performative wink, pointing at her as he passes his putter back to his caddie. Male spectators whistle and whoop, while Hillary can hear a few distant *awws* come from the women around them.

It's corny, but all women love a taste of corny romance in their lives. At the very least, it's good entertainment for Steven's loyal fans.

"You really have him fooled, don't you?"

The bite of Gwen's comment isn't a shock, but her volume is.

"Keep it down. You'll get kicked out for being too loud," Hillary fibs. In between players standing over the ball, the fans can chat at a normal decibel. Gwen is just intent on embarrassing her.

"Please. At my age, I can say whatever I want. Just try and stop me."

"Wouldn't dream of it."

The crowds are getting denser throughout the day, with early tee times completed and the leaders having passed the first few holes. Hillary moves through them with familiarity and ease, while Gwen struggles to find space for herself. She's never been in fantastic shape or anything, but the all-day walking in the heat is probably the most Gwen has ever exercised. Hillary doesn't understand how she's still going.

When Gwen stumbles over a tree root, Hillary reaches out to help her only to be slapped away.

"I'm fine," she barks.

"I was just trying to help," Hillary says. Gwen's feet drag as she tries to find her footing. Her pace is sloppy, different from regular exhaustion. "What's wrong? You look drunk."

"Shut up," she slurs back. "What did you do to me?"

"What do you mean, what did I do to you? I've been with you all day," she says. Hillary's gaze darts back and forth, searching for witnesses. A few tournament attendees saw the exchange, but nobody stopped to ask what was wrong or to help. She pulls an unwilling Gwen behind her to seek privacy.

She fights back, but only nominally. Her half-sister must be aware that she needs shade, or water, or something.

Hillary finally sees an empty grandstand, abandoned after the leaders finished the hole. No longer swamped with crowds or media, the towering white tent structure is the perfect place to hide Gwen's unexplainable state. She needs to find her shade and water, at least.

Hillary has never seen heat stroke up close, but she imagines this is what it looks like.

She opens the Velcro flap and pulls the other woman in behind her. "Seriously, what has gotten into you?"

Gwen leans on a metal pole and drags some of the melted ice water left-over from her Coke through the straw. When the liquid is gone, she opens the top and scoops out the leftover ice, rubbing small handfuls across her forehead, ignoring the dribble down her front. She closes her eyes and attempts a deep breath before replying. "I think I'm having a migraine."

Finally, an answer. "I can handle that," Hillary replies. She zips open her small bag and rummages for supplies. "Fan yourself with this while I dig up some pain relievers," she says and hands Gwen her tournament brochure. She finds the small bottle of ibuprofen and her own water bottle. Shaking two pills into her hand, Hillary turns to pass the pills and room temperature water along only to see Gwen keel over and vomit the entire contents of her stomach on the ground in front of her.

"Jesus Christ," she passes the water over with more urgency. "That must be some migraine."

Gwen snatches the bottle and pulls deeply from it, but it doesn't seem to be helping. In between gulps, she tries to catch her breath. Her grip is white around the pole, her chest heaves with shallow gasps.

"Are you sure this is a migraine?"

Gwen glares at Hillary, her stance weak, but there's no mistaking the hatred in her eyes. "What did you do to me?"

She doesn't respond, because her answer would be the same.

Nothing. I never did anything to you.

Gwen falls to her knees, unable to avoid landing in her own vomit. As she gasps for air, Hillary realizes something is truly wrong. This is an emergency. Watching her half-sister gasp for air, she knows this must be time sensitive, that calling for help now might be the difference between life and death for Gwen.

Yet, she stays still.

She stares at the woman who raised her, exploited her, coached her to manipulate, and she cannot bring herself to move in any direction for help. Not toward Gwen, and not toward a paramedic. She knows she should, more for own self-preservation than the woman on the ground, but she doesn't.

Gwen is on her side now, still lying in the contents of her own stomach, but her breathing isn't as regular. The gaps between a steady rise and fall of her chest, the wheezes, the moans, are growing. It won't be long now.

Only the tear of Velcro coming from behind Hillary is able to pull her out of her trance.

"Oh, crap," Sarah Farmer's voice croaks behind her.

39

BARTENDER #3

This day is going to kill me.

I've never been this worn out and the tournament isn't even over yet. People continue to filter in and out of the clubhouse, but the lunch rush has slowed, and it seems like most people are making their way to the leaders' final holes. This would lessen my workload substantially if I had more than one person helping me in the dining room. I'm down to one substitute busboy who got called in at the last minute and he's not nearly as reliable as Bryce.

"Cody, I've asked you three times already to take out the trash for me," I say more to myself than to him, since even if he was anywhere that I could find him, he still wouldn't be listening to me.

I sigh, then fill the last of table ten's beer order and set it on the delivery counter before removing my apron, resigning myself to the trash duties. I once got fired from a waitressing job in my late teens for taking the garbage out while wearing my serving apron. Apparently, it's a giant health code violation but no one had told me. In hindsight, it's kind of obvious why, but it was my first job so how was I supposed to know?

Lesson learned. I haven't forgotten to remove my apron before handling waste ever since.

This load is only bar trash, mostly cups and napkins, thank God, so at least I don't have to smell old food. I tie the top corners together and heave it out of the bin, hoping no new customers come in while we're empty of staff. It's not my fault that Cody is playing games on his phone in a bathroom stall or that Greg killed himself, but I always take customer anger personally and would prefer not to deal with it at all.

The dumpster, instead of being conveniently behind the clubhouse where it usually is, was deemed unsightly by the tournament commissioners and moved to a spot on the other side of some white tents and spectator seating along the front nine. The trash slaps against my backside as I wander through the empty grass and unpopulated areas of the golf course. Everyone is on the back nine, watching the winners.

After flinging the bag over the side of the dumpster, I begin my walk back to the clubhouse, adding a little jog here and there to quicken the pace.

"What do you mean what did I do to you? I've been with you all day."

The agitated female voice surprises me. I thought I was alone. Instinctively, I stop to hear the rest of the exchange and hide behind one of the tents, peeking my head out to see what's happening.

Hillary Torre is dragging an older woman behind her, the latter stumbling around as if drunk. I recognize her as the one I had to kick out of the clubhouse this morning.

Huh. I guess she wasn't lying about being connected to Steven Torre. I'd feel bad about removing her, but she wasn't exactly charming in her interactions with me. Whether or not she deserves to be pushed around by Hillary is really none of my business.

Hillary rips open a tent flap across the lawn from me and shoves the woman inside. "Seriously, what has gotten into you?"

Not my monkeys, not my circus.

I wince after glancing at my watch and begin to run back to the clubhouse in earnest. I've left the bar unmanned for almost ten minutes.

40

SARAH

Sarah doesn't know why the woman is heaving over what is hopefully her own vomit, but Hillary Torre is staring at her in blank terror, not moving to help at all.

"Is it heat stroke? We need to get a medic here as soon as possible," Sarah says.

Hillary snaps out of her trance enough to control her expression and look down at the woman on the ground. Whoever she is, Sarah thinks she doesn't have long.

"Did you hear me? What's wrong with you? We have to get her some help!"

Hillary shakes her head, staring at the ground. "No," is all she whispers.

"No, what? Are you crazy?"

"No, it's too late."

Stunned, Sarah takes a closer look at the woman on the grass. Where just a second ago, there was labored breathing, there's now no movement to speak of. The woman appears to have passed away.

The full weight of what she's seeing doesn't hit her right away, but when it does, it hits with vengeance.

"Oh my god, oh my god, oh my god," Sarah repeats. She's never been around a dead body outside a funeral before, and certainly not one that she had recently seen moving around. A woman died of heat stroke or something and they were both just staring at her. She might have to literally call outside the tent for help. In the midst of this emergency, she wonders quietly if this event will get the cell phone ban lifted from the Desert Invitational in the future, then shakes herself out of the unhelpful line of thinking.

It's not long before Sarah remembers she isn't alone. "What happened? Did you know her?" When Hillary still doesn't answer, staring at the dead woman, Sarah asks the most important question. "Why didn't you get help sooner?"

This seems to pull the other woman out of her trance. Glaring at Sarah, she responds, "This is not what it looks like," before grabbing Sarah and pulling her through the white flap into the open air.

Hillary doesn't seem motivated by direction as much as speed when guiding them away from the tent. After a short distance, she pulls Sarah around behind a tree and looks into her eyes with desperation.

"I need you to keep this between us."

Sarah thinks she heard her incorrectly. "I'm sorry?"

"I don't know what happened to her, but I didn't do anything."

"I didn't think you did," Sarah says. "Wasn't it heat stroke?"

"I don't know," she repeats.

"Why do I need to stay quiet?"

Hillary sighs, as if she wants to be exasperated but knows she has no right. Sarah can see the vulnerability in her face. For someone who had previously expressed only confidence to the point of arrogance, this small glimpse into another side of this woman forces Sarah to consider what she's asking.

"There's no saving her now," Hillary says. "I don't know what happened and I'm worried. Let me figure out some things and I'll bring the police to her myself. I promise."

"Fine," Sarah replies. She doesn't even think about what she's agreeing to, she just wants to get away.

Satisfied with her answer, Hillary nods and removes her hands from Sarah's shoulders.

"Ok, thank you."

~

It takes Sarah too long to return to Cassandra, and Jared stands over his tee shot in the fairway. From her angle, it looks like he has a good chance of hitting the green. Her natural reaction to his talent, her pride in her husband, is such a comfortable and familiar feeling that she feels bolstered by it. She feels that maybe she'll be able to make it through this day.

"What took you so long?"

"Got lost." Sarah has lied so much this weekend, she wonders if she's getting good at it.

Or not. Cassandra looks skeptical but doesn't push. Her own husband missed the fairway, but just barely, and has the first attempt at the green between the two men. She's focused on his practice swing and won't bother to follow up on Sarah's obvious fib.

This gap in Cassandra's scrutiny and Jared's playing leaves her with the perfect amount of time to second guess the decisions she's made in the last fifteen minutes. She watched a woman die, for Christ's sake. Shouldn't she be screaming for the police? Or hyperventilating? Sarah has always thought that she wouldn't handle these things well. She pictured herself behaving like the cleaning lady on an episode of Law and Order, screeching in theatrical terror over a man bleeding out in a parking garage somewhere.

Secretly, she's a bit impressed with herself for not breaking down publicly.

Aside from that, though, Sarah doesn't have much else to be proud of herself for. Why did she agree not to tell? Hillary had seemed so scared and desperate, that Sarah would have done almost anything out of pity. With even the small amount of distance she's gained since then, she sees the whole scenario with clarity.

Hillary needed to "figure some things out," why, exactly? If it was an accidental death, then an EMT should be called to handle it, and no one is at fault. While the death was tragic, that woman was far from the only heat stroke case at this tournament, or even this morning. They should have gone to get help.

Andy appears to be opting out of swinging straight for the green, taking a shorter club than would be needed to hit the green from his angle. It's probably a smart strategy. It's a par five, and he will still have a chance at birdie if he hits the green after his next shot. Jared looks at his competitor quietly, having stopped his conversation with his caddie, as is standard golf courtesy.

Sarah is only partially paying attention.

And what if the woman's death wasn't accidental?

Hillary wasn't a saint, but Sarah couldn't fathom her committing random murder, especially not of an older, homely woman. She almost gives up trying to make sense of it when something else occurs to her.

How much under the stands did I touch?

The staff and volunteer foot traffic alone would make any fingerprints useless, Sarah hopes. The same probably goes for footprints and hair. Sarah thinks they were completely alone in the area, but this entire course is surrounded by cameras, some manned by a person, others left stationary for commercial cuts. Any film of the three women going under the stands, followed by only two leaving would incriminate both Hillary and Sarah.

"We have the perfect angle from here," Cassandra interrupts her thoughts.

She's right. From the small hill where they stand, Sarah can see Jared standing next to his caddie discussing options. In fact, they're close enough that she can almost discern their conversation, not because she can hear it but because she knows her husband. The uptick on one side of his mouth means he has confidence over the shot, while the pinch between his brow means that he and his caddie might be disagreeing on which club to use. After drying his face and hands on a towel, Jared decides on a strategy and holds his hand out, waiting for it to be filled by a wood, indicating he doesn't plan to lay up like Andy did. His caddie obliges, says a few more words, and steps back.

As he tightens the glove on his left hand, his eyes don't leave his target. He chooses a line and places the clubhead behind the ball, skipping a practice swing. The frustration of having to wait behind a slow group must be getting to him if he's truncating his routine.

There's a price to be paid for short cuts, though. Jared's swing bottoms out early, and as his ball flies towards the green, it is followed distantly by a huge chunk of grass.

Sarah doesn't bother to watch the ball and keeps her eyes on Jared instead. She can hear the disappointed "oohs" from the crowd as his approach shot lands short of the green into one of the trickiest bunkers on the course. She sees her husband fix the divot, cursing himself.

They stomp along, and Jared's caddie hands him a wedge while he removes his glove, all the while he ignores the spectators, including his wife.

41

HILLARY

"Mrs. Torre, your husband is in the press tent."

I must look lost, Hillary thinks. Not an unfair assessment from the volunteer. Without another plan, she follows the young man through the packed open area filled with merchandise and concessions, allowing him to cut through the throngs of sweaty people in her stead.

If she thought there was freedom in despair, there's an unnatural jubilance now that Hillary knows her life might be truly over. She can't even comprehend what had happened to Gwen. Plenty of people with worse health conditions than Gwen hadn't expired from the heat. Maybe Gwen had taken something, a new medication, a too strong cocktail, some bad food. Yes, food poisoning makes the most sense. The old cow must have eaten a bad sandwich that went unrefrigerated for too long. Hillary grasps at an excuse that could possibly exonerate her from the death of her half-sister.

But that wouldn't cut it now, because even assuming her death was a total accident, if Gwen told Hillary the truth about releasing evidence against her, then it was all over. The things she did would be brought to light, and there wasn't anything she could do about it.

Lie, lie, lie, chants a voice in her head. *You needn't take the fall for it after all this time.*

I think I do, replies a tired Hillary. The burden is too heavy.

The volunteer opens the door to the press tent for Hillary as she enters toward the back.

"Mrs. Torre, would you be willing to answer a few questions?" A reporter has moved towards her with a pad, abandoning the main job of interviewing the golfers in favor of a quick piece of gossip from her.

Hillary simply glares at him until he scurries away uncomfortably.

Cameras flash amongst the reporters, all pointed at her husband, who sits at an elevated table in front of a microphone. Steven answers questions from various news outlets about his scoring this tournament, specifically his sudden improvement on Sunday.

The first question she hears is from CBS. "You bogeyed hole eight every day except today, when you birdied it. How do you explain struggling with it for several days, then your sudden improvement?"

"That one is easy. I finally shelved my pride for the day and admitted that my seven iron doesn't carry long enough for that par three," Steven says. "It was a simple case of being stubborn and pig-headed, which I happen to be very good at."

A chorus of laughs filters through the small crowd at his self-deprecation.

"You were exceptionally dialed in today," says one reporter from Fox Sports. "What did you change in your warmup or mindset today that lent itself to that performance improvement?"

"Nothing new in the warmup," Steven says. "I don't like to overcomplicate things for myself, especially since I wasn't technically in contention today. No, I just had a reframe this morning, really thought long and hard about why I do this. When it came to me, it was so clear: I play because I love golf, and I compete to win for my wife and the kids we want to have in the future."

At this comment, Steven's gaze seeks out Hillary's with a huge grin that she tries to return. A chorus of *awws* floats from the media personnel and Steven stands to leave, announcing that he needs a beer, which adds some laughs to the room.

Her husband moves quickly to the back of the tent, taking Hillary's hand. He's saying something, maybe he's hungry or excited, but she can't hear him, not really. She squeezes his hand, to reassure herself that he's still holding it, thinking that she'll miss this hand when he finds out.

All Hillary hopes now is that her past actions haven't ruined everything.

42

HILLARY
ONE YEAR AGO

July 5, 2021

"Hey. Where the fuck is my next drink?"

The waiter dropped his hands from the busboy's arms and glared at Hillary. She wiggled her empty glass in the air for emphasis, trying to get the man to move faster. She didn't need or want another drink, but she didn't like the waiter, and she really didn't like the way his eyes followed the young teenager around the room.

More perceptive than people gave her credit for, Hillary could see the discomfort on the boy's face. She was selfish and materialistic, but she wasn't a sick monster, and she drew the line at pederasty.

Not that she expected to be rewarded for that uncontroversial moral stance.

Her eyes roamed the desert vacation house owned by their hosts for the night. Andy and Cassandra Bell had a vacation home in Sante Fe larger than the primary home for most average people. Hillary couldn't tell if she felt envy or respect toward the opulence. Probably respect. If Steven had a good season, maybe he would buy her a place to relax as well. Frugal habits were hard to break, and financial anxiety wasn't something that went away overnight. Even several years into their marriage, she had to fight against walking straight to the clearance racks. Steven wanted her to have nice things and didn't like when she was stingy with herself. She was still getting used to it, the idea that scarcity was behind her.

She had no plans of returning to it, either.

The party was to kick off the week of the 2021 Desert Invitational, the resort being only two hours from Sante Fe. The Bells opened their home every year before the major, though this season the guest list was sparser than usual, which was probably how Hillary and Steven finally managed an invite. A swift alliance had been made between the players loyal to the PGA after many big names defected to the new league. Seen as anathema in their decision, men like Andy Bell, formerly favorites among players and press, saw some longtime friendships dissipate. Luckily for the Torres, this left openings in the social roster for people like Steven.

Hillary had a harder time merging with the men's wives. Walking around the perimeter of the room, she saw little pockets of women whispering to each other over cocktails or hanging on their husbands' arms. Being alone made her feel vulnerable, but she'd rather die than admit it.

That didn't mean she had to stand there and face scrutiny, so she went outside onto the balcony. Even after twilight, the oppressive desert heat meant most people were staying in the air conditioning. She hoped for solitude, a minute to breathe away from prying eyes. With no light to illuminate the patio area, she ran her hand along the railing to guide her farther away from the windows before she realized she wasn't by herself.

"Hillary."

She paused, debated whether to pretend she didn't know her companion, then decided against playing coy. She wouldn't be fooling either of them

"Hello, Rowan."

As her eyes adjusted to the darkness, she could see the outline of his shoulders leaning over the patio gate while he held a glass. Glendronach on the rocks, though she didn't like remembering why she knew that.

Rowan didn't rush to fill the silence. It wasn't his style. He chose his words carefully, so they always felt like they meant something more than they did. Hillary had fallen for that trick more than once, enough that she should know better, but being prepared didn't lessen the impact when he finally spoke.

"I miss you."

"Not here," she bit back, trying to gain control of the situation. "Don't do this now."

Rowan swirled his glass, clinking the ice together as if she hadn't spoken. "I mean it."

Hillary stood her ground. "And I meant it when I said it was the last time."

She could finally make out his face in the dark, masculine and shadowed. His confidence in her eventual acquiescence, the skepticism at her words bothered her. She wasn't lying or putting on a show. Hillary had ended their brief affair broken hearted, not because she would lose Rowan, but acutely disappointed in her own behavior.

She had let herself become what everyone thought of her.

It had been six months since their last encounter, so what he said next shocked her.

"My marriage is over."

"What?" Oh, God. "Did you tell her?"

Rowan brought his glass to his mouth, finishing it off. He swayed slightly before placing the glass on the table beside him. He must have been halfway through a bottle at that point, since Hillary had never known him to show drunkenness.

"Not because of you," he amended. "It's been over for a while. I think I used you as an excuse or something. I don't know," he sighed, "I'm sorry."

She didn't tell him it was okay, because it wasn't. "I'm sorry, too."

With the new information on the table, Hillary felt more comfortable with the silence, so she was surprised when Rowan spoke again.

"I told Whitney this morning that I would start living in my condo instead of the house."

"How did she take it?"

He closed his eyes and swallowed. "She didn't. It's like she didn't hear me. She just started talking about this week, our plans for tonight. I think she's in denial."

Hillary didn't say anything to that. She felt connected to Whitney in that moment. If Steven asked her for a divorce, she didn't know what she would do. She'd probably begin planning her next outfit, discussing schedules as well.

Rowan tried to take another drink then seemed to remember his glass was empty and laughed at himself. "Probably a sign I should call it, right?"

"Probably," Hillary said. She wasn't sure how to handle this. She hadn't been lying when she said she didn't want him anymore, but it would feel wrong to leave him like that.

"Where are you staying?" At his expression, she amended, "I could drop you off. You know, so you don't have to drive or wait for Whitney."

He set his glass down and nodded. "Sure. I'm not far."

"Our rental is the last one in the driveway. I can make some excuse, and you can meet me around front."

Though nothing had changed about the party inside, the exchange on the patio left Hillary off kilter. She technically hadn't done anything wicked —that night, at least—but any time spent around Rowan unnecessarily exposed them to prying eyes. She waded by the same groups she passed before, smiling and saying hello when appropriate. No sign of Steven, another bullet dodged. The fewer people she had to answer to about this errand, the better.

Hillary approached the foyer table holding everyone's purses. A butler of some kind insisted everyone drop something off at the door, the Bell's attempt at a coat closet despite the heat. Maybe it was their way of welcoming them inside, but no matter. It gave Hillary an excuse to grab the key and leave her purse behind. Anyone looking for her would see her accessories still lying around and could be convinced that she'd been in one of the many bathrooms while she was gone.

Key in hand, she moved toward the door but paused when she saw a man blocking it. The waiter she yelled at earlier stood in her way.

"Can I help you?" he said, his words a direct contrast to his expression, which was decidedly unhelpful. His shiny name plate reflected the chandelier in her eyes briefly, and she noted his name was Greg.

Easy enough to forget later.

Hillary shoved any indecision from her posture and placed herself in a believable and familiar role.

A rich woman who was bitchy toward service workers.

"Actually, yes," she replied. "I'm going to get some Midol out of my car. Maybe you could help with that? Run to the store and get me a box of tampons? A heating pad and a back massage to go with it? Or maybe," she tapped her finger on her chin, feigning introspection, "Maybe I'm not your type."

To his credit, the waiter didn't immediately shrink away, staying to hold her gaze for a moment. Eventually, he gave in and walked down the hall without a retort.

A quick glance over her shoulder to make sure no one followed her, and Hillary was out the door. The driveway was long, but she and Steven arrived later than the others. She'd taken her time getting ready and didn't want to appear overeager for their first invite to the Bells'. Though she needn't have worried. Steven excelled at making people around him comfortable, so he was well into the inner workings of the party before she even left the sidelines.

Hillary used the porch lights to guide her way through cars along the gravel drive until she reached the rental. Rowan leaned against the passenger door in the dark, hardly visible.

Without a word, she unlocked their doors and slid into the driver's seat. "Can you guide me there? I left my phone behind."

"Smart girl," he replied, and she preened at the compliment. Flattery for her appearance came a dime a dozen, but she rarely received acknowledgement for strategy. The fact that Rowan knew this and was likely playing to her weaknesses was secondary, if it mattered at all.

"Take a left out of the drive," he said. "We're only a mile away on the right."

She drove slowly, using the sparse lighting for the road to guide her until she could turn on her headlights. Once on the main road, she flipped the switch and illuminated their way.

Rowan was quiet until they were halfway to his rented condo. "Do you have any regrets?"

"Doesn't everyone?"

She could see him shake his head in her periphery. "No, like a big one."

"Besides you?" Hillary joked, but Rowan was silent again. He didn't seem to think it was funny.

When he spoke again, his voice lowered, almost as if just speaking to himself. "There are a few things I would have done very differently, knowing what I know now."

At this statement, she turned to look at him directly and saw his head in his hands. It would occur to her later that she never insisted that he wear his seatbelt.

When light flooded her vision, Hillary's eyes shot back toward the road just in time to see a single headlight in her lane coming directly towards her.

Breath in, breath out.

Hillary's head pounded as she shook herself free of an airbag. Her seatbelt was tight across her breasts, holding her up at an angle. From her vantage point, she could see that she had driven them into some kind of ditch on the side of the road to avoid the oncoming car.

A car that had kept driving, not bothering to stop and see if they were all right.

She pushed the airbag farther away and looked to her right. "Rowan?"

The man next to her wasn't moving, his head bent unnaturally. She couldn't see any sign of breathing.

Cautiously, she turned his head, trying to be gentle but knowing in the back of her mind that it didn't really matter. When she saw his face, she wished she hadn't. His eyes were still open, but unseeing, like some kind of horror movie.

There's no preparation for a situation like that one. No way to know how one will react when they find themselves alone with a dead body until it happens, but Hillary surprised herself with her efficiency. She didn't freeze up or hyperventilate. She probably could have handled the scene herself, but she made one mistake.

Fumbling around, she finally released herself from the seatbelt and narrowly avoided landing on the horn. When she opened the door, she was able to stand to the side, digging around for anything that could help her, what? Call for help? Give her a lift back to the Bells'? All she knew was that she needed to be far away from this vehicle when it was found.

During her desperate search of the car, she found Steven's phone in the glove compartment. Without thinking, she unlocked it and dialed the only phone number besides her husband's that she had memorized. Unsurprisingly, she answered on the first ring.

"Gwen? I need your help."

Of course her sister had been nearby. A major tournament in their home state? Gwen would not have been able to let Hillary enjoy her new life and freedom without trying to watch from the sidelines. She was less than five minutes away when Hillary reached out for help.

Outside the car, the ramifications of what she did hit her with force. She'd be caught at the scene with a man who wasn't her husband, something the press would run away with. Rowan, a man she didn't love but for whom she'd developed a complicated affection, was dead just minutes after admitting regrets. Well, those weren't worth anything in the grave.

Hillary, still alive, had a shiny new regret to carry with her forever.

Headlights approached the crash site, but Hillary didn't bother hiding. A not insignificant part of her hoped it's not Gwen, but a stranger or a police officer, so she can admit to being the driver. She could already tell that the weight of hiding this secret would probably be worse than getting caught and paying for the consequences. Would it be prison? Was the wreck her fault? That, she could handle. Then she thought of Steven's reaction when he heard the news and visibly winced.

Steven's reaction might break her heart.

It didn't matter. Gwen was the one in the car, and when she stepped out into the brush, hobbling delicately, Hillary could almost swear she looked excited.

That excitement was tampered slightly when she caught sight of Rowan's body in the passenger seat, but she maintained a blasé professionalism about the scenario when she spoke.

"You did this?"

"Yep."

"Figures."

Hillary wanted to roll her eyes but refrained, already in Gwen's debt. "Well, can you help?"

"Tell me what happened."

Hillary detailed the brief drive, as well as the oncoming headlight that pushed her off the road.

Gwen nodded, looking at the front of the car. "Were you drinking?"

She shrugged back. "Not really."

"Then what's the problem? It sounds like this was just an accident. You shouldn't be in too much trouble here."

"Gwen," she replied, her voice tightening. "I cannot be found here."

Gwen frowned then rounded the front of the car again to look closer inside. "Ah, I see," she sighed. "The corpse isn't your husband. I can see how that would create problems for you and the nice little life you've found for yourself after ditching me."

Hillary ignored the underhanded comment. "So, can you help or not?"

"Sure can," she said. "Give me the keys."

Gwen moved closer to the vehicle. "How long since you left the party?"

"Maybe fifteen, almost twenty minutes?"

"Hmm. We'll be pushing it a little. Was everyone drinking?"

Definitely. "It was an open bar."

"Good, good. Here's what you're going to do," she explained. "Go back to the party. Side door if you can. Fix yourself up in the restroom then mingle. Talk to as many people as you can for as long as you can. If you can swing it, make sure you and Steven are the last to leave the party."

"And what are you going to do?"

"Better if you don't know."

The walk back was quick since Hillary could move across yards without using the road. Her shoes in one hand, Steven's phone in the other, she made it to the Bells' and opened a lower-level door to their basement, which by some miracle was both devoid of guests and had a restroom. Ensuring she didn't track anything with her, she locked herself in the half bath and looked at herself.

Hillary was relieved that she looked the same as when she left the party, yet appalled at the notion. Her make-up was still flawless, not a single hair out of place. Her eyes were bright and during her walk back to the house, she had managed not to snag her dress on any branches. She was responsible for a man's death. She should be wildly disheveled, and there should have been guilt etched across her face or a nasty glint to her eyes, but no. She looked like regular, pretty, simple Hillary.

After patting sweat away with some tissues and cleaning her feet with paper towels, she replaced her shoes and opened the bathroom door.

In front of her, hand ready to knock, was Rowan's wife Whitney.

The woman appeared shocked to see her but closed off her reaction swiftly. "Where have you been?"

"Not that it's any of your business," Hillary said, impressed with her own ability to behave as she usually would, "but I had a stomachache." She emphasized the point while moving out of the doorway and slamming it shut behind her.

Whitney frowned. "You've been here the whole time?"

Hillary shouldered past her and walked up the stairs. "If you cared about my wellbeing, Whitney, all you had to do was ask."

The night continued much like it had before the accident, except Hillary made it a point to be seen instead of walking the edges. She spoke to each small clique of both men and women as she moved through the rooms, saying something memorable, good and bad, to everyone. A backhanded compliment here, a beguilingly stupid statement there. Everyone might have been drunk, but they would all remember her being at that party.

Toward the end of the night, she stood beside her husband as he spoke with Andy and Cassandra. They seemed like genuinely kind people, which made Hillary hate them a little bit. You don't get to have everything in the world and be well-liked. It wasn't fair, but she couldn't hold on to her contempt for too long.

Everyone liked the Bells.

"Steven," she mentioned during a pause. "I found your phone in one of the bathrooms," and she slid the device in his pocket.

He patted his thigh as if ensuring its security. "Good catch, babe. I thought I left it in the car?"

"No," she said. "You brought it inside."

"Most of the guests have been filtering out for the night," Cassandra interjected. "But it seems that most of them have had to call the cab service and now there's quite the delay. If you guys need to, we have a couple extra bedrooms for you."

Before Steven could deny their hospitality, Hillary answered for them, "How generous! Now that you say that we actually might need to stay. I can't find my rental key anywhere," she said, digging through her small bag she'd picked up from the entry way earlier. "I bet it slipped out when my purse tipped over and someone must have grabbed it by accident."

"Not to worry," Cassandra said. "I'm sure it will turn up in the morning when everyone remembers what their own keys are supposed to look like." She motioned for them to follow, showing Steven and Hillary into a guest room with a supposedly lovely view during the daytime, one she couldn't wait for them to see in the morning.

"We'll have coffee and some breakfast ready around eight in the morning if you need a snack before leaving," Cassandra said before leaving them alone to get sleep.

It was 4:51 a.m. when the investigating officers for a nearby car accident rang the doorbell.

43

SARAH

"You need to relax. You're even making me nervous, and I've been doing this for eight years," Cassandra says to Sarah.

"Sorry," Sarah replies. "I guess I'm just really invested."

The other wife gives her shoulder a quick squeeze, letting her know she understands. She doesn't, but it's a nice gesture.

Jared bogeyed the last hole. His first attempt out of the sand bunker failed, then his second shot landed within ten feet of the pin, but he failed to sink the par putt, dragging him two back from the lead to Andy. Alex Garcia isn't faring any better, despite wasting time like he owned the course. According to the leaderboard and the spectators, this final group has the action. Whether that means Andy will win outright or Jared will refocus and give everyone a good show remains to be seen.

Sarah wants her husband to play well. His performance in golf is important to him, so it is important to her. That's just part of being married. Jared's happiness is inextricably tied to hers for the rest of their lives.

It's this thought that makes her wonder if her own pain and anxiety are affecting him right now. Sarah knows this is ridiculous, of course; it's not like their relationship gives them telepathy. But she also knows that she sucks at monitoring her own expressions, and while she hasn't made eye contact with Jared the whole day, he is so attuned to her at this point in their relationship she wouldn't put it past him to check in on her when she wasn't looking. Sarah uses this thought to force a polite smile on her face.

It's not Jared, but someone notices. "Much better," Cassandra admires.

"Is there a way to get closer? It's so crowded now."

"Ah. This is where we can pull rank," Cassandra says with a conspiratorial eyebrow raise. "If you want, we can get a volunteer escort to clear out the best spots for us since we're the wives of this group. Though, I don't like to disrupt spectators like that until about the last four holes. We'll have to be more assertive in the meantime."

She grabs Sarah's hand and yanks her closer to the green. It's a par three, so they'll be watching Jared and Andy approach the hole from behind its terminus. It's a smart idea, one that will have them closer than the other fans when time comes for the important stroke: the putt.

Cassandra finds them a place on the hill behind the green. From here, they can see the tee boxes and they have a couple minutes before the men tee off. It gives Sarah too much time for her thoughts and eyes to wander.

She looks around, searching for any sign that the woman's body has been found. Sirens, screaming children, an announcement about suspended play, something. But there's none of that, with everyone's eyes on the final round of the Desert Invitational. It occurs to Sarah that the body might not be found until the course begins breaking down its grandstands in a few days. She winces, thinking of the decay that would undoubtedly be rapid in this heat. Guilt quickly replaces disgust, though.

It wouldn't take days to find her if Sarah tells someone the truth.

"Here they come," Cassandra says.

Andy is first, having scored lower than Jared on the last hole. His iron strike is crisp, clean, and lands gently at a respectable distance from the hole. It's a lag putt, but not the kind that's unmakeable.

Jared is next. Sarah can't see his face from here, but his stance is as confident as ever, though he'd never reveal if he was struggling. It isn't in his nature.

Spectators around her cheer as he lines up his shot, taking a practice swing again, back in his routine. Sarah suddenly feels out of place in her melancholy. This is a place of triumph, celebration. All these strangers are cheering for her husband, and she can't even muster a smile? Cassandra has had no problem appearing unfazed for Andy. Why can't Sarah just be happy for Jared?

Ignoring the note, and Hillary, and all her other issues, Sarah lets herself start clapping.

44

CASSANDRA

Cassandra watches Andy's iron shot land on the green and she cheers eagerly with the people around her. She never tires of seeing him in his element, strong and focused, able to drown out all the messes around him and pay attention to what's important. It's a skill vital for golf, but not wasted on his role as a family man as well. Whenever Cassandra finds herself spiraling into an anxious mess about something or another, kids carpooling to school, missed dentist appointments, he centers her.

Andy wipes his hands on the towel offered by his caddie. As their mouths move silently in tandem discussing strategy, the spectators' applause begins for Jared while he decides on a club.

The brief reprieve allows Cassandra to pay more attention to her new friend. Sarah started the day distracted and miserable, but something new upsets her. She's behaving like an invalid, needing to be guided sightlessly to each spot from which they can cheer. If there's been a new threat, another of Whitney's useless and depressing attempts at keeping Rowan alive, then she believes Sarah would have told her. They were in it together yesterday, and Cassandra likes to think she's earned a modicum of trust from the younger wife. She would have confided had she been in the same position.

But they are very different people, and Cassandra possesses a far more cutthroat upbringing than Sarah. With these thoughts, she scans the horizon from her vantage point as if someone in the crowd will volunteer themselves as the person who upset the other woman.

Nothing obvious jumps out at her, as the entirety of the people at the tournament are now following her husband's group. Despite the waves of interchangeable professional golf fans, the trees on this course are sparse, and Cassandra's line of sight casts farther than it normally would.

Atop a hill in the distance, she sees a still figure standing near the exit. She can't be sure from this far away, but it looks to be a familiar pale woman clad in black, red hair flowing behind her. It should be impossible, but it feels like that figure in the distance has been staring right at her, waiting for acknowledgement. Maybe she's imagining it, but she thinks she receives a dip of the head in return before the figure turns and disappears over the hill.

Somehow, Cassandra understands that this sighting will be the last she sees of Whitney Silver.

The crowds are gearing up again, this time in preparation for Jared's approach to the green. Surprisingly, Sarah's tentative claps grow louder. Cassandra looks towards the woman—maybe she's had some kind of mental breakdown? But no, she seems a bit more relaxed, genuinely excited for her husband. As Sarah's smile grows, Cassandra returns her attention to Jared. If he sees his wife, he doesn't reveal it, but his posture is steady, confident. She would never cheer against her husband, but she finds herself needing this shot to change the course of the day.

The crowd goes silent at the request of the volunteers and Jared stands over the tee. After a slow swing arc bringing his left arm parallel to the ground, he rips his momentum forward and it's as if the snap of the club's contact with the ball is what moves everyone's gaze toward the green.

The trajectory couldn't be more perfect, but nobody would dare to celebrate prematurely. With a thump, Jared's shot lands six feet behind the pin, its back spin allowing it to trickle slowly closer to the hole while the spectators erupt with applause.

"That's what we call a 'gimme' putt," she hears a man beside her explain to his young son. "In a more casual setting, you would let your friend pick up the ball because everyone would assume it's going to go in."

"Will Andy give Jared the 'gimme'," the boy asks his father.

"No, he's not allowed to. This is their job, so they have to finish everything."

With Sarah's excited cheering, Cassandra gets a little smug about the fact that she knew they would have a good show today.

45

HILLARY

"I think I'm really tapping into a new level here, Hil."

Hillary squeezes Steven's hand as they walk to the clubhouse. She plasters on a smile, kissing his cheek for the cameras. The ever present and all-consuming need to put on a show has been her life since she can remember, and will continue to be part of it, especially when everything comes out —that is, if Gwen was telling the truth. Not that she can worry about it now. She and Steven are still on display.

"I think so too," she says, grinning wide for him, but also anyone else who can see them.

He's already signed his scorecard and only needs to collect any items he left in the locker room, but Hillary wants to get ahead of any plans he thinks he's made.

"Steven, when you get finished, let's head out. I want some time just for us."

His eyes dance, Steven immediately picking up on what she's implying. "You got it. I'll just be a minute."

He doesn't take long in the locker room. Motivated by his baser instincts, Steven avoids the bar and his friends and the press to shove his belongings into the trunk of their rental. Apparently feeling chivalrous, he even beats Hillary to the passenger door so he can open it for her.

As he pulls out of the parking lot, he puts on his blinker to turn in the direction of the resort. "Let's go for a drive," she insists. "Somewhere private."

Steven can't keep his right hand off her as he drives. It rests on her thigh, but she can't make herself touch him back. She knows what's coming and he doesn't. It doesn't feel fair to use him for comfort in this moment.

The desert doesn't offer much in the way of privacy, but Steven finds an empty place to park behind a stack of rocks. A small hill? Certainly not a mountain, but she could almost believe he'd already scouted the place. It was too perfect of a hiding spot.

Steven unbuckles his seatbelt and leans over her, his mouth finding her throat without hesitation. "Wait," Hillary says.

"For what?" He ignores her.

Hands to his chest, gently pushing him away, she thinks about how easy it would be to lie. What are the chances Gwen was even telling the truth? This could all go away. Her secrets could die with Rowan, she and Steven could move on, live happily. She would be loyal this time. She could make herself the best wife he could ask for. It would be so easy to keep lying.

But Hillary is tired. The truth is going to hurt, but waiting to be found out is its own hell.

"We have some things we need to talk about."

Steven stares through the windshield, not actually seeing anything, his arms crossed. Having said her piece, Hillary waits for his reaction. It feels like a longer wait than is the reality, but she knows this is the least of her penance.

"How many times?"

Intuitively, she knows he's not asking how many times she's accidentally killed someone. "Four. It was four times."

He nods once, as if she had just said she balanced the checkbook or cleaned the toilets. It's quiet again. Hillary picks at a fingernail while she waits.

"This sucks."

She doesn't look up. "I'm sorry."

"I think I'm supposed to ask for a divorce now."

"I wouldn't blame you."

Steven looks at her directly, probably trying to look jaded but he can't cover the pain. "Why?"

Hillary has never been able to answer that question for herself, but speaking to her husband now, something resembling the truth slips out. "He was there, and I was weak."

They stay silent after that statement. The sun shining down on them feels like a betrayal. Her marriage is ending; shouldn't there be rain or thunder or earthquakes? There should be a natural disaster, something devastating and life altering.

But it's just sunny.

"Do you know when I fell in love with you? I don't think I ever told you."

Steven's comment is so unexpected Hillary doesn't respond at first. She thinks she dreamed it. When she looks at him, and he's clearly waiting for an answer, she gives the only one she knows.

"When you first laid eyes on me?" It's what he always says in interviews. Whenever asked, Steven would tell the story about seeing her at work that afternoon, having the wind knocked out of him because she was so beautiful. Love at first sight, he often declared, followed by a cheeky, *look at her! Can you blame me?*

"No," he says. "It was our fourth date. You were always so capable, I guess. I don't even know the right word for it. Independent, maybe? I was captivated by you, but I didn't know if it would last. You didn't seem to need me."

He exhales loudly but keeps speaking. "I couldn't think of why you were there with me. Sure, I had some money, some fame, but you could have found those somewhere else. I remember we were sitting there, at this fancy place. I kept wondering if it was nice enough for you, if I should be spending more to keep you around when the waiter came.

"You looked over at me and asked me to order for you. It was a small thing, but you let me take charge. And in that moment, I loved you."

The menu was in cursive, Hillary thinks. *I couldn't read it.*

"And what sucks the most," Steven keeps going, "is that I think I could have loved you my entire life. Shit, I think I still will, despite everything."

Hillary's thumbnail is bleeding now. She needs to stop picking it. "So, what now?" It's a stupid question, but one she must ask.

"I should ask for a divorce. But I don't think I can yet," he says.

His next question surprises her. "What do you want?"

Hillary doesn't have to think about it long. "I want to take back a lot of what I've done. I want to avoid jail, though I doubt that's possible. But mostly," she says, "I want to stay married to you. I fucked up, but I don't want a divorce. I don't want to lose you."

"Well, I didn't want you to cheat on me," Steven replies. "But we can't have everything we want."

Hillary doesn't say anything to that. What can she say? He's completely right.

"Regardless of what happens to us," he continues, "I'll get you through whatever legal stuff comes up. Pay for a lawyer and all that. It sounds like you're in a world of shit, but I can help. I've got a guy."

"A guy?"

"Yeah, a guy," Steven says. "For the right price, he can get your case in front of a good judge. A lenient one. One that can be reasoned with so to speak. I've used him before."

Hillary is somewhat shocked by the admission, but it makes sense. So, Steven has a fixer. She wasn't the only one keeping secrets in her marriage. It would also explain how, despite his increasingly delinquent behavior over the years, Steven has never had a legal charge stick to him.

"Ok," she says. "Thank you."

Steven puts the car in reverse but says nothing.

46

SARAH

A month after their first date, Jared invited Sarah to watch him compete in one of his summer junior golf tournaments. He was paired with two young men who had just graduated and committed to play at the collegiate level: one for the University of Florida and one for Rutgers. Sarah had thought that both men were considerably larger than golf required of its participants, and Jared was dwarfed by them as a result. She knew, because he had explained it to her, that yes, size and strength were a factor in golf as it was in all other sports, but practice, precision, strategy, and mental strength would almost always beat the muscular meathead who didn't have them. So, Sarah trusted him and was excited to watch him in his element.

But still. Why get emotionally invested in the long shot? If they were both going to be disappointed, why bother with hope?

Jared, conversely, did not appear concerned. He knew the young men from previous seasons and while they weren't sociable or friendly on the tee, neither were they behaving as if the final trophy was owed to them. Everyone was in the zone, assessing the course for traps and points of exploitation.

The following four and a half hours wore on Sarah in ways to which she was unaccustomed. A gasp of fear when Jared missed the green only to be followed by an elated whoop when he chipped into the hole afterwards was an adrenaline drain like she'd never experienced. If watching was that stressful, Sarah couldn't imagine the fortitude required to compete, although Jared showed no signs of exhaustion when he accepted his award for first place that day.

Sarah had let herself forget how fun it could be to cheer for her husband.

Today, she is sixteen again and watching David face Goliath. Andy is still the clear favorite, but Jared is finally playing to win. He briefly held the lead by one stroke between the holes of ten and thirteen until Andy birdied again, bringing them back to a tie. Fourteen, fifteen, and sixteen were ties as well, until seventeen. In an implausible feat, Andy had dropped a forty-foot putt for birdie, bringing him one stroke ahead of Jared going into hole eighteen.

Sarah can barely breathe.

"I'd tell you to relax," Cassandra says as they walk to their position mid-fairway to wait for their husbands' tee shots, "but I can barely contain myself either."

"Tell me about it," Sarah replies, wiping her hands on her skirt in a futile attempt to dry them. She hasn't been this invested in Jared's performance in a long time, but it's also his first year really competing against the best of the best. "Is it always like this?"

Cassandra considers her for a moment before answering. "Yes and no," she admits. "I'm always devoted to Andy. It's like I'm connected to every shot he takes, even when he isn't top of the leaderboard. I feel every putt, missed or made," she looks around at the hordes of excited fans, the cameras, and the course, "but this is something else."

"I think I get it," Sarah says.

The men are on the tee box of eighteen. With the sun finally behind all the manmade structures surrounding the competition, there's a collective relief from the desert heat, swiftly replaced by the intensity of the final hole. Roaring cheers erupt once, then twice, as both Jared and Andy's tee shots find the fairway. The cheering continues as they walk with their caddies, waving at fans along the way. Behind the men, on the ground already passed, spectators flood onto the fairway, creating a wave of adoration to surround the final strokes of the tournament.

Even with their elevated status as wives of the two leaders, Cassandra and Sarah are shoulder to shoulder with anyone smart enough to park themselves at the finish line. As they make their way toward the green, a volunteer sees them and waves them over to the cords holding fans away from the green. Here, they can stand and watch their husbands' approach shots.

"Thank God for that," Cassandra whispers.

Despite special treatment, fans are still pushing against their backs. "I'll be glad when this is over," Sarah says.

"Now none of that. You'll look back on this with fondness, believe me."

Sarah doesn't disagree, but she'll still be relieved to get off her feet and finally get a shower. There's something about the heat that makes her feel perpetually dirty, like the dried sweat follows her around. Combined with the dirtiness of seeing that woman die...

No, now is not the time to think about that. She's here, watching Jared, and she's never been more proud of her husband.

Jared's drive is several yards behind Andy's, and he stands over it with a long iron. His caddie says a few more words, then retreats to give Jared space. As he swings, the multitudes remain silent. It's a miracle, really, that so many people can sustain this kind of quiet, even for one shot.

Sarah watches as her husband's approach makes the familiar thump ten feet from the hole, leading to an eardrum shattering roar from the crowds.

He waves, gracious as ever. Andy, with the confidence only a veteran golfer can muster, stands over his shot without waiting for the noise to die down. His practice swing is noticed by many, leading to a dimmer roar, but the fans don't quiet down completely. His approach only reinvigorates the crowds' screaming, his shot landing just two feet outside of Jared's.

Both men strut toward the green, removing their gloves as the spectators behind them continue to close in on the final shots. Andy and Jared are both smiling and waving, paying attention to hungry fans. Thousands of people surround the final hole, millions more watch from television sets at bars and in homes.

"It's like something out of a movie," Sarah says.

"Sure is," Cassandra agrees. She's nibbling at her thumbnail, the first sign of true nervousness that Sarah's ever seen from her. They both know what comes next. Jared needs to make his putt, and for Andy to miss his to force a sudden death playoff. The men would replay hole eighteen over and over, until one of them wins, or until the sun sets and they have to come back tomorrow.

Spectators are unable to stay quiet for any meaningful length of time, requiring volunteer intervention with signs demanding silence. Andy and Jared are both on the green with their caddies, all four men kneeling in various positions around the pin to read the potential breaks in their putts. A gentle breeze moves the flag briefly, still too hot to offer reprieve for the masses of people. Finally, Andy stands behind his putt.

Sarah isn't looking at him though; she's looking at Jared. He stands away from the other man, arms crossed, staring at the green without seeing.

Please look at me. Let me know we're ok.

Andy moves to stand over his putt. Cassandra holds her breath with everyone else as he takes one, then two practice strokes before moving his putter directly behind the ball. Before he takes his shot, Jared looks away, finally finding Sarah's eyes.

How silly of her, to think anything else mattered. It was all so pointless, worrying about the make-up and the shapewear and the cameras. She was a fool for letting those things become more important than her marriage. Knowing Jared, she could see he held similar sentiments, that he didn't want her anywhere but by his side. Neither of them was watching the green when an ear-splitting roar encircled them, with hats and promotional pamphlets getting tossed about in celebration.

Andy Bell has won the Desert Invitational.

Excerpt from the *All Things Golf* Podcast with Drake Jones
Released on July 17, 2022

Drake: You know I hate to say it—
    Britney: No, you don't.
    Drake: I told you so.

Britney: There it is.

Drake: In all seriousness, I don't see how the outcome of this weekend can be seen as anything other than a resounding rebuke of the PGA's narrative about the new league. Plenty of the guys who were written off as being past their prime were decidedly competitive this weekend, including my spot-on pick for winner, Andy Bell.

Britney: Resounding rebuke might be an exaggeration. Eight of the top ten players are still PGA members, the only exceptions were Andy Bell and Alex Garcia.

Drake: If you were talking about a percentage of each member group, though, that makes it about an even split.

Britney: That's fair.

Drake: I do have to give you props for your call on Jared Farmer. He was basically off my radar until you mentioned him last week and I can see your logic. This guy is going to be big.

Britney: Yeah, I really like this kid's future. As I said, he's young, healthy, and has the rest of his career in front of him. I think if he stays focused on fundamentals and keeps his head in the game, then there's nowhere to go but up.

Drake: I still think he has some growing up to do when it comes to his mental game. The scoring doesn't necessarily reflect it, but for most of Sunday I don't think we were getting a champion fight out of him. Or, how am I trying to say this, it looked like he wasn't all in it, you know?

Britney: Right, I saw that too. It seemed like there was something going on in his head that wasn't helping him compete for sure. But I still think that's something he can grow out of eventually. Newer players always go through some kind of mental strength reckoning in their early years. It mostly comes down to getting the reps in, playing in so many majors that the nerves fall behind and competition becomes second nature.

Drake: Right, maybe just something that comes with maturity.

Britney: That's a hurdle all pros have got to cross in their career. It's what separates the champions from the weekend warrior guys.

Drake: Do you think Jared can do it?

Britney: Absolutely. With the right practice regimen and a supportive family to come home to, this guy can do anything.

47

SARAH

After Jared sinks his birdie putt, the men shake hands with each other and their caddies. With all the bodies moving around her, Sarah has only a small window of opportunity to reach her husband. With the media mostly focused on Andy, it shouldn't be too hard, but the fans have other priorities.

Priorities like, apparently, standing in her way.

This won't do. Sarah straightens her spine and follows Cassandra into the fray. She notices and tries really hard not to be bitter about the fact that everyone moves out of the way more easily for the other woman now, but her singular focus is still on her husband. She won't have much time—he still needs to sign his scorecard to complete the round—but she needs to see him, needs to touch him and make sure he's real.

As Jared comes into view at the edge of the green, she picks up speed. There're no cameras, no viewers, nobody but Sarah and her husband. Jared has an oddly relaxed demeanor to him, the weight of the tournament behind him. She knows better than to assume he's satisfied with second place, but this day came with its own unique stressors for both of them. When he sees Sarah, he moves quickly to embrace her, holding her close despite the sweat and grime of the day that still coats them. She blinks back her tears before whispering in his ear.

"I'm so sorry."

"Shhh," he returns, squeezing her somehow even closer. "It's time to go home."

~

"Congratulations," Sarah says to Cassandra. Their husbands are signing scorecards, and soon Andy will be presented with his award. While she wishes it was her husband, Sarah finds she can't gather the energy to be jealous of the other woman. She's been too friendly and supportive these past few days. Mostly, Sarah is just relieved that she can finally put this weekend behind her, relieved that she still has Jared after all the mistakes she made.

"Thank you," Cassandra replies. "I hope our husbands are paired together in the future. You would likely be unsurprised at how difficult it is to befriend other wives on tour. The competition doesn't exactly stop with our husbands."

"I didn't think I'd hear anyone admit that out loud."

"And you probably won't hear it again," Cassandra offers a knowing and sardonic look in Sarah's direction before they both descend into giggles. It's the kind of laughter that mostly comes from a liberation from tension. Neither woman is immune to helping carry the stresses of their husbands.

"What does a Sunday night spent celebrating a win look like for the Bells?"

"Hopefully just a long shower and some room service. I don't have the energy for anything else."

First place celebrations don't sound that different from Sarah's second place plans. "That sounds marvelous."

They make their way to the standing areas surrounding a temporary platform where the awards ceremony will begin in a few minutes. A majority of the spectators are leaving, trying to beat the crush. Maybe less than half will stay for the awards ceremony, but those would be the diehard fans, the ones who would pay any price to get close to the contest and its winners. Volunteers setting up and moving people into place are a familiar scene to Sarah. What's new is the emergency service lights moving from the front nine to the exit.

An EMT vehicle tries to make it through, people slowly recognizing its presence and getting out of the way. Whispers are filtering through the crowd now, asking questions about the ambulance. Has it been here the whole time just in case? When did it arrive? Is anyone in the back, and what happened to them? Having emergency response personnel on hand for huge events like this one isn't uncommon, but the fact that it's moving through sanctioned areas means that something's happened. Despite its emergency status, the drivers seem to be in no real rush to get to a hospital. The sirens aren't on, and the guys operating the vehicle appear content to trickle out at a speed reserved more for elderly drivers than two young men rushing someone to safety.

There'd be no point in rushing if the person is already dead.

Sarah must be doing a terrible job of schooling her face, because Cassandra notices. "What's wrong?"

"Nothing," she lies. "I just hope everyone is ok."

48

BARTENDER #3

I fill another cup of water for one of our last patrons. I was supposed to be able to leave earlier this afternoon, but thanks to Greg, I am forced to work open to close today. I'm essentially dead on my feet, but luckily, my permanent manager is an understanding guy, and he's giving me the week off after this.

It's the only thing keeping a smile on my face right now.

Cody left a few hours ago, replaced by another set of eager teenagers, ones I don't know as well because we usually don't work the same shift. At least they're competent, keeping all the stations clean so I don't have to worry about side work as I try to politely get everyone to leave.

Andy Bell should be getting his award soon, and after that I'll be able to officially close. Anyone who wants a drink will have to go somewhere else.

Coverage is playing loudly on the television across from my bar, and I hear some of the analysis.

"In my opinion, this is something of a fluke. I don't think this is a referendum on the PGA tour at all, and in fact most of the men on the leader board were PGA tour members. I stand by recent assessments, that most of the new league players are past their prime," says one of the commentators.

"Glen," the woman next to him says, "Andy Bell won pretty decisively. I think he's still extremely competitive in his own right."

I smile to myself. There would be a lot of commentators stumbling over themselves to explain how they're still right even when, quite literally, everything they predicted for this weekend ended up being wrong. I've never understood why admitting you guessed something incorrectly was a point of embarrassment. It's a guess. Sometimes they're right, sometimes they're wrong. I think the viewers of these commentators would respect their opinions a lot more if they were more honest about their predictions. As it stands, continuing to defend his incorrect assumptions is only going to make Glen a huge joke in all the golf fan Reddit boards.

When it comes to the PGA drama and its new competing league, I have no thoughts on it in either direction. As long as one or both of the tours brings a major tournament to my place of work, I'll happily take tips from whoever buys drinks.

My musings are interrupted by two men in suits who approach the bar. Immediately, my guard is up. Only the very upper management would wear a suit to this kind of golf tournament, and I wonder if I'm in serious trouble for some reason.

Then I remember that I've worked almost all my waking hours for the past two days and decide that I can't possibly be in trouble.

"Good evening, miss," says one of the men.

"You, too. What can I get you gentlemen to drink?"

"Two waters are fine," the other one answers. Neither moves to sit down, and as I pour their water, they don't fill the silence either.

"Have you been working here all day?"

I raise an eyebrow. "Do I look tired or something?"

"No," the first man chuckles and I find I'm relieved by the levity. That is, until he removes a large billfold, flips it open, and shows me a gold badge. I'm not well versed in the different types of law enforcement, so I have no idea if he's local or state or something else, but it looks official. When the second guy shows me a matching one, I start to worry.

"I'm Detective Brody, and this is Detective Grossman. Do you have a few minutes to answer some questions for us?"

Is this about Greg? I don't see how I could be connected to his death in any way. It was a suicide. And even if he went out wanting to punish me one last time, what would he say?

I need to kill myself because that one nosy bartender stopped me from flirting with teenagers.

Ridiculous. That, and he never bothered to learn my name. Something else must have happened today.

"If you guys want to grab a seat at the corner table, I just need to find someone to cover the bar for me while we talk."

~

Since the hostess and busboy aren't old enough to serve drinks, I have to pull a disgruntled cook from the kitchen before I can meet with the detectives. He grumbles, but I think he's secretly grateful to skip out on the clean-up duties that are normally reserved for him.

As I approach the table, I take in as much about the two men as I can before I sit down. Detective Brody is clearly the senior detective, the younger man deferring to him in his mannerisms. Brody is older, with some paunch around his face and stomach. He looks like a stereotype, a corrupt cop with a drinking or gambling problem. Maybe both. I don't know any of this for sure, so my best course of action will be to interact with him as if this is all in good faith.

Hopefully that is true.

Detective Grossman is, ironically, extremely attractive and looks to be only a few years older than me. Maybe he's still training with Brody, or if they're true partners then it seems to be a new relationship. Despite his junior rank, Grossman sits without slouching and appears confident in his position at the table.

I sit down and note that Brody has a well-worn, classic yellow-gold wedding band, while Grossman's left hand is empty. If I weren't sitting down with the police, I'd find that interesting.

"Miss, before we get started, we just want to let you know that this interview is entirely voluntary, and you can stop at any time if you don't feel comfortable," Brody says, opening our conversation.

"Sure," I say. "Can I ask what this is about?"

Grossman answers this time. "Two people have died at the resort in the last twenty-four hours," he says, pausing to wait for my reaction.

When I don't break down in tears or pass out at the news, he continues, "Regardless of the fact that one seems to be a suicide and another of heat stroke or food poisoning, two right on top of one another warranted a visit from us. We're just taking some proactive steps to avoid losing evidence. If something does come up, either with the suicide last night or the woman on the course today, we don't want to have lost access to any on site witnesses."

"I understand, but I've been here all day, and certainly no one died in here."

"All day? That seems like a long shift," Brody says.

"I wasn't supposed to, but we were understaffed. The suicide was actually one of my temporary supervisors, Greg. Plus, it's not like I can complain about overtime wages."

"When was the last contact you had with Greg Yeager?"

"We both worked the gala last night. Then he texted me about updating the systems here around midnight."

The detectives look at each other before Brody continues, "You might have been the last person who spoke with him."

"Not in person," I insist. I can't tell if that statement makes me look guilty or not, so I shut up until they ask for more.

"Did he seem sad or in a different mood than usual?"

"Not that I could tell, but I only knew him for about a week." I'd rather not dive into who he was as a person. Even if he creeped everyone out, I have no proof that he actually did anything illegal, and the man is gone. I figure even he deserves a little rest now.

Luckily, they move on, and Brody pushes a driver's license photo of a middle-aged woman on the table in my direction, "At any point today, did you serve this woman?"

"I saw her," I explain, "but I didn't serve her anything."

"What do you mean?" Grossman interjects.

"Well, she didn't have the correct wrist band. Fans pay a high price for access to the clubhouse, and if someone didn't pay for one of those tickets gets served here, I get in trouble. I told her she had to go to one of the outside vendors."

"Was that the last time you saw her?"

They aren't giving me enough information. "Why her? What happened?"

Grossman speaks again, "She was the other death on site today."

Damn. I should've been nicer to her.

"Did you give her anything free, maybe a to go cup of water?"

I shake my head. "Nothing, sir." Not that I feel great about it at this point. If we end up finding out that she died of heat stroke because I didn't give her a stupid cup of water, then I'd be really annoyed at myself.

"Let's circle back," Brody says, "was her intrusion into the clubhouse the last time you saw her?"

"Yes. Wait, no." Crap. The news has thrown me, and I'm not thinking clearly. I take a deep breath, slow down. This interview is more serious than they originally implied. "I saw her later this afternoon. I was walking the trash to the dumpster, and she was outside one of the tents. She was with another woman, and they walked under the shelter together."

"Was this the tent off hole number five?"

"Pretty sure, yes."

Brody nods, putting the picture away. "Did you recognize the person with her?"

"Yeah. It was Hillary Torre. I think they're related, somehow. They were arguing about something before they went inside."

The detectives look at each other.

"What is it?"

"Nothing," Brody says. "To the best of your ability, can you tell us everyone you served today?"

My face must reveal my reaction to that question, because Grossman has to fight to hide his smile. I wish he wouldn't, it's a nice smile.

"Sir," I reply, trying to be patient, "I served hundreds of people today, most of whom I never received a name from. What you're asking is impossible."

"What if you just gave us the names of people you recognized?" Brody offers as a compromise.

I sigh, hoping it doesn't get me in trouble. "If you're looking for someone specific, maybe you could just ask about them and I can tell you whether or not I served them?"

"Let's start with Hillary Torre, then." Grossman explains. "Did you serve her?"

I begin the process of pulling the impossible information. Prior to the detective's arrival, I had been looking forward to forgetting this entire week-end. I'd gone through the day only halfway observing anyone who passed through. Now, I must recall everyone I served?

Criminal.

"She was here in the morning, just after the first tee times. But I don't remember her ordering anything."

"Who else? As many names as possible," Brody demands.

"Let's see," I start, stalling for time as I bring myself back to when I opened the bar. "For the players who came in before they teed off for the day, I served Jared Farmer, Alex Garcia, Matthew Price, Pat Bannen, and Ryan Sayer. There were a few other guys who I recognized as players but never got their names. If you show me a picture of the roster, I'd be able to point them out to you."

"That's fine. Keep going, please," Brody says.

"Then there was one guy who, again, his name I don't know but I think he was from the press tent getting drinks for everyone there. I'd be able to pull him out of a line up if needed. I also served Sarah Farmer and Cassandra Bell, who came in after their husbands. Another wife, Patricia, was in here too, though I can't think of her last name."

Grossman writes everything down while Brody stares at me. "This is all great. Anyone else you can think of, before we go?"

Whitney Silver, I want to say, but something stops me. First, now that I'm thinking clearly, I don't even respect this line of questioning. Why don't they just pull security footage, or, I don't know, declare an actual crime committed before they start collecting suspects?

Second, Whitney's probably had to deal with the police far too many times last year, without the closure of having her husband's death even resolved. That sounds like hell. Was I really going to punish her further with an accidental death of someone she probably didn't even know? Over, what, ordering soda on a hot day?

Plus, she's a very generous tipper...

"Nothing else right now. If you have a card or something, I can call if I remember anything," I say, ending the interview.

Brody begins the clearly painful process of leaning his girth to the side so he can access his wallet, so the younger Grossman beats him easily, sliding his card across the table toward me first. I pick it up, reading the information.

"Your full name is Neal Grossman?"

His face reddens slightly, though he appears used to the teasing. "Sexy, right?"

I stand up, sensing that Detective Brody has had enough of me for the night. I'm happy to stand up for myself, but there's no need to push my luck with local law enforcement.

"If you guys don't have anything else for me, I need to get back to work. I think I mentioned this before, but we're understaffed here, and I need to help out."

"That's fine," Brody replies as he stands up. I walk back toward the bar area, when Grossman calls out.

"Were you brought in to help with the tournament? Or are you from around here?"

I face them to answer his question, thinking they need to know for follow-up purposes, but the look Brody is giving his partner lets me know this was not a sanctioned question.

"Local," I say, as I try to make my smile as charming as possible. I probably look horrendous after the workday I've had, but I won't let that deter me. "I work full time at the club here."

Grossman smiles with his whole face, his eyes framed by mild laugh lines that will inevitably deepen with time. "That's good."

～

Sante Fe Herald: July 18, 2022
Woman Dead of Presumed Heat Stroke

This weekend's exciting Desert Invitational was marred by tragedy when one of the spectators, Gwen Hicks, was found dead of a presumed heat stroke on Sunday evening. Her body was found underneath the bleachers on hole five. It is assumed by local investigators that she was seeking shade at the time. No foul play is currently suspected, but an autopsy has been requested by her life insurance provider.

While Hicks was the only heat stroke death this weekend, many other specta-tors were treated for dehydration and other side effects of local weather. The Santa Fe Herald would like to remind its readers about the importance of staying hydrated, especially as we get deeper into the summer months, and there's no better way to do that than with our sponsor, HydrAlpha^{TM}. HydrAlpha^{TM} is the fastest working hydration tool with the longest protection against heat and exer-tion. Please follow the link at the bottom of the page for 10% off your next purchase.

<This is a breaking news story. Please refresh the page for updates.>

49

CASSANDRA

"Mrs. Bell, we've reserved a place for you in the press tent with air conditioning and other amenities. You can watch the acceptance speech from there."

The volunteer means well, but Cassandra has no intention of leaving her place several yards from the stage. She wants her eyes on Andy when he accepts his award, not the commentary from sports analysts about what his win means for professional golf and the dueling leagues. His win is sure to open discussions concerning those who joined the new league and whether they can participate in the PGA tournaments. Fans of professional golf want to watch the winners, and Andy has proven there are plenty of winners in the new league. If it makes them money, they'll probably say yes.

"No, thank you," she answers. "I'll stay right here."

The crowds have thinned, many leaving to get dinner with their families or get a prime position in line for the shuttles. Cassandra has plenty of room for herself along with the diehards and super fans.

"May I have your attention, please," begins Frank Delonago, the tournament's facilitator. "First, I want to thank Santa Fe National for hosting the Desert Invitational. Every year, I'm blown away by the quality of the facilities and volunteers, thinking there's no way you guys can beat this, and every year I'm proven wrong."

This statement is met with a small pattering of claps and polite laughter while he continues. "I also want to thank the USGA for its tireless efforts…"

For all of the award ceremonies and tournaments she has attended since her marriage, Cassandra could probably give this speech herself. Thank the course, thank the volunteers, thank the association. She doubts they will memorialize Rowan Silver, having done so more privately last night.

She also knows that if they do, Whitney's absence might be noted. The widow likely asked them not to say anything today.

Frank moves on to congratulate one of the amateur players who participated this weekend, Matthew Price, a junior at UCLA, giving him a small trophy for his hole in one on Saturday. As he shakes the young man's hand, he speaks at length about his future, "We cannot wait to see you on tour someday, Matthew."

Finally, Frank moves on to the final award, and Cassandra stands up straighter, the tiredness and sore feet gone without a trace. Andy makes his way up the steps to stand next to the podium. "Without further delay, I present your winner of the 55th Annual Desert Invitational, Andy Bell. Andy, congratulations on an impressive weekend, sir."

The men exchange a handshake, followed by some glad-handing back pats and half hugs, a masculine greeting somehow no champion escapes when they accept their trophy. Andy handles it amicably and stands before the microphone.

"Thank you everyone, especially Sante Fe National and the USGA, for hosting one of my favorite events every year. I think everyone can agree this was an outstanding weekend."

More light clapping follows Andy's words while his eyes scan the crowd, finally landing on Cassandra. He always finds her for these speeches. He made plenty of successful public talks before her, but he hasn't made one without seeking out her gaze since they met.

"I'd also like to thank my swing coach, Ed Sheppard, for tirelessly pushing me to improve beyond what I thought were my capabilities. I owe you so much for both my swing and my mental focus throughout the game. I could not have risen to the level I have in my game without you.

"I want to thank my parents, who continue to be some of my biggest supporters. I think a majority of the merchandise with my name on it has only sold because they purchased it," he says to a round of laughter from onlookers. "I know my kids aren't wearing it."

"I also want to thank my friends in the league, both new and old, for making me love the game more than I already do. Golf can be a competitive and isolating sport if you let yourself become too internally focused, too self-involved, so I thank you guys for keeping the sport fun and keeping me humbled by your own talents.

"Lastly," he pauses to swallow, and Cassandra feels her own chest grow tight, "I want to thank my wife, Cassandra.

"I couldn't do any of this without you. Seeing you behind the green makes these tournaments brighter, and coming home to you after a day spent practicing is still the highlight of my weeks. I couldn't ask for a better partner or mother of my children. In all ways possible, and some I can't even measure, you've made my life better just by being in it. Every trophy, every championship, every putt I make, it's all for you.

"I love you, Cassandra."

50

SARAH

"Why didn't you tell me?"

Sarah lays in Jared's side on the bed, both fresh out of the shower after the official end to the tournament. Normally, they try and return home as soon as possible, even if it means taking the red eye or driving through the night. But this time, Jared extended their stay for another two nights. He said that they needed some time together before returning to the routine of living in Ottawa.

"I don't know," she says. "I was scared, I think, and I just froze up. I didn't want to distract you."

He pulls her chin up, forcing her to look at him. "Never keep something like that from me again, ok?"

"Ok."

She had told him about the note, and how everyone reacted to it. It bothers her to not have more information about who wrote it, but other worries have overshadowed it. If her new friendship with Cassandra holds up, maybe they can join forces to discover who wrote it, but it's not a priority anymore. She told him about the dead waiter, then eventually the woman under the tent who died and how Hillary might have been involved.

"I mean it," he insists. "The idea of you carrying that around by yourself pains me. We're a team. Even if you suspect something, we need to talk that stuff out. I knew some of the new media exposure was hard on you, but I didn't realize how bad it had gotten."

She looks at him, confused. "What do you mean?"

"The make-up on hot days, the camera paranoia, starving yourself. I assumed it would pass, but I didn't understand what was happening. I thought you'd get used to it, but I should have confronted you sooner. I let you struggle with it all alone and it led to everything crashing this weekend.

"If you're having a hard time or feeling insecure, I want you to talk to me. It's never too much or too little for me to take care of my wife."

Sarah sighs and snuggles back into Jared. "It won't happen again." In hindsight, she feels silly for believing the note, but he's right. If she hadn't been so stuck in her own head, so aggressively comparing herself to every other woman, the note would not have even affected her. It was an insecurity in herself, not their marriage, that caused her reaction to it.

He pets her arm and stays quiet, pensive. She is beginning to think he's done talking, that they won't discuss it further when he speaks again. "I think that maybe you think I don't notice."

She sits up. "Notice what?"

"All the stuff," he replies, looking up at her from his spot on the pillow. "You do so much. I never have to think about dinner, or laundry, or bills. And those things are small, but they say something more to me than that. It is like you trust me."

Sarah feels shot through the heart. "Jared, about the note—"

"Not that kind of trust," he interrupts. "Well, yes, but different." He lifts himself up, leaning against the headboard. He sighs as if he can't explain what he's thinking. Sarah knows the feeling well.

"Do you have any idea how many times my own dad told me to give up?"

"Give up?"

"On golf," Jared explains. "Almost weekly before I made my first cut on tour, I would get a call or a lecture from my dad, sometimes my mom too. They would insist I give up golf and get a real job. That it was shameful for me, as a man, to let my wife go to work while I chased my silly little dream. And a lot of days, I would believe them. I would head home after another

failed qualifier or a frustrating day at the range and wonder why I was wasting your time.

"Then I would get home, and everything would be perfect. You would smile at me and ask about golf and what the next milestone is and when you could watch me play again. There was never a question of, like, 'when are you going to get serious,' or 'I'm worried about money.' It was like you knew I was going to make it, and in my mind, I was like, 'Holy shit. Sarah has no backup plan. She believes in me. She actually thinks I can do this.'"

Sarah looks at Jared, beginning to understand. "Of course, I believed in you. Still do. I mean, look at you and how good you are. It was obvious."

He pulls her closer and kisses her temple, giving her a squeeze. "It was only obvious to you."

The weight of her sorrow and regret threatens to pull her away from Jared, but Sarah ignores it and leans in to kiss him instead. It's healing for both of them, coming together like this. As tempting as it was to move on from the conversation into happier, safer territory, Sarah needs to acknowledge her mistake to Jared.

"Never again."

"Never again," he agrees, and pulls her beneath him.

Excerpt from Reporter's Official Transcript of Proceedings
Criminal Pretrial Hearing
The State of New Mexico vs. Hillary Torre
August 16, 2022

Before: Honorable Christopher Brown, Associate Judge and a Jury
For the Prosecution: John B. Brighton, Attorney
For the Defendant: Francis Morgan, Attorney; Theodore A. Washington, Attorney

The Clerk: All rise for the honorable Judge Brown presiding.
Judge Brown: Please be seated.

The Clerk: Criminal Case 09-1698, The State of New Mexico vs. Hillary Torre.

Judge Brown: Let's hear from the State.

Mr. Brighton: Your Honor, the defendant has been charged with obstruction of justice in the death of Rowan Silver last year, and murder in the first degree of Gwendolyn Hicks.

Judge Brown: In the case of obstruction of justice, how does the defendant plead?

Mr. Morgan: My client pleads guilty to the obstruction charges, your Honor.

Judge Brown: In the case of murder in the first degree, how does the defendant plead?

Mr. Morgan: Your Honor, in the case of murder in the first degree, my client pleads not guilty.

Judge Brown: Is your client prepared to face a jury of her peers?

Mr. Morgan: Yes, your Honor.

Judge Brown: Very well. In exchange for a guilty plea for obstruction of justice, Mrs. Torre will be serving a prison sentence of six months, plus three months' probation including time served. <Gavel Bang> Next case, please.

51

HILLARY

"Thank you for meeting with me."

Hillary wishes she could backhand her lawyer. Thanking her for her presence, right after her sentencing. As if she has a choice, sitting here across the table in a heavily surveilled prison conference room, head to toe in orange. A shifty, litigious stereotype, Francis Morgan is a total scum bag. If someone were to ask Hillary what she thought a greedy ambulance chaser or a corrupt prosecutor looks like, she would describe the man sitting in front of her. She hates everything about him, even his name (*Francis?*), except that he's crafty enough to keep her out of prison for longer than she deserves. Steven is here too, which should help, but she has no idea where they stand as husband and wife.

"Sure," Hillary says.

Francis doesn't acknowledge any animosity from her and keeps speaking. "I'm friends with the prosecutor here, which is why he was so willing to work with us. There was no evidence that you were impaired driving that night or at fault for the wreck, so he only charged for obstruction of justice, leading to the deal we just got for you."

Hillary sneaks a glance at Steven, but he won't look at her. "Mr. Morgan, I understand that you're talented, but this all seems too good to be true. From what I understand, I should be going to jail for several years."

"Perhaps you deserve to," Francis soldiers on, not softening any verbal blows. Why should he? She needs him more than he needs her. "But I am, in fact, very good at what I do."

It's far more likely that Steven helped grease some palms along the way. "Wonderful."

"I'm more concerned about the murder charge of your half-sister."

"And like I told you: I didn't do it. I thought it was heatstroke or a food borne illness. I had no idea she was poisoned with some chemical."

"Unfortunately, you were the last one to see her alive and you didn't report it immediately. Also, with everything else that's come out, you had a clear motive for wanting her gone."

On that, Steven had kept his promise as well. The two separate deaths on site at a major golf tournament had made it easy for his people to bury most negative press about Hillary. Gwen hadn't been bluffing when she said she would release all the secrets from that night. She'd gathered enough evidence that Hillary had been in the car, and Gwen had also lifted Rowan's phone from the wreckage which had all their old text messages still saved. Had the package been released during a slower news cycle, Hillary would have been dealing with a way larger media shitstorm.

She presses her torso against the metal table and looks directly at Francis. "Or maybe I had a motive to keep her alive. After all, if she was still here, I wouldn't be in prison, and she'd be bilking me for cash instead of you."

"You make a compelling point," Francis says with a twitch at the corner of his mouth. He's the kind of conniving person that doesn't respect ethical behavior or wisdom. He would never appreciate honesty or innocence. He only cares about power, and when Hillary challenges him, it is the first time he glances at her with anything resembling admiration.

"My most compelling point is the fact that I didn't fucking do it," she continues. "Why would I be carrying around antifreeze? I've never even refilled the windshield wiper fluid in my car."

"So, you didn't know antifreeze has an overly sweet aftertaste, making it easy to hide in flavored beverages?"

"Obviously not."

"Fortunately," Francis is back to business now, "you were attending an event with no shortage of cameras. My investigator was able to get his hands on most of the footage. It was a live streamed event, so we didn't have to fight the network at all. They've already made their money, you see."

"So, you're going to comb through well over twelve hours of golf coverage to see if anyone looking like a mechanic handed something to Gwen?"

He grins across the table. "That's exactly what we're going to do. Is there anything you can give me that would make that process easier?"

"You already know what I'm going to say," Hillary replies.

"And you know what I'm going to say," he says. "Even if Mrs. Silver is the one who gave Gwen the last thing she ever consumed, you can see how that accusation would appear vindictive, coming from you?"

Right. Because the whole world now knows I banged her husband.

Almost as if he can hear her thoughts, Steven tenses in his spot at the table, but still doesn't say anything.

"I'm not asking you to blast her in the media or even send the police her way. Just have your investigators keep an eye on her when they're looking through the tournament footage."

"I don't see why we can't accommodate that request," he says, not really promising to do it. Francis stands, collecting his notes, even though she didn't see him pick up a pen for the entire meeting. "Steven, you ready?"

Hillary expects him to leave with the attorney, but his eyes stay glued to the table. "Can I have a minute with my wife, please?"

Hillary freezes. She hasn't been alone with Steven since her arrest, and she fears what he will say. That he hates her? Doesn't believe her? That he's going to ask Francis to throw the case, so she gets the maximum amount of time in prison?

The metal door slams behind Mr. Morgan and Hillary sits before Steven without supervision. Well, alone together physically but likely still being surveilled by prison security.

He plays with his hands, spins his wedding band around his finger before speaking. "I practiced on the way over here."

He still won't look at her. "Practiced?"

"Practiced saying what I thought I was supposed to say," he nods, still to himself. "I was going to ask you for a divorce. Very straightforward, with no room for arguments."

Here it is. Hillary thought she would feel relief in this moment. It's what she felt when everything else fell apart, when she found out Gwen had blackmail materials on her, when she knew the truth about Rowan was coming out. She inaccurately assumed that waiting for Steven to ask her for a divorce would be worse than when he actually did it, but she was wrong.

Instead of a burden lifted, she feels sick to her stomach. She realizes she didn't really believe that the divorce was inevitable. She had been pathetically holding onto a tiny shard of hope, somewhere deep in the back of her mind.

Well, here it comes.

"If that's what you wanted," Hillary swallows, "then I wouldn't have argued."

Steven almost laughs, then finally looks at her. His eyes are red, his skin sallow. He might be sleeping less than she is. "Why not?"

"Why not argue?"

"No," he responds, "why not fight for us?"

"Because I deserve for you to leave me. After everything, this is what I deserve."

"Yeah, well, I deserve a hell of a lot worse than what I have. I've lived far from a perfect life, Hillary."

"Yes, but—"

"Do you love me?"

His question is like a slap to the face. Does she love him? It seems like such a simple question, but it's been so low on her list of considerations. Don't get caught, find a way to get away from Gwen, run from her past. She'd been image conscious for so long, she forgot to account for how she felt about anything. Her marriage to Steven has been so insulated and poisoned by the baggage she brought with her, that she hasn't even thought about him as a man in years.

What if it was just them? If Steven weren't Steven Torre, PGA winner and chronic partier, and she wasn't Hillary Torre—formerly Hicks—what then?

"Yes," she says, "I've always loved you."

He blinks, perhaps not believing it. "Ok," he replies. "Ok, we can work on this then. I don't know what comes next or how we will fix this. Maybe we don't, I don't know."

Steven takes a breath and finishes, "But we don't give up. You can fight with me, and we'll make mistakes, but don't you dare quit on us."

He exits the room, met outside the door by a guard. He didn't touch her the entire time they were together, but Hillary is too grateful for another chance that she doesn't notice. Steven looks back briefly, then she loses sight of him as he turns a corner.

A different guard brings her out, pulling her back to her cell that she shares with a woman doing six years for credit card fraud. She's on trial for murder and should obviously be in a rougher part of the prison, but from what she can tell compared to the other women, she has comparatively cushy accommodations.

Another gift from Steven, she assumes.

On paper, Hillary's life has almost never been worse than it is now. She walks in an orange jumpsuit with no privacy or trust on the walk back to the communal areas, waiting for a trial that she has no guarantee of winning, despite her innocence. There will be no more make-up, eyebrow threading, expensive haircuts. No more Instagram followers, fame, or expensive clothes.

But when the women's prison guard drags her by the arm deeper into incarceration, Hillary smiles.

Gwen is gone.

Steven wants to fight for their marriage.

She's out of the public eye.

For the first time in her memory, Hillary sees a path, maybe not to happiness, but at least toward contentment.

～

Interview Excerpt with Whitney Silver, CBS News
August 24th, 2022

CBS: I imagine the news breaking this week has dredged up a lot of bad memories for you.

Whitney: Of course it has, but that's to be expected. The pain is more bearable now that I know Rowan will get justice. Not knowing what happened made everything worse.

CBS: Were you surprised when the driver's name came out?

Whitney: I was no less than blindsided. I have always considered Hillary a friend, and I don't want to think about why they were in the same car together, but I suppose people are speculating anyway. I don't expect the guilty party to tell the truth, and we can obviously never ask Rowan. But at the end of the day, I'm just grateful to finally have some closure.

CBS: Have you been keeping track of the trial?

Whitney: Not really, it's still too raw for me. I did see an update about sentencing and I was really shocked at how lenient the judge was. I don't think it's fair for her to get so little time, but apparently, she has other charges pending as well.

CBS: Now that you have the information surrounding your late husband's death, what's next for Whitney Silver?

Whitney: I'll still oversee some of the projects for Silver Linings Golf Group, but I no longer have an active role. It's Rowan's legacy, but it's outgrown my capabilities. Honestly, I just want a quiet and private life.

52

SARAH

"It's not too late to change Farmer back to Wilson. If you insist on playing the kept woman, you could at least keep a piece of your own identity."

Sarah rolls her eyes. She is on the phone with her mother, her once every two-week obligation to the woman who raised her. While she loves her, she also knows the value of boundaries. It wasn't the older woman's fault that her advice came from a place of trauma, but that didn't mean Sarah had to sabotage her own marriage by taking it.

"Sure, mom. I'll just stick with keeping Dad's last name then. Is that what you want?"

The unintelligible muttering on the other end of the line is her answer.

Sarah hangs up after a few more pleasantries, with a promise to call again soon. Fall is on the way, and she's enjoying the first tolerable day of outside weather after July made it unbearable to be even near a window.

She's playing hooky from her household responsibilities today. Instead of cleaning or cooking or folding the laundry she knows is waiting for her, she followed Jared to the golf course for fun. From her spot on the club patio, she watches him use a chalk line on the practice green to line up a straight putt. It never gets old, seeing him in his element.

With her glass of lemonade under an umbrella, Sarah is just about to have the perfect day.

After the Desert Invitational, she and Jared didn't go back to normal right away. He was still hurt by her secrets, and they had to work through some underlying issues. Her perfectionism in the house and in public when Jared only needed affection and support wasn't going to heal itself overnight, but they were getting much better. She was finding it easier to read him when he needed to really focus on practicing rather than relaxing, and now she could pick up on when he needed a light distraction or a rest day.

Her friendship with Cassandra helps. Andy and Jared have gotten closer too, albeit with the wall of constant competition between them, but men tend to be better at bridging those social gaps than women. In the weeks since the last tournament, Cassandra confided in her that she's relieved to be closer to them with all the tumult coursing through the professional golf world. Apparently, she'd been struggling with friendships since Andy's decision to leave the PGA, but what came after the Desert Invitational was when things really started to heat up.

First, there was the earth-shattering news that Hillary Torre had been responsible for Rowan Silver's death. Any updates from court immediately became front page headlines, as well as the somewhat shocking fact that Steven hadn't said anything publicly about divorce or separation. The gossip rags speculated wildly on why that is, from an already finalized private divorce to the truly ludicrous accusation that Hillary is an actual witch and has cursed Steven to never leave her. Ignoring all of them, she decided to give them a small fraction of privacy by not entertaining herself with the drama surrounding their lives. Sarah knows well that there's more to a marriage than what everyone sees.

Cassandra also admitted readily that Whitney was the one responsible for the note. While the widow's reasons for giving it to Sarah weren't explained in detail—much to her disappointment—that conversation also included a brief coaching session on how to handle the media better in the future. Jared and Sarah have since enlisted the help of a freelance public relations expert, which both prepares Jared for interviews, and alleviates most of Sarah's stress when it comes to being in the public eye. It's really been a huge weight off her shoulders, for multiple reasons.

Less deadly, but no less dramatic was the sudden rise in young, popular players joining the new league, even players who had publicly criticized their opposition to the point of slander. It seemed like a business decision for most of the players, but that didn't stop sports commentators from hinting at hidden injuries and impending falls from grace.

Sarah doesn't let herself think too deeply about any of these things.

No, she's found her own slice of paradise at her home with Jared in Ottawa. They've kept their permanent home here, although they still travel most weeks for tournaments. With the sun high, and her eyes on her husband, Sarah has no complaints.

Things are only going to get better, she thinks, with a hand over her growing abdomen.

BARTENDER #3

I tie my hair away from my face before getting back behind the bar. It's not the golf course bar, much to my disappointment. After the Desert Invitational wrapped up and I came back from my week off, the property manager announced that all facilities were getting a remodel. The resort, the country club, even parts of the golf course. According to management, the renovations will increase revenue, will have no downsides whatsoever, and will pull us up in the national rankings for tour courses.

My opinion was not requested, but if it was, I would have mentioned that if all those things were true, maybe they should have happened before the major tournament instead. The relaunch could have maximized its advertising power with the free press from everyone following the players that weekend, and the costs could have been recouped much earlier with all the spectator foot traffic.

Another thing I noticed, and one that probably hadn't factored into their decision making, was the obvious downside of my being out of work for three months while the construction was going on.

"I'll do one more before I head out," the lone man at my bar waves me down before pulling out his wallet. I pour him another double and swipe his card, both of us oblivious to the people outside the airport headed to work on a weekday morning.

I really can't complain too much about my interim gig. Like golf courses, airports are one of the places where it's acceptable to drink at all hours of the day, which means I'm never bored, and I haven't had to see a decrease in my tipped wages.

While the man finishes his drink, I pretend to work at my POS system. I'm not quite unprofessional enough to text on the job, so I pull out my wallet, and with it my main form of entertainment these days.

Detective Grossman's card is well-worn from all the attention it's gotten from me these past few weeks. At least once a day, I pull it out and play with the corners. Sometimes I get really close to calling him, maybe seeing if he wants to get coffee. Once I had his number all typed out on my own phone, ready to dial, only to quickly delete it in embarrassment. Something always stops me from reaching out.

I put the faded business card back in its home when I hear the clicking heels of a new customer.

For a moment, I double take, thinking I'm back at the course because Whitney Silver is sitting at my bar. She's not as made-up as last time with her hair in a ponytail, and she's wearing a black blouse instead of a dress but it's her. I walk over, hoping she'll appreciate being recognized.

"Diet Coke, right? Fountain, not bottle?"

The look she gives me can only be described as utterly confused. "No," she says, "I don't drink soda. I'll have a glass of your sparkling rose."

I'm too professional to let her lie affect me. "Of course," I reply. "Where are you headed?"

"Abroad, hopefully to a few different places," she says. "I think I need a change."

Once I pop open a new bottle and slide the glass in front of her, I decide to admit I know who she is. "Yeah, um, I'm sorry about that. If anyone deserves a break, it's you."

Whitney raises an eyebrow as she takes her first sip.

"Sorry, I'm not trying to be weird or anything. I used to work at a golf course."

"Ah," she nods and smiles, but doesn't concede to recalling our interaction. "That explains it then."

I pick up a rag to wipe the counter on one side of her just to give myself something to do. "That's sort of exciting, though. Getting to travel."

"I don't know if it's exciting so much as necessary," she finishes the glass and pushes it back toward me, so I refill it without needing to be asked. "I'll still be alone, just in prettier places so I can ignore the solitude, at least during the day. Nights are the hardest part, you know."

Passing the glass back, I resume my counter cleaning and clear my head. I'm used to all kinds of patrons. There are the ones who moderate their intake and the heavy spenders. There are the sports fans and the readers. Then there are the quiet types and the chatty customers. I didn't take Whitney for someone talkative, so I moved down the counter, assuming she was done, when she spoke again.

"I just need to move forward."

That phrasing stops me immediately.

I'm not all that confrontational. I'll never be accused of being bold and I lean more toward passivity. But something wriggles in the back of my mind, and I decide to engage with her, despite what I may learn.

"How did you know Greg?"

Whitney freezes, just long enough to confirm my suspicions before finishing her current sip. "Who is Greg?"

"Greg Yeager. He used to work around golf, too. You might have heard about his passing recently."

She sets the glass down while her eyes dance with humor. "I remember you now," she says. "The girl from the VIP area at the Invitational. I bet they left you to deal with the aftermath of that weekend. You probably just wanted to go home, and they wasted your time with a bunch of questions."

I laugh but it sounds more like a cough. "They didn't keep me long."

She raises an eyebrow. "I'll do one more glass, then settle up my tab with you."

As I turn to print her receipt, I'm feeling dismissed, but she surprises me by continuing to speak. "Greg used to do a lot of work in the golf world, even some freelance projects here and there for the players. He even did me a favor once."

I slide the tab into its small, black booklet and move it to her while she keeps speaking. "He didn't do a very good job, though."

"Oh really."

"Completely bungled it, if I'm being honest," she says as she rummages through her purse. "Rowan was not supposed to be in the car that night."

I freeze over the glassware I'm placing in the sink, wondering if I heard her correctly. My back is to her this way, and it feels unsafe.

"I suppose it's like the old saying goes," she says while I hear her moving around behind me, "you can only do something right if you do it yourself, and all that."

Turning back around, I almost expect her to be pointing a weapon at me, but she's only sitting there with her glass, the tab's booklet pushed back in my direction.

She smiles at me, with her teeth this time, and it's jarring. "Though that's not right, either. I didn't exactly do that job correctly, myself."

I connect the pieces in my mind before I can stop myself from speaking. "What did she do to you?"

Whitney stands up and collects her purse and her small carryon, getting ready to leave. "Please. You're not that stupid."

Of course I'm not. News anchors and golf podcasts have spoken of little else since the Desert Invitational came to an end. Hillary and Rowan's affair, her involvement in his death, and her subsequent murder of her own sister have been everywhere, repeating the facts of each case with mind-numbing repetitiveness.

Apparently, they had it all wrong.

"I don't understand why you're admitting this to me," I say. "I could share this with anyone if I wanted to."

She shakes her head as she speaks, "You won't, though. You didn't say anything at the tournament, either."

"You don't know that," I say, indignant.

"I guess you can do whatever you want, once I leave."

I cross my arms, watching her move with as much fascination as fear. "Why would you do any of it?"

Whitney's smile is sad now, though I'm mad at myself for noticing. "Have you ever been married?"

I shake my head.

"Then you wouldn't understand," she replies. "I promised to love him forever."

With that, she leaves, and I wait until she is fully lost to the terminal, out of sight before I pick up the little black booklet.

I'm both surprised and not surprised at what I see. Inside, there are ten, crisp, hundred-dollar bills. A quick swipe of the counterfeit cash pen from my drawer reveals them to be real, or at least as real as they need to be for me to use them. I've already made my decision, but that doesn't mean I'm proud of it or that I won't regret it later.

Quickly, so I don't have to think about it, I pull out my wallet and remove Detective Grossman's card, toss it in the trash, and replace it with the money before going back to work.

AUTHOR'S NOTE

If you can't tell, I grew up in a golf family. For those of you who are new to golf, I hope you enjoyed the story enough to learn more about the game. For those of you already invested in the professional golf world, I hope the creative liberties I took for the sake of writing fiction are not too offensive to you.

Besides a few allusions to professional golfers throughout the story, there is only one name that belongs to a person who existed in real life. Andy Bell's swing coach, Ed Sheppard, shares the name of the swing coach I used all through high school.

Ed was a fantastic coach, if not a little taken in by all the new golf technology that came about during his time teaching. Any new launch of a swing aid or putting mat or a new club head shape, he was going to try it, and he was also going to make my sister and I try it. Square drivers? He had one. An arm brace to stop my over-extended back swing? I wore it. A medicine ball under your left foot while swinging, ok now your right foot, now could you try it blindfolded? You bet we did it.

For all the merchandise we swapped out under his instruction, my sister and I did get much better at golf during this time. Was it because we had access to the most expensive new toys? Probably in part, but I know it was something else.

Ed had all the technical skills to pass along while he was instructing, but where he really excelled was in coaching for the mental strength of the game. Golf is extremely taxing mentally, and the mind games that happen on the course are what separates people who practice and are pretty good from those who can truly become winners. I can't think of another sport or game where one is forced to socialize with their competition for over four and a half hours.

I often let the other girls I played against get in my head, but Ed had a way of talking me down and training me to expect bumps in the road. I think the metaphors helped; he would always refer to your mind as your "kitchen."

"Don't let that girl in your kitchen, Clarice."

"Take a breath, that girl is making an omelet in your kitchen right now."

"Close the kitchen window, Clarice."

It might sound weird, but it really worked. As a teenager, I was under the impression that protecting my kitchen was a skill I could master eventually. I thought someday I would be able to completely seal off my mind from foreign intrusions. When I brought this up to Ed, he kind of laughed and said that it was impossible. Not even the pros, the best in the world ever fully seal off their kitchen.

I got a good example of this later when we were talking about a major tournament, and how someone I thought for sure would win ended up falling behind in the last days. I brought this up to Ed, and his answer was simple.

"He's going through a divorce. What did you expect?"

I don't even remember who the player was, but this statement opened a new door for how I watched professional golf. Admittedly, there might have been a feminine draw to the dramatics involved in following golf gossip, but I couldn't deny the real world correlation between a chaotic personal life and an inability to focus during tournaments. I started to see men fall apart in competition, and my immediate assumption would be, *there must be trouble at home.*

This is, obviously, a generalization and perhaps an overly romantic view on how much wives can affect their husbands. There are likely tons of players who compete well no matter what's happening at home and plenty of men with lovely, near perfect home lives who don't win very often. But I have to insist that a supportive home to return to after a long day can only be a net positive for the men who have them. This "Law of the Good Wife," so to speak, formed the basis for many of the themes throughout my novel.

Around the time I completed the first draft of this story, I received the news that Ed had passed away at age seventy. While I had not been coached by him since high school, he remained close with my family and we all stayed in touch throughout the years. I think he had this relationship with everyone he met, this easy familial closeness that brought you in. Every other person I know who was coached by him considered him to be a part of their families or even a father figure.

I don't have anything romantic to say about death. It sucks. The world was a better place with Ed in it and now he's gone. But I consider it a blessing to have known someone who had so universal of a positive effect on those around him.

So thank you, Ed Sheppard, for sharing some of yourself with me while you were here.

ACKNOWLEDGMENTS

I'd like to thank my mom and sister for always being my first draft editors. Specifically, thank you Mom, for loving everything I write because I'm your special princess, and thank you to my sister Holly, who is capable of being mean enough to tell me the truth when something in my story doesn't make sense. And thank you to Dad as well, because without the lessons you gave me in responsibility and discipline growing up, I'd never have been able to finish writing a single book.

Thank you to Andrew Watts and Ten-Hut Media for taking a chance on me as a writer. I'm grateful for the opportunity and couldn't have moved forward with this manuscript alone. Another thank you goes to my publisher, Julia, and my editors, Randall and Amie.

I also want to give a special thanks to all the golf coaches I had growing up: Steve Purtell, Scott Varner, Tab Griffin, Ed Sheppard, Mike Clary, Sam Kern, and Paul Tretnor. You guys helped me love the game of golf, or at least kept me from hating it enough to quit after a bad round.

Lastly, and most importantly, I want to thank my husband, Russell. Every day I count the minutes until you come home. You make everything brighter and more fun, make every moment more meaningful. I love you so much, and without your love and support this book would not exist.

ABOUT THE AUTHOR

Clarice grew up in the American South and now lives in the Midwest with her husband. *The Keepers of Men* is her first novel.

To learn more about Clarice's books, visit:
severnriverbooks.com/collections/clarice-montgomery

𝕏 x.com/authorclaricem

◎ instagram.com/authorclaricem

ⓐ amazon.com/stores/Clarice-Montgomery/author/B0DYQ777J1

www.ingramcontent.com/pod-product-compliance
Lightning Source LLC
Chambersburg PA
CBHW020358030726
47496CB00007B/2191